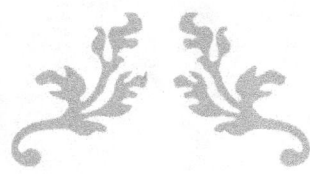

HOW (NOT) TO GRIEVE

Kristie Higgins

Allegro Publishing
AllegroPublishing@yahoo.com
        ひ
How (not) to Grieve/ Kristie Higgins.
Print ISBN 9781718060081

You cannot find peace by avoiding life.

–Virginia Woolf

Acknowledgements

I have to thank my beta readers first. You guys are the best! Thank you so much for proofing, putting up with my changes, reading and rereading for me, and for encouraging me to keep going on my writing. Thank you, Ashley Singer-Falkner, Cathie McManus, Debbie Layton, Lori Bolt, Debbie Hinely! I couldn't do this without you guys.

I also need to thank the women riders of the era of this novel, when they pushed their way into a man's world, the Sport of Kings, thoroughbred horse racing. Your bravery and strength should be remembered and emulated. I hope my books help bring to light some of what you did for racing and women's liberation.

Lastly, to my small and loyal group of fans, always asking for the next book, thank you for your support and encouragement throughout this journey. I hope my new books live up to your expectations and more!

Thank you!

Kristie

CONTENTS

PROLOGUE

Elmont, New York, 1955

In the slight breeze, Julia's hair tickled her face, so she swept one side behind her ear. Her heart sank as she scanned the room for husband, only to find the room bare and empty, void of furniture other than her bed, void of trinkets, void of color. The scene mirrored how she felt – nearly empty. At least she got to talk to him from time to time.

"How have things been?" His voice came from her right and she turned to find that he wasn't showing himself. Only his voice pierced the emptiness. It was frustrating accepting things out of her control, but what choice did she have?

"Okay, I guess," she answered, torn between the excitement of talking with him and the heartache of not being able to see him.

"The kids?"

"Fine." Her voice cracked. The heartache was winning.

"What's the matter?"

Tears trickled down Julia's ruddy cheeks. "You know what's wrong. This isn't fair."

"I know, darling, but it has to be this way."

"Why?"

"How are things at the track?"

Julia relented with a hint of a sigh. Her husband never answered that question. She wasn't sure why it was such a big secret, but she didn't have much of a choice in the matter. He wasn't giving. "Okay. I mean, actually, I had fun there today."

"Yeah?"

"Yeah, I finally got to ride a horse."

"Oh! That's wonderful, Jules."

Julia's eyes lit as she wiped a stray tear. "They put me up on Snaps. I was so scared, but he was patient with me; he barely moved. When we started walking, oh, I fell in love with him, with riding, and I wanted so badly to run like the wind."

"Did they take you to the track?"

"No." Julia scoffed. "Just around the backstretch. First, up and down the shedrow, then around the barn. The others were laughing at me. Some were mad, though. There were a few of the guys who thought I shouldn't be up on a horse." Julia shook her head. "As if women had never ridden a horse before. They're so ridiculous."

Robbie chuckled in response and let her continue.

"I clucked, and he started trotting, and they taught me how to post, but I never went any faster than that. They said next time I could."

"Were the kids there?"

"Rachel was. She was begging to ride. She's always begging to ride." Julia pictured her tiny four-year-old jumping up and down, curls bouncing in every direction, excited that her mommy was finally riding a horse. Once Julia was through with her lesson, Rachel wanted a turn. She begged and begged, but the others would not let her. "You're too young," they had told her. She had stomped her foot and crossed her arms in defiance. Julia laughed as she wondered where Rachel had learned that move, as Julia had never done that before.

"Do you want to see the babies?" Julia asked her husband.

"I see them, Jules. I see them very often."

Julia nodded, and the tears started again. "I wish you could be here with us."

"Me too, Jules."

"I miss you so much." By now, tears were flowing like rivers and she was shaking as she tried desperately to stay quiet and not wake the kids.

"I miss you, too. But you know I'm always here whenever you need me."

"But you're not here."

"I know, honey. It has to be this way."

"Why?" she begged, then sobbed and hid her face, knowing he would never answer. "Why?" she asked louder, hoping maybe this time she'd get a response. "Why? It's not fair."

Then, she saw him. He was there. He was sitting on the foot of the bed. There was even an indent from the weight of his body. *Could he really be here?*

She wiped a tear and slid from under her covers to the middle of the bed. He wasn't looking her way, and she feared if she moved too fast, he would disappear. Every movement was miniscule as she made her way down the bed toward her husband. "Robbie?" Gingerly, carefully, she lifted her hand toward him. Her whole body ached to touch him again. It had been so long. It had been a little over a year now since his accident.

"I love you. Tell the kids I love them, Jules. I have to go."

"No!" She leapt toward him but landed on the covers at the foot of the bed.

He was gone.

Julia loved yet almost hated these dreams of hers where she would talk to him. He visited occasionally, usually after something big happened. She wondered if perhaps he knew what was going on, but asked her about it anyway, so she could talk about it. Still, each time he left, it broke her heart all over again because it reminded her that she was alone.

A twenty-two-year-old widow.

"It's not fair," she said aloud, then slammed her fist into her pillow. "It's not fair," she shouted, throwing her pillow from the bed. As she gasped, she realized it was *his* pillow and covered her mouth with both hands. "No." It came out a pitiful whine. She crawled out of bed and ran to get his pillow again. Cradling it in her arms, she brought it back to the bed. She pressed her nose against it, hoping to catch a whiff of his leftover scent. She could almost sense something but wondered if it was her imagination. She had washed the pillowcase, but not the feather pillow. She took off the pillow case in search of a hint of her husband.

Underneath, she found tearstains, hers, from all the nights she had held his pillow and cried desperately for him. She wished she could die so she could be with him again. But the kids... She could never do that to the kids.

Rachel was only three when her husband had died and hadn't fully understood the situation. It took a good two weeks for it to sink in – Daddy wasn't coming home from the hospital. When it finally hit her, for Julia, it was like losing him all over again.

Billy, of course, as a baby, was oblivious to the entire situation, which helped. Dealing with two grieving kids might have broken her. One was bad enough.

They had spent months at home doing absolutely nothing. Julia's parents had begged and begged her to find work, but she couldn't do it. She didn't know what to do. All she knew was the track. She was desperate to go back to the horses yet knew it would only remind her of her husband. Go? Stay home? Each day the two sides waged war against each other inside her mind, making her dizzy, nauseous, wearing her out, and adding to the depression from losing her husband.

Her mind fought within itself as she stared at the walls of her home, the home Robbie had bought for her. Meanwhile, Rachel watched Howdy Doody or some other kids' show on their new television set. They had recently bought it with the money Robbie had brought home from winning a big race. They'd had a promising future, one with joy, comfort, love, but now...

Now their money was running out, and if she wanted to keep the kids in their home, she was going to have to force herself to work. She knew her parents would help, but she didn't want to burden them. And Robbie's parents? Vanished. They had cut off all contact with Julia and the kids, making it even harder on them.

Rachel had asked several times about Grandma McMahon and begged to see her or Aunt Janet, but they had simply vanished off the face of the earth. They had sold their restaurant, moved, and never told Julia where they were going.

"When they see us, they probably think about Daddy, and it makes them sad," Julia had told Rachel. Of course, Rachel didn't understand that, either. Then again, neither did Julia.

Six months after Robbie's death, Julia finally mustered up the courage to go back to the track for work. She had been a groom there while dating Robbie, and once they were married, almost immediately, she became pregnant with Rachel and had quit her job.

She had rubbed horses for two years before that, though technically, women were not allowed to work on the backside at Belmont Park. She had hidden her feminine features as best she could with only her boss knowing she was female. Soon, everyone had figured it out, but since she had been doing so well with the horses and cleaning, women's work, they never enforced the rule about kicking her out.

After Robbie's death, several co-workers and her boss had called to let her know she was welcome back any time and could get her old job back. However, she did not want to go back there to be reminded of all the good times she had spent there with her husband. Still, it was all she knew, and she loved and missed the horses terribly. She knew they would be a source of comfort, as would her old friends.

She sniffed and took a shaky breath of the cold New York autumn air on her way back. A squirrel dropped his acorn next to her and she jumped, catching sight of the diminutive animal before he vanished into the trees. Once on her way again, she stuck her hands in her pockets to keep them warm. The sidewalk was covered with red and orange oak leaves. She had always enjoyed the satisfying crunching sound they made and made sure to step on at least one leaf with every step. At least something felt better in her life.

It wasn't very far to the Belmont Park backstretch gate on Plainfield Avenue; she'd only had to pass a few houses and head across the street. Once she was at the gate, she stopped as she saw Pete, the security guard at his post. Pete's eyes were as big as the Jolly balls the horses played with in their stalls. They stood staring at each other in somewhat of a standoff – Julia, afraid of moving forward, Pete wanting to encourage her but afraid to scare her off and ruin everything.

Finally, Julia swallowed a giant lump and decided to force herself to walk. It was like pulling off a Band-Aid or jumping into an ice-cold pool. Pete held the gate for her without a word as she passed through. Once she was on the other side and on Belmont grounds, she froze again in place as she absorbed everything.

Everybody had gone on with their lives as if nothing had happened. There were people talking, joking, laughing, walking horses, riding horses to and from the track, grooms washing horses, hanging up laundry. It almost insulted Julia, but she reminded herself that they had to go on. It was all for the horses, just as she'd had to go on for her kids. Besides, they had seen this before. Many men had lost their lives racing horses, as did many more horses. Despite the loss and pain, they always had to go on.

Somehow, she had found herself back in barn eighteen, her old barn, her husband's barn, the Hanover Farms barn. She had to go on, too. She didn't have any other choice.

CHAPTER ONE

"Mommy, I want to ride, too," Rachel whined for the millionth time. Julia's nerves were on their last thread as she wished she hadn't brought Rachel to the track again.

Rachel absolutely loved it here, loved the horses, and helped wherever she could. She had been very sensible, staying clear of the horses' hooves and teeth, only handling equipment and tack she could handle easily. She might carry a saddle for someone or help polish one, maybe help hang bandages on the clotheslines after they'd been washed. Rachel was very careful to do everything right because she knew if she didn't, she would get hurt or Mommy would make her stay home, and she didn't want either one of those options. Most of all, she desperately wanted to ride a horse just as her mom had done yesterday.

"Sweetie, I'm sorry, but you're just too little. They would never allow it. It's too dangerous. What if you fall? It's so far down. Do you know how tall Snaps' back is? Look." Julia placed her hand on Snaps' gray and slightly swayed back, then brought her hand over toward her eyes. "Look. His back is way up here where my eyes are."

Rachel moved closer to her mother and looked up, tilting her had back awkwardly. Julia almost laughed, but managed to hold it in. "Yeah. That is pretty far up."

"I just don't want you to get hurt, okay?"

Rachel lowered her eyes and stuck out her bottom lip.

"You have to eat all your vegetables and grow up to be big and strong, so you can ride, okay?"

"Let's go get some spinach, Mommy. Like Popeye. If I eat spinach, can I ride?"

Julia heard someone laughing from the other side of Snaps and looked up to grin at him. Then she spoke to her daughter again. "No, honey, it doesn't work like that in real life. That's only in cartoons. In real life, it takes a lot longer for it to work. It'll take years."

"How long is that?"

Julia dropped her shoulders and let out a whoosh of air, wishing she had all the answers. She was saved when the man came around to their side and attempted to explain.

"Well, Rachel, how old are you?" Kenny squatted in front of her.

"This many." She held up four fingers.

"You're four years old. I think you'd have to wait at least another four years before you'd be allowed on a big giant horse like this."

Rachel's eyes bugged, though she still had no idea what that meant. "Is that a long time?"

"Yes, honey. I'm afraid it will be a long time from now. You have a lot of growing to do first."

"Don't they make smaller horses?"

Julia looked at Kenny, the assistant trainer. He looked at Julia, too, and neither were sure what to say. Finally, Julia came up with something. "Yes, but we don't have any ponies here, sweetie. I'm sorry."

"Can we go buy one?"

"I don't have the money."

Rachel stomped her foot in defiance again. "We never have the money."

"I know, baby. I'm sorry." Julia's heart burned inside, knowing the reason why they never had the money for things. It was because she didn't have a husband anymore, and she was the only breadwinner in the house. Yet another reminder of how alone she was.

In reality, she wasn't completely alone, and she knew it. Her parents were there for her. Her mother watched the kids while she worked and was practically raising Billy by herself. Julia felt awful about it and had apologized to her mother, but knew at the same time, she had to work every day, sometimes twelve or more hours. Julia wondered why they even kept the house, why they couldn't live in a track apartment. However, Julia's mother would never allow her daughter and grandbabies to live in a one-room dormitory. There were roaches there, and she would not allow the children, at the very least, to be around roaches. Grandma had given Julia the old, "You'll thank me later," line. Julia knew it was true.

"Come help me with the laundry, Rachel." Rachel took her mother's hand and they walked to the laundry area. Laundry was a disgusting job and Julia hated it. She wished desperately they would get a washing machine like the rest of the world. Everything here had to be washed by hand with a washboard, as if they were in the mountains of West Virginia. "It's nineteen fifty-five. When are they going to wake up and come into the twentieth century? It's half over and they still don't have washing machines."

Rachel shrugged, pretending to understand her mother's complaint. After helping her mother scrub the bandages for the horses' legs, she helped her mother hang them on the line to dry. Then it was time to have fun. With her mom distracted by her work, Rachel sneaked away and into the tack room.

She'd had this idea a few days ago while watching a rider practice his form on a stack of hay bales. She couldn't move the hay, but she could move the saddle, and knew of a stack that would be perfect to put it on. It was just outside the front door. Without a care in the world, she went into the tack room and surveyed the saddles. With one finger pointing, she compared sizes, then chose the smallest one. Hooking her arm under it as she had been taught to do, she lifted it from its post and carried it to the hay bales. She wasn't sure whose saddle it was, but it didn't matter, anyway. She silently promised to have it back in the room soon. She just needed a little practice first.

Carefully, she slid it onto the stack of two hay bales. Biting her lip, she wondered how to fasten a girth around it, but decided she didn't need it. She needed reins, though. Back in the tack room, she found a lead rope and yanked it from its hook. She tied each end of the leather rope to a chair and slid it closer to her makeshift horse. Going to the left side of her horse, she gathered the reins as she had seen other riders do, then hopped a few times. She wished for someone to give her a leg up but did not want to bother anyone. Instead, she found a way to climb up without using the stirrups.

Then, carefully, gingerly, she slid onto the saddle. She put her feet in the stirrups and lifted herself up, balancing so as not to slip off the hay bales.

The stirrups were too long, and her legs weren't bent like a jockey's legs. She had watched them tie the stirrups in knots before, so she tried that. Several attempts later, and after almost giving up, she finally figured out how to shorten the stirrups. They were still too long, but they were better.

She stood again, balanced herself on the balls of her feet, and bent over, still holding the reins. Her knees bent as she tried to focus on keeping her back straight and flat. Then she shook the reins and chirped, telling her horse to go.

Her black beauty took off running at full speed and Rachel balanced like an expert in the saddle. She gathered the reins tightly against the horse's neck, forcing it to arch like a beautiful show horse as they ran around the track for their warm up. "Easy, boy," she told him. It wasn't long before it was time to let go for their blow out. "Heeya!" she shouted as she shook the reins loosely against the horse's neck. He took off like a bullet. Rachel absorbed the movement of the horse with her knees, keeping her body still and her face buried deep in the horse's mane. That's how the others did it, and it looked swell. She hoped she looked the same.

Their workout was a long one, and they must have gone around the track ten times before she finally gave in and let the horse rest. With a soft thump, she sat in the saddle. "Whew." She wiped a dusty sleeve over her brow, leaving behind sand-colored streaks.

"Rachel, what are you doing?" she heard. It was Mommy. She twisted in the saddle to see her mother standing against the wall of the barn with her arms crossed. Rachel was glad to see her mother smiling and not upset at her for doing this.

"Mommy! I worked a horse!" Rachel jumped with her exclamation and the saddle slipped. She fell to one side, onto the ground. As her mother ran over to her, she stood up again, brushed herself off, and straightened the saddle. "I'm okay, Mommy. I'm okay."

"Okay. Okay." Julia stopped and raised her hands.

"Did you see?"

"I did. You are a natural." Julia firmly believed her own words. Rachel's form had been excellent, especially for a beginner, and especially for having the stirrups too long. Her back was completely flat, and she held the reins properly with them between her fingers, as she had seen the other riders do. Julia couldn't believe Rachel had picked up so much by watching.

"What's this? A new jockey for our stable?" An older man approached and slipped his fedora from his balding head, revealing messy white hair. Rachel knew him as the head trainer, the boss.

"Yeah. Watch this." Rachel balanced in her saddle, bent her knees, and showed off her best jockey stance. She pushed the reins forward and back. "Heeya!"

Walter chuckled. "Not bad, little filly." Walter patted her back before moving on to his office.

Julia wished she could get her daughter on a horse.

Julia ran into Walter later that day, as Rachel was still on her makeshift horse, practicing her riding skills. She had been there for a few hours now and Julia couldn't get her to dismount.

"I'm surprised at how good she looks," Julia said casually.

"Rachel? Yeah, she's doing pretty well. Maybe she'll gallop our horses when she grows up."

Julia nodded. "Would be nice to put her on a pony. She's a natural."

"How you gonna manage that?"

"Not sure. I can't afford to buy a pony."

"You could pick one up pretty cheap. Could keep him around here as a mascot."

Julia caught his eyes and tried her hardest not to look too excited. "Really? We could keep a pony here?"

"I don't see why not. We've got the whole barn to ourselves. Always an empty stall somewhere."

Julia's face beamed with joy at the thought. It was something she had always wanted for herself, but it would be a dream-come-true for her daughter as well. "Can you help me find one?" Though, she wasn't sure where she would get the money, even if it were only "pretty cheap."

"Of course. I've got an idea or two." He winked and then walked off.

Julia suppressed the urge to hop up and down.

The next day, Julia brought Rachel to the track in the afternoon. Rachel went right for the tack room and grabbed a saddle. Julia was tickled with her daughter's eagerness. At least it was something to keep her out of other people's hair for a while. Normally, Rachel begged them to let her help them with whatever they were doing.

Before Rachel could tack up her horse, she heard the roar of a truck with squeaky trailer wheels. She and her mother looked up to find the truck pulling up right outside the barn door. "Looks like we're getting a new horse." Julia tossed her brush into a bucket and grabbed her daughter's hand. Rachel finally let go of her saddle at the idea of seeing their new steed. They walked toward the door as a man was putting the ramp on the side of the trailer. Rachel and her mother stood patiently as Walter poked his head out of the door.

"Hi, kids. We've got a new one today."

Rachel cheered. Walter disappeared back inside, and a minute later, he appeared holding the rope attached to a small chestnut pony. Julia put her hand over her mouth. She watched Rachel, who saw the pony with huge green eyes and her jaw dropped in surprise. Rachel pointed. "Mommy, look how small that horse is."

Her mother beamed as she looked at Walter. "My goodness, Walter. Is he... Will he be our mascot?"

"You betcha." Walter led the pony toward the girls. He handed the rope to Rachel, who was hesitant at first, but held the rope with one hand and the halter with the other, as she had seen Mommy do. "Where should we put him?"

"How about this stall? This looks good right here." Walter led them to an empty stall as Rachel led the small horse with her head held high. She sparkled with delight that no one had seen in over a year now.

They walked inside and closed the metal bars behind them. "What's his name?" Rachel asked as she unclipped the rope.

"Whatever you want to call him, Rachel. You pick the name."

"Me? I get to name him?" Rachel jumped once with joy.

"Yup. You'd better come up with a good one, too. He has to live with it for the rest of his life, you know."

Rachel thought about it with narrowed eyes and one hand on her chin while Walter and her mother stood by patiently.

Julia turned to Walter. "Thank you, Walter. How much was he?"

He shrugged in reply. "It was nothing. Mr. Hanover had a couple up at their farm and he decided to send one down. I told him we needed a mascot like every other stable, and he agreed."

Still partially in shock, Julia continued. "That's swell of him. I'll have to thank him."

Walter nodded, then asked Rachel, "Think of anything yet?"

"Goldie."

"Goldie, it is."

"Mommy, can I brush him?"

"Of course." Julia grabbed a brush from a bucket outside the stall and gave it to her daughter, who held it with the strap around her hand. Rachel brushed her pony as she had seen her mom brushing the bigger horses. She was gentle around his face and legs and made sure to brush with the direction of his hair. Goldie closed his eyes, completely relaxed in the hands of his new owner.

ᴖᴖᴖ

The late morning summer heat mingled with the pollution, making the air thick and heavy. It didn't faze Rachel one bit; she couldn't wait to get back to the track and her new pony. Eagerly pulling her mother down the path from gate seven that backstretch workers had nicknamed Man O'War Ave, she yelled, "Come on, Mommy. Hurry!"

Julia stumbled, narrowly missing a pile of manure. "Calm down, Rachel. He's not going anywhere."

When they finally reached the pony's stall, Rachel stood at the door for a second to admire him, holding both hands over her heart. She then grabbed a carrot from her mother's pocket and tried to break off a piece. After a short struggle, she handed it to her mother. Julia handed her daughter a small chunk of the carrot and reminded her to keep her hand flat.

Rachel sighed and rolled her eyes. "I know, Mommy." She fed Goldie his carrot, and while he was still chewing, she opened the stall door and quickly grabbed his halter as he pushed forward. "Not yet, big boy. You're not going anywhere yet." That was something her mother often said to the bigger horses.

Julia gathered the feed and vitamins for the horses as Rachel combed Goldie's mane and tail. It wasn't long before Julia heard the question she had been dreading. "Mommy, can I ride him?"

"We, um, we don't have a saddle or bridle, yet, honey. I guess we will have to order, um, maybe just a bridle." She scratched her neck and looked around. She was grateful that the farm had ponies and that Mr. Hanover was so kind as to send them one but now there were additional costs. How could she afford the expenses? She had seen rope halters before, but if her daughter were going to ride this pony safely, he would need a bridle with a bit, and there would be no way to make one from rope. Julia internalized a groan.

Later that morning, she searched the tack room for the smallest saddle and bridle she could find despite knowing it was futile. There were plenty of small racing and exercising saddles, but even they might be too long for the pony's short back. As for the bridles, they were all too big, with bits easily two inches too wide. It would never work. Then, in one corner, she saw a tack box she hadn't seen before. As she heard angels singing, she rushed to the box, hoping it had come with the pony from the farm. Inside, she found everything she could ever want for Goldie. There was a small western saddle, saddle pad, breastplate, bridle, grooming supplies, and even a pony-sized blanket.

She was so excited, she couldn't help but call Rachel into the room. Rachel skipped in when she heard her mother calling. Rachel found her mother smiling and standing over an open box, so she looked inside and found the tack.

"Is this for Goldie?"

"Sure is."

Rachel clapped and cheered as she jumped up and down, then reached into the box and grabbed a handful of leather, tangling it into a jumbled mess. As she pulled it out, she couldn't tell what was what. It became too heavy for her, so she put it back down and looked up at her mother, clasped her hands behind her back, and dropped her gaze to the ground.

"Now, see? You got over excited again and acted before you thought about it. First, you think, and then you act. How am I going to trust you to ride a horse unless you learn that?"

Rachel winced and frowned in shame. "Sorry, Mommy."

"It's okay. Let's get this untangled." Julia reached inside for the jumbled mess and pulled it out.

After sorting everything out and making sure all chores were done for the morning, it was finally time to tack up the horse and try a riding lesson. Julia had called on Kenny, one of the stable's assistant trainers for help. Kenny had helped her ride Snaps the other day.

After bringing the pony outside the stall and tying him up, Rachel helped tack up the pony and then stood back to admire her work. "He looks so pretty." The pony looked at her for a second, then reached up for another horse's hay as it hung in a net on the outside of the stall.

Kenny tested the saddle by wiggling it, making sure it was secure. "Are you ready, Rachel?"

"Yes!" She jumped, making the pony flinch and jerk his head. Rachel slapped her hand over her mouth.

"Oh, now, you know better than to scare him like that. You need to talk to him nice and soft and gentle, and he'll be gentle with you."

Rachel nodded without a word and stepped closer to the pony. *Nice and soft and gentle.* Kenny told her how to hold the reins and the saddle and showed her which foot to put in the stirrup. He helped her leg over the saddle, and she settled in.

"But that's not how you get up on a horse. Someone grabs your leg and pulls –" Rachel started.

Laughter interrupted her. "No, honey, this is different. He's not a race horse. He has a western saddle. See how big it is? This is how you get into a western saddle."

"Oh. Okay." She allowed Kenny to help her get up onto the pony's back and when she found herself safely in the saddle, she held the horn and reins as she looked proudly at her mom. Julia had her camera and took a few pictures of them.

Kenny showed her how to hold the reins with one hand, which confused her since she had seen other riders use both hands. Nevertheless, she quietly listened and learned all she could from him, so she could be a good rider. "This is how cowboys ride, so they can throw a lasso around the calf."

Julia nodded.

Rachel lit up. "Oh, and the outriders use one hand, too!"

"That's right. They need one hand to grab the loose horse. Good observation, Rachel," Kenny praised.

Rachel nodded as she made sure not to touch the horn in front of her, letting them know she was good at this and could stay balanced without holding on in case she had to grab a loose horse. Or a calf.

Her mother kept a rope clipped to Goldie's bridle, but stood back, giving Rachel some room to work and learn how to steer her horse. They practiced going left, right, stopping, forward, even going backward. She begged and begged her mother to unclip the line, but she wouldn't. Goldie seemed like a very sweet and docile pony, but Mommy said she didn't know him all that well yet and thought it better to be safe than sorry. Still, despite being tied to her mother, Rachel was having the time of her life riding around in front of the barn.

A few people stopped to look as they passed by, some joking about how she might be the next big jockey in town or be the stable's "pony girl." Rachel loved both labels, but most of all, she wanted to be a jockey. Mom wouldn't let her shorten the stirrups like a jockey, which frustrated her, but she was still glad to be able to ride – finally.

Every day, she got better and better at riding, until finally her mother decided it would be okay to unclip the rope. The pony stood still for a few seconds, eyeing Julia as he wondered why. When Rachel chirped and kicked him lightly, he took off in a quick trot. "Mommy...I...don't...like...trotting," she said between bounces as she steered Goldie in a circle.

Julia told her to lift herself every other bounce. "It's called posting."

Rachel got the hang of it quickly.

After a few more days, Rachel thought she was ready to run. With the lack of useable space in front of the barn, Julia told her she wasn't allowed to run yet, though she knew she could always take them to an enclosed paddock.

The thought of running scared Julia, as the picture of her husband's accident always loomed in the back of her mind.

Without warning, Rachel decided she would make him run anyway. She clucked, kicked, and yelled until Goldie was cantering and Julia was running after them in a panic. Rachel kicked and clucked again, and Goldie went even faster. Petrified, with her curls bouncing in every direction, she held the horn of the saddle tightly with one hand and the reins in the other as she realized it was faster than she thought it would be. Having enough of that after a few seconds, she pulled the reins and slowed her pony back to a walk. Goldie wasn't keen on running anyway and eagerly slowed for his rider. Julia caught up and slowed as she neared them.

"Rachel," she scolded quietly, so as not to scare the pony into taking off again. "I told you no running."

"I know, Mommy. I'm sorry. I didn't think it would be that fast."

"Not thinking again," Julia muttered as she grabbed the bridle and led them back to the barn.

It broke Rachel's heart to disappoint her mother. Several tears slipped down Rachel's face as they walked. She was thankful her mother couldn't see her crying, but when she sniffed, her mother turned toward her.

"Oh, Rachel. I just don't want you to get hurt. Okay? If you listen to me, you'll be safe. That's my job. To keep you safe."

Rachel suddenly thought about her father's accident. He was running, and he had gotten hurt. *Worse than that*, she thought, as she remembered hearing that he had broken his neck. Jockeys ran races five, six, or seven days a week without getting hurt, though. The exercise boys, too. They were all fine. It would never happen to her again. What were the chances?

ᕔᕔᕔ

After only a week with Goldie, it was time for kindergarten to start. Rachel cried, not because she would miss her mom, or would be without

Mom for several hours in a strange place, but because she couldn't ride Goldie to school. She wanted to show her classmates her pony. To get her through the day, Mom made sure to send Rachel with a photo of her and Goldie. Rachel soon learned to count the hours and minutes until she saw Goldie again. It made for great inspiration for learning to read a clock.

Mom always took her directly from school to the track, as she knew Rachel would never stand for going home to eat first. Her priorities were to make sure Goldie was okay and not lonely. Rachel knew he had to have missed her while she was gone, just as she had missed him. She wouldn't even eat her lunch, no matter how hungry she was, unless she checked on Goldie first. Mom decided she would always bring Rachel's lunch along, so she would eat soon after checking on Goldie.

After lunch, she would immediately tack up her horse by herself, mount up, and roam around their barn's area.

Julia shook her head as Walter laughed at Rachel's eagerness. "Little girls and their ponies. I bet you wanted one, too, huh?" he asked.

"You bet, I did. And to this day, here I am working with horses for several years and I've only ridden once."

"Really? You should ride Goldie sometime. If your daughter lets you."

"Yeah, right. She'd never let me." Julia shook her head. "I'm too big, anyway. I could ride Snaps again, though." Julia hoped her statement did not sound too presumptuous, but she was almost as eager to ride as her daughter was.

"It makes me nervous to see you ride. What if you get hurt?"

"Everybody takes that chance, don't they?"

"I guess. I guess you're right. Not right now, though. We have work to do." And with that, he walked away. It was one thing to have a little girl riding a pony and another to have a woman riding a stable pony, one of the regular-sized horses they used to lead the runners. Other stables never allowed women to ride any of their stable ponies, and most stables wouldn't even allow women to work with them. Julia wondered if Walter had gotten in trouble for letting her ride that time.

Sudden and quick galloping got her attention. Was it a runaway horse? Julia heard the galloping get closer and closer and she looked out to see Rachel running toward the barn on Goldie. Rachel pulled the pony up, but he stopped too quickly for her. Lowering his head, Goldie deposited Rachel on the ground in a cloud of dust in front of him. Julia ran toward the pair as she yelled her daughter's name. She came too close to the pony and scared him. As Rachel tried to get up, the pony shied and stepped over her.

Rachel screamed in pain as the pony's front hoof solidly hit her forehead. Julia was there at that point and grabbed the pony with one hand, Rachel with the other. Blood poured from Rachel's cut and down her nose. She screamed at the sight of the blood now dripping into her open hand. Kenny was nearby and ran up to help. He held Goldie as Rachel leapt into her mother's arms, splattering blood onto her shirt.

Julia mentally bashed herself for allowing Rachel to roam around by herself. After all, she was only four years old. She shook her head at herself as she grabbed a rag from Kenny's hand and pressed it against Rachel's forehead. Kenny unhooked her helmet, which was too big anyway because it was adult-sized, and took it off. He pulled the rag away from Rachel's head for a second, so he could look at the cut. The area filled with dark red in an instant.

"I'll take you to the hospital. Looks like she'll need stitches, Jules."

Julia hid her face in her daughter's curls and cried as silently as she could. It was probably only going to need a few stitches, but it could have been a lot worse. She was glad that she had at least made Rachel wear a helmet. But the pony's hoof had hit her right below the rim. He didn't do it on purpose, and she knew she couldn't be mad at Goldie. It was her own fault. She ran too close to him, for one. Secondly, she should have never allowed Rachel to ride by herself. Rachel wanted to run so badly that she didn't think about the consequences. She wasn't old enough to make decisions like that. Julia was disgusted with herself.

Kenny put Goldie in the stall and quickly removed the saddle and bridle while Julia sat in a chair with her daughter on her lap. Rachel's tears had slowed to stuttering breaths by now, and Julia was still trying to curb her own tears. There was nothing worse than an emotional female in a man's world, and the men here were seemingly always looking for excuses to get rid of her. She knew there would be complaints now, and she could be banned from the track. What would she do without a job?

Soon, they were in Kenny's car on the way to the hospital. Rachel sat in front with her mother as she kept pressure on the cut. Julia didn't want to look to see how big the cut was.

The nurse took them back within a few minutes. Rachel was scared because the last time she was here in this emergency room, something awful had happened to her daddy – he never went home again. Mom's face was pure white, and Rachel wondered if Mom was thinking about it, too. Fortunately, or maybe unfortunately, something changed her focus from that tragic day to today.

A needle.

A nurse came in with a cold, metal tray, and on it lay a syringe and needle, gauze, and what looked like black thread and a curved sewing needle. Rachel eyed the tray nervously.

"We're going to numb the area first, Rachel," the nurse stated firmly as she fiddled around with things in the room. Rachel had no idea what that meant. Mom was holding gauze against her forehead now, and Rachel looked up at her mother.

"It's okay. It might hurt for a second, but then it will go away, and you won't feel a thing."

"I don't wanna hurt for a second," Rachel cried, then squirmed as she tried to get off the bed. Her mother's arm kept her in place.

"It will hurt less than the pony hurt you, Rachel. Stay put. Trust me." Julia said calmly, as she tried to keep her daughter on the bed.

Rachel still cried, although silently now. Her little body heaved with occasional sobs as she tried to be stoic and trust her mommy. *It will hurt less than the pony hurt you*, she heard as her mother's words replayed repeatedly in her mind. She didn't remember feeling any pain from the hoof. It was the blood that scared her. So much blood! Rachel shivered.

Soon, the doctor came in, and the nurse was coming at her with the needle. It was way too close to her eyes. Whimpers escaped as she tried to be brave again, but the fear was beginning to take over. "I'm right here, Rachel. Hang in there. You'll be okay in a second. Trust me," her mother was saying, though she could hardly hear it. The needle touched her skin, pinched, and she felt it hit bone. She screamed in terror and the nurse pulled the needle from her head.

"Stay still, or it will hurt worse," bellowed the nurse. Rachel's eyes bugged with even more fear now as she saw the anger in the woman's eyes. Julia shot a warning look at the gray-haired lady, who sighed and quickly stuck Rachel again with the needle, trying to hit a spot that was already numb. Rachel closed her eyes and tried to stay still so it would hurt less, and sure enough, it did hurt less. In fact, she hardly felt anything at all. After only a few seconds, there was absolutely no pain as the medicine took hold of her skin.

As Rachel lay on the bed, the doctor came forward with his rubber gloves and explained the situation to Rachel. "Now, this won't hurt a bit. You must stay still so I can do a good job. If it doesn't heal up properly, you'll have a scar, and I know a pretty girl like you wouldn't want a scar on her forehead."

"What's a scar?" Rachel took a stuttering breath, leftover from crying.

"It's a mark. Hmm." He searched his arm and found a white scar, obviously from long ago, and showed it to her. "Here's where I had stitches when I was a kid, and it leaves a mark. I hope not to leave a mark on your forehead. I want to put it together carefully, okay? So, stay as still as you can. You will feel tugging, like someone's pulling your skin, but it won't hurt at all, okay?"

"Mm-kay." She shivered from fear but took a deep breath and closed her eyes. She hoped it would be over by the time she opened them again, like falling asleep and waking up the next morning. Her mother held her icy cold hand as Rachel thought about happier things – her new pony, her dream of becoming a jockey, feeding the horses treats, even helping to muck stalls.

Finally, the doctor was done, had put a bandage over her cut, and they were on their way home.

As Kenny drove them, Julia asked Rachel, "So now will you listen to me and not run with Goldie? He's not a thoroughbred, you know. And you're not a professional rider."

"Yes, Mommy." But Rachel knew now that when the pony stopped suddenly, she would have to hold on tighter. It wouldn't matter if they ran now. She could handle this, even if it happened again.

∪∪∪

"Robbie? Are you there?" Julia waited as she sat in her bed, alone, with her arms hugging her bent legs. She knew he would not answer her this way. "I want to talk to you. Visit me in my dream, okay?" She had never asked him to do this before and wasn't sure if it was something he could control.

"Rachel had a little scare today, huh?" Julia heard his voice and looked around for him. She saw his face in the distance and relaxed.

"Yeah. Did you see? She was running, and Goldie dumped her when he stopped. Then, it was my fault. I scared the poor thing, and he stepped on Rachel's forehead. It was my fault because I was only thinking about Rachel and forgot about the pony."

"Something like that might get you kicked off the backstretch."

"Are they going to do it, Robbie? Are they going to fire me and kick me out?"

"No. They've considered it, but they think of you as a family member now, and you can't fire family. Besides, they know you need the job."

"Can you tell what they are thinking? Can you tell what I am thinking?"

"Yes."

"That's pretty neat. I wish I could do that."

Robbie chuckled. "I wish I couldn't."

"Me too, baby. Me too."

"Rachel's proud of her stitches. I'm sure she will be telling everyone at school and at the track."

"She's not afraid of Goldie, is she?"

"A little. You might have to talk to her about getting back up on the horse after a fall. All great riders get right back up on the horse as soon as they can."

"I'll tell her that. That's good."

"She'll be fine. She is a natural."

"You're right. She is. Think she'll be able to gallop horses one day? Or even be a jockey?"

"Hard to say. But I can't help but think that she will do it."

"Jockey?"

"She will fight with everything she's got to be a jockey, I know that much."

Julia nodded. "That's Rachel. Hardheaded and persistent. I wonder who she got that from."

"From you, of course."

That night, they had had a good conversation, like old times when they would sit at the kitchen table or in their living room. She was overjoyed that she was able to talk to him like this and wondered if other people ever talked to their deceased relatives. No one had ever mentioned it.

Then, she wondered if all this really happened or if it was only in her imagination. Maybe she wanted to talk to him so badly that she conjured him up in her dreams so she could have the chance again. What if it was not real? What if he wasn't there and she was losing her mind? Did he really watch over them like an angel as people often said? Or was that something to make people feel better after losing someone?

"Don't doubt me, Julia. I'm with you," she heard audibly as she dressed the next morning. She looked around the room. He wasn't there.

"Am I going crazy? Or did I just hear you?" There was no answer. Billy cried from the other room, so she quickly finished dressing and went to his room. Billy was out of his crib, standing on the floor and crying. He looked confused, as if he couldn't figure out how he had gotten there. Julia noted that the railings were still up on his crib. "Well, you are almost two now. I suppose you're about ready for a big boy bed, aren't you?"

"Bi- boy bed?"

"Yeah!" Picking him up, she feigned excitement, but knew it would cost her money she didn't have. Yet another expense to add to the pile that had recently quadrupled in size thanks to Rachel's emergency room visit. The weight of that pile lay heavily on her shoulders, making them droop.

For a moment, she wondered if she should try to find another man to marry for financial reasons. Of course, she could never love anyone the way she had loved Robbie. As she imagined herself with someone else, perhaps in this house, her stomach instantly twisted painfully, and she knew she couldn't do it. Not even to save herself from the grips of debt.

Occasionally, men from the track had asked her on dates, and she would politely decline, stating that she wasn't ready yet. She knew she was never going to be ready. There was never going to be an appropriate time to date again because Robbie was the one and only man for her. Anyone else would only be a substitute, and she would feel tremendously guilty because she knew it would be a loveless marriage of convenience. And no one could replace Daddy for Billy and Rachel.

CHAPTER TWO

"I hear you're not dating anybody," Kenny said as he approached Julia as she stood watching workouts along the rail. She jumped at the sound of his voice.

"No. I'm not ready yet. I'm still in mourning." Her standard answer.

"I see. Well, you know, you could go out with, uh, someone as a friend." He pushed some of the sand back under the fence with his foot. "You know, to get a drink or something to relax, or have a good time. No pressure."

She looked at him, puzzled. "You?"

"Yes, me." He put his hands on his hips. "I'm not so bad."

"No, I mean, you're not. I mean, yeah. I guess that would be okay." Julia shuffled her feet. "I don't know. I haven't been..."

"No pressure, Jules. I won't even try to kiss you." He winked.

Julia lowered her face to hide her red cheeks. She wished she'd left her hair down, but it was always pinned up so she would look more masculine, like the others. "Um, yeah, I could handle that. Just friends," she said finally as she looked up at him again.

Rachel held her brother's hand as they stood behind her. Rachel and Billy were watching the interaction between the two silently, so silently that Julia forgot they were there for a second. Kenny nodded at the kids and asked, "Uh, when could you get a babysitter and go out with your friend?"

"Huh?" Julia asked as she glanced at the kids. "Oh, it doesn't matter. My mother watches them."

"How about tonight?"

"Sounds good."

"Pick you up here at the shedrow at seven?"

"Sure." The blood rushed from her head. *It's not a date,* she reminded herself. *Just a friend trying to get me out of the house again. That's all.*

Kenny nodded with a smile, winked at the kids, then walked away. Julia knit her brows in thought. *No pressure, huh? Sure, he says that, but what will really happen? Would Robbie approve of this?* Wouldn't he want her to go out with people again? It had been a little over two years now. Was it time? *But it's not a date!*

Rachel interrupted her thoughts. "Mommy, will he be our new daddy?"

"No, honey. No one will ever replace your daddy. Ever." Julia immediately burst into tears before she could think about holding them in and hiding them from the kids. She hid her face with her hand and sobbed a few times. But when her kids each grabbed one leg, she found her bravery again, took a deep breath, and stopped her tears.

She had to change the subject. "Let's watch how they ride." The kids were all for that idea, as they loved watching and learning what they could.

Rachel wanted to ride Goldie like the men rode the thoroughbreds, but her mother wouldn't allow it. She hoped one day to ride a thoroughbred. For now, Goldie was good enough until she was big enough to ride one.

Mom always made her stay near the barn with Goldie, but she was fine with that because she didn't want to wind up falling off again away from her mom. She rode Goldie in counter clockwise circles as she pretended she was riding around the track, riding in a race. And she would always win.

All afternoon, Julia worried about her date, or whatever it was. What would Robbie think? Was she ready for this? Was it even a date? He had said it was only a drink with a friend but was that his true intention? Did he think that when she asked for help with Rachel's riding that she was flirting? He *had* been very friendly to her since then. It seemed he was her best friend all of a sudden. She hoped he wasn't getting his hopes up, because there was no way she was ready for someone else.

Two years. Is that really enough time? How much is enough?

After taking the kids to her mother's house and getting an encouraging word from Mom, Julia went back to the track. She had changed her clothes and was now wearing a dress, but she felt extremely self-conscious. She wasn't used to wearing dresses anymore and she also hoped that he didn't think it was a real date. She merely wanted to look nice out in public and not the way she dressed at the track. Looking down at the skirt of her dress, she sighed and shook her head. *Too formal*, she thought, but it was too late to change now.

Kenny arrived at exactly seven, wearing a baggy suit and wing-tipped shoes. He took off his hat as he drew closer.

Well, I'm not the only one over-dressed here, she thought. What were his intentions?

"Jules. Wow. You sure clean up nice."

Blushing slightly, she tittered and thanked him. He held out his elbow for her, and instinctively she hooked her arm around his and allowed him to lead her to his car.

Oh my. He thinks this is a date. This is too much like a date. I can't do this.

She didn't want to disappoint him, so she tried her best to play the part. It had been so long since she dated that she wasn't quite sure exactly how to play that part, though. It wasn't like when she was first starting out with Robbie. They hardly went out anyway. They mostly spent time together at the track.

Finally, they made it to an Irish tavern and he parked the car, got out, and opened the door for her. She thanked him but could not smile. It was too much like a date for her taste. Kenny sensed her uneasiness and reminded her, "Jules, remember. No pressure, okay?"

Julia nodded as he led her inside and found herself fighting tears. When they sat down, she couldn't look at him for fear he would see her moist eyes. Reminding herself that she was good at controlling her emotions, she scolded herself for possibly ruining the evening for Kenny. Maybe he was the one that needed a friend. She could do that much.

But once Kenny asked, "Are you okay?" she lost all control of the tidal wave. He handed her a napkin and she hid her face as she blotted her tears.

"Oh God, I'm so sorry. I'm causing a scene," she managed to choke out as she dried her face.

"No, no, Jules. No one's looking. It's okay. Look. I know this is hard for you. If you want to go, it's okay. I just thought you might like to get out and have some fun, but if it's too much –"

"No," she interrupted. "I can do this. I can do this." Taking a deep breath, she put her napkin down and bravely faced him. He had given her an out, and she knew she could use it any time. She had options. "I can do this."

In the past, focusing on an object or two had helped in situations that made her nervous. Fortunately, the decor of the restaurant was warm, inviting, and interesting. The intricate woodwork, the dark colors, the tin ceiling, the bartender laughing with a patron were plenty to keep her occupied.

The waitress came to their table and handed them bar menus. They ordered drinks and appetizers, then sat in silence for a minute after the waitress left. Julia knew it was her fault things were so tense, so she tried to lighten the mood.

"Rachel's having a great time with Goldie. She's really a good rider. Thanks to you." Her forced smile somehow made her relax a bit and it turned into a genuine smile as he answered.

"Thanks. Yeah, she loves that pony, that's for sure."

"She's proud of her stitches, too. It didn't seem to faze her one bit that she fell. She's a tough little girl."

"Yes, she is. You think she'll be a gallop boy, I mean girl, when she grows up? Maybe by then, girls will be allowed."

"I hope so. If not, then she'll pretend she's a boy and do it anyway. Stubborn little thing." She re-centered her drink on her bar napkin. "You know, I've always wanted to gallop the horses in the morning, too. Walter won't let me, though."

"Ah. Yeah. I think he wouldn't mind if it were legal, but only men are permitted to be on the track. Then again, women aren't allowed to work on the backstretch, either." Kenny chuckled as he thought about Julia and her kids spending so much time there, despite the rules. He pictured her hanging up towels next to a sign that read, "No women or children permitted after dark." Every morning, she came in before the sun rose, and every morning she laughed at that sign. She claimed one day she would take a hatchet to that sign.

She shook her head. "That seems so ridiculous. Women have been around horses for thousands of years. What's the problem these days?"

"Not sure. Could be because thoroughbreds are a little tougher to handle? Or maybe the guys just want their own little club. You know, like one of those lodge groups. Maybe they feel threatened by women. I don't know. I don't feel that way. I don't see a problem with it. You've been doing such a great job as a groom and you have learned so much since you started working there. You're smart. I know lots of women who are smart and have a way with horses like you have."

The corners of Julia's mouth curved upwards, but only a little. It was sort of a strange compliment. "Thanks. I do love working there. I never had any experience with horses before R... Well, you know. Before I started working there."

"Really? And you've never ridden a horse besides that one time on Snaps?"

"Nope. I'd love to ride more, though. I'm so jealous of my daughter." She laughed loudly, surprising herself in the process.

"Oh, we've got to get you back up. Maybe you could take riding lessons."

"I can't afford that. I'm only a groom. I have bills, you know. I'm on my own now."

Kenny made a discouraged face. "I would love to show you, but you'd have to ride Goldie. Word got around about you riding that time and the stewards weren't too happy."

Julia frowned. "I know. I figured. Well, maybe one day. One can always hope, right?"

Kenny nodded and raised one corner of his mouth, discouraged, and not knowing what to do about it. He certainly couldn't change the minds of all the men at the track. It was even too much for some to have her working there.

After a while, the two fell into more comfortable conversation, and he made sure never to get too close or pressure her in any way. On the drive home, she wondered if he would try to kiss her, and she was worried, but her worries quickly dissolved as he kept his distance from her, even while holding the car door for her.

"Thank you for the wonderful evening, Kenny. I had fun," she stated from a safe distance.

"Any time, Jules, and I mean that. Any time you want to go out again, you know, for a drink or something, just let me know."

"Thank you." After flashing him a polite smile, she walked up to her parents' house to pick up the kids.

As Kenny drove away, she looked down the street and locked her eyes on a house a few doors down from her spot on the front porch. That house was where she had seen Robbie for the first time. A clear memory replayed in her mind - the moving truck and several men moving furniture into the house. There was a girl about her age followed by what appeared to be a younger boy. He did not matter, though. She was more excited about the girl, a possible new friend.

The next day, she and her mother had baked cookies for them and brought them over to welcome them to the neighborhood. It was then that she had gotten a good look at the brother. He was smaller, yes, but older, and gorgeous. She was hooked. His eyes! Those big, green, round, Irish eyes. She had been mesmerized and had stammered over her words.

"Hi. I'm Julia. I live downstairs," she had said. He had bent over, laughing, while her face turned fifty shades of red. "I mean, down the street," she corrected with a shake of her head. Then she wiped her wet hands down the front of her dress.

"I'm Robbie and I live upstairs," he had cracked.

Janet appeared then, coming from the kitchen with her mother. Julia saw a girl who looked to be the same age as she, and her eyes had widened with expectation.

"How old'r you, lass?" Janet's mother asked. She had a strong Irish accent and Julia could barely understand her.

After staring at the older woman for a few seconds processing the words, she finally answered. "Uh, sixteen." Her mother nudged her. "M, ma'am. I'm sixteen, ma'am." Julia glanced at her mother, then curtsied slightly.

"Janet here is sixteen, too. You'll be goin' t' school together."

Julia's face lit up, as did Janet's. Giggling in a flurry of bobby socks, saddle shoes, and circle skirts, they bounced up the stairs to Janet's room.

"I'll show you my records. Robbie has a girlfriend." Janet plopped onto her bed as she picked up a record album.

"What? What do you mean?" Julia's face tinted, and she lowered her gaze, hoping it was not obvious.

"He's taken." Janet put down the album and picked up a book from her nightstand. "Do you like 'Little Women'?"

"Um, yeah. Yes. I like that one. B—"

"Her next book was so boring."

Julia forced herself into conversation but part of her kept going back to those big green eyes greeting her at the door. She felt that queasy feeling she always got whenever she had a crush on a boy. She also felt warm all over, as if she had jumped into a warm pool. She suppressed a sigh as she relived her first exchange with him at the front door where he smiled at her. She had been embarrassed, but she'd had his attention. She wanted more.

Months went by without seeing him and it drove her batty. Every so often, she would casually ask Janet about him. "He's at the track," Janet would always say, and usually change the subject. Rarely, she would elaborate. "Papa wanted him to work at our restaurant, but he didn't want to. He's small, so he wants to be a jockey."

A jockey... Julia sighed audibly.

"He got a job there but he's grooming and hotwalking now."

"What's hotwalking? Walking a hot horse?"

"Yeah. After races or works."

Julia wanted to do that. She loved horses. She wondered if she could get a job there, too, and see him. Two birds with one stone.

"No women allowed to work there, though, sorry," Janet said, as if reading her mind.

Julia knit her eyebrows at Janet. "I wasn't going to try to get a job there."

"Uh, huh. Sure. Girls always want to go out with him." Janet rolled her eyes.

"What's that got to do with —"

"I know what you're thinking. I've done this before. It doesn't work, by the way."

"What doesn't work?"

"Going out with him."

"Why not?"

"He's too into his work and won't ever pay enough attention to you. Even if you worked there. Which you can't. He's focused on becoming a jockey."

"Why do you keep assuming I want to go out with him?" Julia stood and turned toward the window to hide her face.

"All my friends want to. It's a given. They all do. I'm tired of it. Then, when he breaks their hearts, they don't want to be friends with me anymore."

"He doesn't really have a girlfriend, does he?" Julia crossed her arms and twirled around again to judge Janet's expression.

Janet lowered her gaze. "It just won't work. Trust me." She looked up, meeting Julia's annoyed glare. "Okay?"

Julia rolled her eyes and relented, lowering her arms. "Fine." But she couldn't squelch the need for his attention again. His eyes were like a drug and she was addicted.

Holding a large wrapped present, Julia walked out of her house, down her steps, and past three houses. The fourth house was Janet's. And Robbie's. It was Janet's seventeenth birthday party, and Julia hoped Robbie would be there for it. After all, he was her brother. Wouldn't he want to be there for his sister's birthday?

As she knocked on the front door, she heard people talking and laughing inside and in the back yard. The door opened and there before her were the same big green eyes she had fallen for.

"It's the girl downstairs."

Julia laughed uncontrollably, bending over and nearly dropping her box. Robbie grabbed it before it fell. Julia stood quickly and nearly lost her balance in the process. "Sorry," she said, then covered her mouth to stifle her nervousness.

"Come on in. The party's out back."

Touching her arm and still holding the present, he helped her through the door. Julia tried desperately not to break down into another fit of giggles as she stepped inside. She was stiff and silent as he led her down the hallway toward the back of the house. She was afraid to speak and ruin this moment with him.

As they emerged into the back yard, they heard the music. "In the Mood" was playing on a record player aimed out the back window. Janet screeched and made a beeline toward Julia. "You're heeeere!"

Before Julia could answer, Janet grabbed Julia's arm and whisked her away from Robbie. Julia glanced back at Robbie as she was led away. Robbie was waving. Julia burst into another fit of giggles.

"Stop it," Janet scolded under her breath.

"What?"

"Let's dance!" Janet said as they reached a group of friends. The two held hands and broke into a swing dance.

After a few songs, Julia had spotted Robbie by the food. "I need something to eat. And I'm tired."

"I'll get you something."

"No, it's okay. I can get myself something."

"I'll go with you."

Julia relented, dropping her shoulders, and the two walked toward the food table together. Robbie was standing behind it, talking with another boy.

"Hi," Julia said casually as she picked up a plate.

Robbie hurried around to Julia's side and picked up another plate, then put a tiny sandwich on it. "I'll get it, if you like."

"No, you won't." Janet took that plate from him, spilling the sandwich onto the table. Julia picked it up.

"I insist," Robbie said with pursed lips and glaring at his sister. He picked up another plate, took the sandwich from Julia, and put it on the plate. Julia snickered, but knew she should stay quiet.

"*I* insist. She's *my* friend." Janet took the plate from Robbie, spilling the sandwich again. Julia caught it before it hit the table. Crumbs fell onto the tablecloth.

"Guys," Julia started, but Robbie interrupted.

"I feel like doing something nice for *your* friend," he said, still glaring at his sister. He picked up yet another plate and Janet took it. Julia wondered how many would be in Janet's hand by the end of this. Thankfully, they were paper plates.

"No. You don't."

"Yes. I do."

Julia held up one finger. "Um..."

Robbie picked up a plate and held it on the other side of him. "I insist." Janet ran to his other side and tried to take it from him. As they continued to fight, Julia crossed her arms and enjoyed the show. It was flattering that they were fighting over her until she looked around to find most people watching the altercation. Julia's cheeks heated, and she turned away hoping they would disappear.

Robbie held the plate in the air, but Janet was taller and snatched it from his hand. He picked up another plate from the table just as Julia tried to pick up the same plate. He didn't seem to notice that he had prevented Julia from picking it up.

At this point, he started to find the fight funny, and he jogged away with the plate and an angry Janet close behind. Finally free of the two, with one corner of her mouth raised, Julia picked up a plate and filled it with food.

Just as Julia finished picking out her food, Robbie appeared out of nowhere and snatched her plate from her hand. Julia was surprised it did not spill.

Janet ran up behind them, now in tears. "She's my friend," she growled to him under her breath.

"I can be friends with both of you. Right? Come on, guys. Don't fight over me." Julia suppressed a grin.

"Oh, please. We're not fighting over you." Janet crossed her arms and rolled her eyes.

Julia glanced at Robbie, who grinned and nodded, looking much like a mischievous little boy. "I agree with you, Julia," he said, wiggling his eyebrows.

"Ha!" Janet scoffed.

"Let's sit down," Julia suggested. She headed for a table and the two followed. Julia chose a seat with two on either side of her, assuming Janet would sit on one side and Robbie on the other. Managing who to talk to first or how to keep a conversation with the two of them at the same time crossed her mind but it was too hard to figure that out right now.

Robbie rushed to hold the chair as Julia sat, but didn't make it in time because Janet was pushing him. "Stop it," he muttered to her.

"You stop it."

Julia chuckled and took a bite of her mangled sandwich.

Robbie tried to sit next to Julia, but Janet sat down quickly before he could. He rushed to the other side of her and sat in the other chair.

Janet grabbed Julia's left arm just as Julia opened her mouth for a bite of her sandwich. "So, what about, you know, um, Jimmy? You said you had a crush on him."

Julia's stomach growled as she glared at Janet. "I did not."

"Well, he said he had a crush on you."

"That doesn't mean –"

Robbie interrupted. "When's the last day of school, Julia? What are your plans for summer?"

Julia opened her mouth, but Janet spoke for her. "We're going to help Mom decorate the house. We're going to make curtains."

Julia was confused and turned to Janet. "Huh? I didn't –"

"Mom said she needed help with the curtains." Janet gave Julia an urging glare, but Julia wanted nothing to do with whatever Janet was cooking up.

"I don't like sewing. I was thinking of getting a job at the track."

"Girls can't work at the track."

"I don't see why not," Robbie chimed in.

Julia nodded at him. "No reason why we shouldn't be able to work there. That's ridiculous that they exclude women. We're perfectly capable. Women worked during the war and did fine. We're tougher than they think."

"I think it's a safety thing," Robbie started, but then recanted. "I mean, not that women aren't safe around horses."

"Why wouldn't we be? Women have ridden horses for thousands of years."

Robbie pressed his lips together as he nodded. "You're right."

At that point, everything changed. Her life had changed forever and for the better. "Moonlight Serenade" started on the record player and Robbie, with his hypnotizing green eyes, asked Julia to dance. Ignoring Janet, they stood and walked to the middle of the yard where several couples were dancing. Julia's breath caught in her throat as Robbie slipped his hand around her waist and took her hand in his. He was slightly shorter than Julia, but she didn't care. They swayed comfortably to the music. Their eyes connected and could not let go. His silly side vanished and as she peered into his eyes, she felt as though she knew what he was thinking. She knew who he was. She knew everything about him.

He was a gentle soul, caring, and generous. He was a hard worker but wasn't a hard person. He had a soft side, as one would have to as a person who worked with horses. He could calm skittish thoroughbreds. He knew how to ride them, to get the most out of them, take care of them, to pet them and love them. She loved that about him.

No longer was she a giggling teenager with a crush. She had fallen in love.

"You could come to work with me," he said, jostling her out of her trance.

"Yes," she said, unable to say anything else.

The next day was a Sunday, so after church, Julia hurried to the subway to meet Robbie at Belmont Park. She could almost fly there, since she was still high from her dances with Robbie the night before. The two had spent the rest of the evening together, angering Janet. Unbeknownst to Julia and Robbie, Janet had burst into tears and had run to her room. When it had gotten too late and it was time to leave, Julia then realized that Janet was gone and that she hadn't opened her presents and hadn't blown out her birthday candles. Julia frowned at the beautifully decorated cake as Robbie walked her to the door. She was going to look for Janet before leaving, but Robbie offered to walk her home. Before thinking, she accepted, and they left. They held hands as they walked down the street and talked. She was afraid he might try to kiss her on her porch. Would her parents see?

When they got to her house, he held both hands, said goodbye and that he would see her tomorrow, and then kissed the back of her hand and bowed. Julia folded her bottom lip in, opened the door, and slipped inside.

She closed the door and leaned against it, sighed, then slipped to the ground to sit, as her legs could no longer hold her.

Robbie met her at Belmont Park's train station, and then they walked to the backstretch together, holding hands. Before reaching the backstretch, he reminded her that she had to look like a boy and they couldn't hold hands. She adjusted the boyish tam on her head and straightened her pants and shirt.

"Do I look like a man?"

Robbie snickered and shook his head, replying, "Maybe from a distance."

"Well, somehow I have to be able to get into the barn with you, right? You were going to show me your horses and how you groom them."

"Yes. I think it'll work. I'll sneak you in when the boss isn't looking. Everyone else will be too busy to notice. I think it'll be okay."

"I hope so. I don't want to get you in trouble."

"What's the worst that could happen? They'll tell me you have to leave, and I'll take you back to the station. They'll never fire me. The boss loves me."

"I trust you," Julia said, then blinked slowly at him.

He blinked in return, then shook his head. "You're so..."

"What?"

Robbie seemed embarrassed as he kicked a rock and took a breath. She didn't want to push him, but before she could change the subject, he continued. "Beautiful." His face tinted, as did hers.

"Thank you," she answered, then folded in her lips. "You're not so bad, yourself." She paused, and then continued. "You're...handsome."

"Are we cheesy or what? Come on," he said, taking her hand again and they hurried toward the gate. They let go as they came into sight of the guard.

Robbie showed his pass at the backstretch gate and they walked through. "Easy," Robbie whispered, but Julia hardly heard him. Her eyes widened, and she stopped in her tracks.

Julia was so used to seeing the city's buildings, cars, trains, and sparse trees, that she was instantly taken with the scene before her. It was as if she had been transported to a different world – a farm or the country, somewhere with trees, birds, bunnies, squirrels, horses, hay, and...*a goat?* Julia pointed and laughed.

"He's a mascot or a friend of one of the horses. They're all over."

"Really?"

"Yes, it helps calm them. They love goats for some reason."

Eventually they made it to barn eighteen. Robbie explained that William Hanover owned every horse in this barn. He also owned a large breeding farm in upstate New York and spent his time divided between the track and the farm. Robbie pointed toward the middle-aged man marching by outside as they stood inside the barn. "That's him."

"Is he rich?"

"Most definitely. You've got to have tons of money to finance a barn like this *and* a farm. He's friends with Mr. Vanderbilt himself, who just got back from the war. He says he worked Man O' War once, but no one can confirm or deny it. Chances are, if it happened, he was dumped and not invited back. That horse dumped everybody. Wouldn't have dumped me, though. I know how to stay on."

"How do you stay on?"

"Hold on for dear life."

He led her to a stall and taught her how to groom a horse. Julia was hooked, and the rest was history. Every day after school, every day during summer, Julia met Robbie at the station and walked with him into her favorite world, the backstretch. She hadn't had much time for Janet, and she tried to explain that she was in love, but Janet wanted no part of it. They hardly talked in school and never talked after school anymore. Julia was sad she had lost her friend but working with Robbie more than made up for it.

When Robbie mustered up the strength to ask if Julia could be paid, the head trainer sighed and relented, taking her on as a groom.

Robbie moved up in the ranks quickly from groom to exercise rider. Once Robbie and Julia were married, the head trainer encouraged Robbie to get his jockey's license. He did so and was successful. For a few short years, anyway.

The race. That awful race. It would be forever burned into her brain. Julia had stood at the rail at the quarter pole at Belmont with their babies, Rachel and Billy in a pram in front of her. Rachel was three and standing next to her brother. Her jumping disturbed the sleeping baby and Julia tried to get her to stop jumping as the horses approached.

"Mommy, which one is Daddy?" Julia heard, but she couldn't reply. Terror replaced everything in her world as they watched three horses fall right in front of them. The other horses raced toward the finish line, but Julia never saw them. Quickly, she scanned the jockeys on the ground, looking for the silks of the owner for whom he had been riding. Two jockeys stood. One did not. It was Robbie. He wasn't moving. Screaming and leaving her babies on the rail, Julia raced toward the gate and past a guard. She stumbled in her heels on the sandy loam but hardly noticed. Her eyes remained focused on her husband, who was still not moving.

Someone stopped her, but she fought him off and fell to her knees next to Robbie. His head was cocked at an angle. "No. No. No. No." Julia hoped that if she said it enough times, it wouldn't be true. She screamed it, but it didn't help. He was still on the ground, unmoving. She buried her head into his lifeless chest, sobbing and repeating, "No. No."

After the funeral, Robbie's parents disappeared without a trace, without a word. Julia only had her parents now, but she was grateful for that much. They had been so helpful. While it was hard to explain to Rachel why she couldn't see her other grandparents anymore, Julia found it to be somewhat of a relief, as it was another reminder that had gone away. In a way, she understood why the McMahons had run from New York.

✿✿✿

"I hope you don't mind. I went for a drink with Kenny. You remember Kenny?"

"Of course, I don't mind, Jules. You should get out and have fun once in a while."

"But I'm not going to go on dates."

"Why not?"

"Not ready. I can't imagine being with someone else." Her heart suddenly caught fire as her eyes welled up, but she managed to stop before it became uncontrollable.

"You can't spend the rest of your life alone, Jules."

Julia folded in her lips, holding it in, desperate not to let that huge tear fall from her eye. When she blinked, it finally dropped. "I'm just not ready. I'll never be ready."

"Yes, you will. I know you will. I don't want you to be alone."

Now she knew it was her imagination. She longed for a companion again but couldn't bring herself to do it. She wasn't ready, like she had said. She knew she had to be making this up in her head to justify her wants. Robbie certainly wouldn't want her to be with someone else. Not that she could do it, anyway. "I'm not ready," she repeated.

"I understand, my love."

That was why she couldn't do it. She was still his love.

CHAPTER THREE

As time crawled by, Julia talked with Robbie about life, the kids, her job. Robbie always encouraged her to try for more. She could move up in the horse racing business. She could exercise horses, perhaps, or become a trainer. Robbie convinced her that just because there were no women trainers, it didn't mean that it would never happen. Julia didn't care about training. She wanted to ride.

Julia had hopped onto Snaps' back several times without permission, and they finally allowed her to walk around the backside to practice. Her fellow Hanover Team members never allowed her on the track, though, so she could not move any faster than a walk unless she was in a small grassy area where she could trot briefly. Since she knew she would not get the opportunity to run free anytime soon, she watched other riders and imagined herself on their horses. The wind in her hair, the horse's mane whipping her face, even the stinging dirt on her smooth skin, were all things she felt from her spot on the rail.

"'Scuse me. Miss?" A man's voice jarred her back into reality.

"Yes?"

"It is...miss, right?"

"Yes, sir." To be polite, she held in the urge to chuckle. She had spent so much time trying to fit in with the guys that she started to look like one of them. She never wore make-up and always had her hair up or tied back. She wore pants that were too big, huge shirts to hide her figure, and of course, no jewelry.

"Sorry," he answered as he touched the brim of his hat. "I'm amazed. I did not think women were allowed to work on the backstretch."

While ordinarily she would have taken offense to his words, she could tell he was not from this area. She'd never seen him before and he had a distinct Kentucky accent. He was a southern gentleman and was merely curious. "Well, this is Belmont Park. We're trend setting."

"Golly. Do you ride the horses, too?"

"Oh, yes. Of course." Well, that was sort of true.

"Really? That's amazing. I haven't read about this. How long you been riding?"

"Couple of years." She was beginning to feel as though she was digging herself deeper and deeper into something.

"Kind of like National Velvet, huh?"

"Pretty much." Julia had always wanted to see that movie but had never had a chance.

"Interesting riding clothes, though."

"Oh. I'm not riding today. I'm here for my horse, to take him back."

"Why don't you come by barn twenty-four tomorrow, hop up on one of mine?"

"Really?"

"Sure. Might as well. You can handle 'em, can't you?"

"Of course." Did he mean to work a horse? Galloping? On the track?

"Great! This will be a gas. See you then."

Dazed and confused, she stood perfectly still as he walked away. She hoped he didn't mean what she thought he meant. On the other hand, it would be fun. What would Robbie say about this?

Grateful that the kids were in school, she tried to work everything out, so she could steal away and visit barn twenty-four the next morning. She did her best to have her horse ready to go, and then asked a hotwalker to meet up with the horse after his workout. Wordlessly, she tip-toed away as the sun peeked over the grandstand.

Thick wisps of vapor appeared and disappeared in front of her face as she walked, reminding her that she was breathing too fast. *What am I getting myself into here?* Wrapping her arms around herself, she suppressed a full body chill that wasn't entirely due to the cold. Well, she would have to tell him that she could ride but wasn't an exercise rider. If the stewards caught her out there without permission, she would be fired for sure.

However, if she could hide in her large clothes, she would finally get the chance to be on a horse running full speed down the track. The thought of the wind and the horse's mane in her face, feeling the strength beneath her as her horse ran free, took over all reasoning in her mind. This could be her chance. She would only ride once and then tell him that she wasn't able to ride anymore. If she had to lie and tell him she was booked solid and was unable to take on any more horses, she would do it. She had to. It was dangerous, above all else. *Just once*, she told herself. *Just once. I have to try it once. Robbie encourages me to be courageous, break out, do new things, and rise up in the hierarchy of this place. I want to see what I can do. Let's give it a shot. I'll hide my face behind goggles and a helmet. No one will know.*

"Hey, it's my new exercise rider. I never caught your name." The older gentleman she had met the day before stood next to a younger one who was obviously stunned. The younger man's eyes drifted up and down as he tried to figure out if Julia was male or female. Julia might have laughed but was too scared.

"Call me Jules." She kept her voice soft and low.

"Oh, like Jules Verne." The younger man relaxed. A man's name. Just what he wanted.

Julia diverted her gaze to the horse two stalls down who was cribbing, chewing on the wood of his stall door. It was a nervous habit for a horse, like biting one's fingernails, something Julia was now fighting the urge to do.

The older man stuck out his hand. "Oscar. Oscar Hilton. This is my assistant, Benny." They shook hands, and Julia was glad for once for her calluses. She gripped his hand as hard as she could. "Where's your tack?"

"I was hoping to borrow yours. I can't afford –"

"Say no more," Oscar interrupted with his hand. "I remember how that was. No problem. Benny, go get a helmet and saddle, will ya?"

"Sure." Benny left as Oscar led Julia toward a dark bay horse. First, she looked him over, then felt his legs for heat, checked his hooves, then patted his neck and rubbed his ears. Gently keeping her face close to the horse's nose, she breathed out, allowing the horse to take in her scent. The bay lowered his head slightly.

"This is Dusty Road. He's here for the big race next week. The Hayfield Stakes." Oscar patted the horse's shoulder as Julia continued to stay at the horse's head.

"We're going for a little run today," Julia told him.

"Actually, keep him under wraps. Just want a slow gallop today. Nothing under, say, fifty-two if you can help it." His time suggestion led her to believe that he wanted the horse to run a half-mile.

"Okay." She knew she had to warm up the horse first but wasn't sure how long he wanted for the warm up. She had seen horses on the track warming up for varying amounts of time. She wondered if trainers gave exercise riders instructions for the warm up as well, but Oscar wasn't giving. Not yet, anyway.

Benny marched up with the tack. He shoved the helmet into Julia's chest, then went right to the horse's side and worked with Oscar to saddle him. Julia slipped the helmet over her head and wondered where the goggles were. Then she remembered that no one wore goggles in the mornings. Some didn't even wear helmets. How was she going to keep her face hidden?

It seemed that only seconds later, they were reaching for her leg. When she had ridden Snaps, they had given her a mounting block. *Oh, Lord.* Her face flushed. Before she could remember what she had seen other riders do, she had moved to the left side and gathered the reins in her hand. She lifted her leg. Oscar bent down and held her leg but didn't lift. He froze in place.

Oh, oh. What do I do? Oh. I have to hop. Julia hopped on one foot a couple of times, then jumped as high as she could while Oscar helped lift her onto the back of the bay. Her emotions swung wildly from elation to panic, back and forth. She was so excited to be on a real racehorse, perched above everyone, ready to soar. *What if I fall?* His muscles rippled under his shiny coat and she could feel the strength of her steed between her legs and she marveled, almost in awe, of his sinew. *What if I can't control him?*

Before she knew it, and before she could get her feet in the stirrups, they were leading her out of the stall. She ducked quickly to make sure she didn't hit the top of the door. Still keeping her head low, she suppressed a nervous smile and snicker. It had almost escaped.

Her feet hung lazily at the horse's side, and she wondered about the length of the stirrups. How could she adjust them if they were walking? As they walked, Oscar handed them off to another man and left her side. Benny walked in another direction, leaving her to her own devices. She had no idea what to do. And no clue as to how long her stirrups should be.

She knew she would be allowed to have long stirrups, not short like the jockeys or more experienced riders. Some riders opted for the longer length, and she opted for the same. She slipped her toes into the irons and lifted herself off the saddle. It creaked as her weight shifted forward a bit and Dusty Road lifted his head and dropped it several times. She sat back down as she realized she had been leaning heavily on his neck.

Then, without a word, they were at the gap and the man let go of the bridle. Julia quickly took up the reins before the horse could bolt. She was glad he didn't take off since she hadn't been ready. With a clucking of her tongue, they began cantering the wrong way, on purpose, as that's the direction horses ran to warm up, down the track toward the grandstand to the left. She wasn't ready for the cantering, either, as she had never been faster than a trot before. Despite that, it was exhilarating! She leaned forward and desperately wanted to go faster. She couldn't wait until she turned him around for his work.

She was fortunate he wasn't a tough horse to handle. He wasn't fighting her at all. She knew if she had been on another horse, it might not have been the same. Out of the corner of her eye, she saw horses speeding past her on her right, but also people in the stands on her left. They were so close. She knew they could see her face. The wind had blown into her shirt, puffing it, and leaving the neck open enough so that she could sink her chin down into it. Then she squinted, hoping people could not see her eyes clearly. *Next time, I'm getting goggles. Wait. Next time? No. I told myself this was it. I don't want it to be it. Wait a minute. Where am I? Where's the pole? Half pole, right?* As she came to the outside of the wide turn, she looked toward the inner rail and found it clear. She looked for other horses on their way, but no one was there. She guided her horse toward the inner rail, turned him, then clucked again as she gave him more rein.

He took off like a bullet, scaring her. This wasn't cantering. This was a full out gallop and he was flying. The wind nearly took her breath away. She couldn't believe how fast he ran. Did all horses run this fast? *Oh! A slow gallop.* Pulling on the reins, she tried talking to him, but he didn't slow at all. She wrapped the reins around her wrists, pulling even harder. It felt like he had the bit between his teeth. Finally, he relented and slowed. When she tried to relax her tiring arms, he moved faster, eager for the tiniest hint of a cue. And the time? She had no idea what the time was.

Mentally slapping herself for not counting, she tried to judge their speed. It was impossible to tell, as she had never been this fast before on a horse. As she saw the finish line fast approaching, she could only hope this was the speed Oscar had asked for.

"Easy. Easy," she murmured. "Shh." Her arms were exhausted and felt like they would be pulled from their sockets any moment. "Whoa. Please?" He was slowing, but it was very gradual. It wasn't until the middle of the clubhouse turn that he finally reached a canter again. At the end of the turn, he was trotting. Julia strongly resisted screaming in pain from her burning arms, and at the same time resisted laughing from sheer joy. She turned him as another horse sprinted by along the rail. Finally, she got him to stop, and she rested her arms with an almost silent whimper. "Walk." She lowered her voice to a whisper. "Please walk." She didn't expect him to listen and follow directions this way, but he began walking. Taking a breath and holding it for a few seconds, she quelled her emotions. She couldn't believe what she had just done, though unethical, illegal, and dangerous. It was all worth it, though. She wanted to do this every day.

"Good job, Jules." Oscar approached, then took hold of his horse's bridle. They started for the barn and a groom jogged up and took the horse from the trainer.

"Thanks. Thanks," Julia said as she huffed to catch her breath.

UUU

It took Julia a long time to fall asleep that night as she looked forward to telling Robbie all about her day. It bothered her that she was not going to get enough sleep and was going to be exhausted tomorrow, but, if she could only talk to Robbie, it would make it all worth it. The last time she looked at the clock, it was midnight, and she grunted, frustrated with herself for getting so worked up.

She had to get some sleep because in the morning, she would be riding Dusty again. Oscar had been so impressed that he asked her to come back the next morning, too. Julia tried, but was unable to tell him the truth, that she wasn't an exercise boy. She wasn't licensed to be on that track. If something happened or if someone recognized her, it could be the end of her career. If she were too tired to handle the horse in the morning, surely, it would not go as well as it had gone today. Anything could happen. The horse could dump her from the saddle, run off with her, run into another horse, anything.

She had to sleep, but the added pressure on herself only made it harder. It took another half hour before she finally dozed off.

"Jules, why did you do that? Do you have any idea how risky that was?"

"Yes," she answered with her head lowered in shame. It was too much fun. It was too exhilarating. It was wonderful, beautiful, joyful. She had been truly happy while guiding her horse in his workout, something she hadn't felt for a long time – sheer joy.

Robbie let out a breath of air as he gave in. "Well, I did tell you to try and move up in the world."

Julia held in a snicker.

"You're working him tomorrow, too?"

Julia nodded. "I think it will be fine. It will be another slow work. I guess my sore shoulders won't like it, but I will. I can't wait to ride him again."

"You could get caught."

"I'll try hard to hide my face. I'll wear goggles tomorrow."

"That will only draw more attention to you because you'll be the only one with them."

"You're right. Okay. No goggles, then. Oh, Robbie, I love riding. I can see now why you loved your job so much."

"I certainly did, but now, I am to become your teacher. There are a few things we need to fix such as your stirrup length, your toes, heels, and your posture. You're back too far and your stirrups are too long."

Robbie went on with his lesson, and Julia wished he could be with her while on Dusty's back, telling her what to do. She tried her hardest to remember everything, though, so she would look better and be a better rider. Her horse deserved it.

ⵣⵣⵣ

Ten days later, she was still juggling her grooming job with exercising Dusty Road. She hadn't worked up the nerve to tell Oscar she wasn't a real exercise boy. Each day, she had hidden her face in her jacket as she rode by the stands, and no one had recognized her. She couldn't believe she pulled it off.

"Nice lookin' horse you got there," Walter said as Dusty flew by for his last workout before the race.

"Thanks," Oscar answered. "He's gonna win on Saturday."

"Looks like it. He's a strong one."

"Yup."

"Who's that up on him? I don't recognize him." Walter squinted toward the horse as he passed the finish line.

"Jules something. Never got her last name."

"Jules?"

"Yeah."

"As in, Julia?"

"Well, I don't know. Might be. It is a woman, though."

Walter dropped his jaw and laughed, but he couldn't speak.

"Yeah. A woman. She's doing great, too. Don't you think? She doesn't get many morning gallops, though. I've only seen her work Dusty here."

Walter couldn't close his mouth and another laugh escaped.

"What?"

Finally, Walter was able to gain control of his mouth and closed it. Then he shook his head. "She...um...." He really wanted to tell Oscar she was his groom, but at the same time, he didn't want to spoil things for her. He somehow managed to maintain control. "She's the first female exercise rider at Belmont."

"That she is."

Suppressing more chuckles, Walter went back to his barn.

When he saw Julia again, working as if nothing had happened this morning, Walter approached her. He wondered how long she had been moonlighting on him.

"Hi there," Julia greeted as she pulled hair from a horse brush.

"So, uh," Walter rocked back on his feet and clasped his hands behind his back. Julia stopped and narrowed her eyes at his strange posture. "Uh," he laughed, then stopped himself as he swiped his hand over his mouth, desperately trying to wipe away his grin. "Are you riding Dusty in the race on Saturday?"

Julia's hazel eyes were as big as saucers, her face whiter than the bandages flapping in the breeze behind her on the clothesline. Walter let out a booming laugh. When she said nothing, Walter continued as he put one hand on her slight shoulder, shaking her from the force. "Look. I don't know how you talked him into it, but you did good."

"Thanks." Julia's expression never changed.

"Yeah, he was impressed."

Julia groaned. "You didn't tell him, did you?"

"Nope. Secret's safe with me."

Julia covered her now reddened cheeks with her hands. "Oh, my goodness."

Walter walked away, laughing again.

CHAPTER FOUR

Julia went to the grandstand, avoiding the area where she had stood just a few years ago and watched her husband die right before her eyes. If she couldn't avoid being at Belmont Park, at least she could avoid that spot on the rail. Fortunately, while riding Dusty in his works, she hadn't had the frame of mind to consider where that spot was when his horse went down, just past the quarter pole. After each work, she had jumped down, gotten her mind back together so she could rush back to Walter's barn, and hadn't had the chance to think about it until she was in the stall, alone, quiet, with her horse. Later, on the first day, she realized she had run right over that spot. On the second day, again, she hadn't realized it until after coming back to the barn. And on each day after that, it was much the same reaction, which greatly surprised her.

But here on the rail, waiting for Dusty's race, she got a good look at the track. Images from that hellish day flashed before her eyes. Rachel and she were jumping and screaming for Daddy. Earl Grey was flying around the outside, had rushed past a pack of horses, skirted to the left and next to another horse, whose rider promptly whipped Earl Grey's nose. The skittish two-year-old panicked and slowed heavily, causing a tremendous pile up of himself, two other horses, and three jockeys. All three horses had broken legs and were put down. Julia had heard the gun shots as she knelt near her husband's prone body, his head twisted in a sickening position, scaring her more than she had ever been scared in her life. She will never get that picture out of her mind, she knew. It was an image she could conjure up at will, or sometimes it appeared without warning. Each time, it broke her heart all over again. That was the end of her perfect marriage and her perfect family.

Of course, she was grateful for her children, even though looking at Rachel was often like looking at a miniature Robbie – the same curly brown hair, big green eyes, and freckles. If Rachel had short hair, she could have been him. Nevertheless, Julia thought, at least she had part of Robbie with her. And he still talked to her...or was that her imagination? Either way, she was grateful for the chance to speak to him from time to time. She had even seen him a few times.

Each time, he was still wearing the silks he wore in that race. She was glad those silks were not at Belmont anymore. The owner and trainer were both so upset about Robbie's and Earl Grey's deaths, that they packed up and moved their horses to Maryland, never to return to Belmont or Aqueduct again. But that was fine with her. It would have been another reminder, which she didn't need. She had way too many already.

Whatever doesn't kill you makes you stronger, she told herself.

It was almost post time. Dusty, ridden by an out-of-town rider from Pimlico, strode to the gate in the post parade. Julia was proud that the horse she had ridden almost every morning for two weeks looked confident and was well-behaved. She was fortunate that her first horse *(first horse?)* wasn't a handful and hadn't fought her much at all. He was easy to rate, as Oscar had said, and Julia agreed, though she had nothing to compare him to other than Snaps.

Coming out of the gate, Dusty bounced right to the front and took the lead. Dusty's rider had a good hold on him, Julia could tell. She practiced counting the time and comparing with the tote board as they flew around the track. She wished she were riding him in this race so badly that she could almost feel the sand and wind in her face. If only women were allowed to become jockeys.

A few women were unofficial jockeys but were not allowed to race in races where bets were placed. These women would race once or twice a year in gimmicky races like the Pimlico Classic, only to draw a crowd. They didn't race at all in New York. Julia did not think they would ever allow a female to race in New York.

As she dismissed her own chances to become a jockey, she wondered about Rachel and her chances in the future. In New York, no, but maybe in Maryland or Kentucky. Maybe Rachel would have to move to another state once she grew up. Though, as she thought about it, Julia did not want Rachel to become a jockey. It was way too dangerous, and besides, that's what took Robbie from her. She couldn't lose Rachel in the same way. It would kill her.

Soon, Dusty was leading the way around the far turn and thundering down the homestretch toward her. "Come on, buddy," she screamed, hoping he could hear her voice over the crowd. His jockey was riding hard now, pumping his arms, using his whip, and Dusty was giving it his all. His huge strides swallowed up the distance to the wire, and Julia was awestruck by his beauty. The announcer's voice rose and caught Julia's attention. As they neared the finish, the others were catching up to him! Julia grabbed her head with both hands as she feared he would lose at the last second, but, he was able to hold off the closest horse by a nose.

Julia dropped her head to the rail for a second with relief. Then she looked up to find Oscar waving at her, asking her to come to the winner's circle. *Oh no! I look dreadful.* She was wearing overalls, of all things. She felt like an old farmer from Wisconsin. Reluctantly, she made her way to meet them in the winner's circle and did her best to stay behind several jovial and excited men lined up next to the horse. Her eyes peeked over the shoulders of two men as the photographer snapped the photo.

Blinded temporarily by the flash, even in daylight, she blinked a few times and tried to slip away unseen. Oscar caught her. "Jules! Hey, Marty! Come meet Jules, Dusty's exercise boy."

Julia closed her eyes with dread for a second, wishing she could melt into the sand. Oscar introduced her to Marty, who eyed her strangely, and she knew why. He couldn't figure out if she was male or female. The thought amused her, and she nearly laughed, but stayed in control. Finally, Julia said goodbye to Oscar and to Dusty, knowing they would be shipping out in a few hours. She wondered if word would spread about her. A girl riding a horse on a race track? *Unheard of! No one would believe him*, she thought, and giggled   as   she   reached   her   barn.

CHAPTER FIVE

"Jules," Kenny started carefully and softly. The way he hid his face worried Julia. They had gone out, though just as friends, several times in the past two years. It wasn't much. He had asked many more times, and she had turned him down most of the time. Occasionally, she had given in and gone out with him simply to pacify him. It was so difficult with him, as it always felt like a date. She didn't want to date. She still had Robbie.

"Yes?" She continued to face her horse as she brushed him, avoiding Kenny's eyes.

It was silent for several seconds, and when he did not answer, she stopped brushing and looked at him.

"Let's get some dinner out tonight. What do ya say?"

Julia could see uncertainty in his eyes. Something was different about this time. "Everything okay?" she asked, pushing for more time.

"Yeah. Definitely. For sure. Everything's fine."

Julia waited, hoping for a clue, but he wasn't giving. "Okay," she heard herself say. She chalked up her feelings to curiosity and knew this was the only way she was going to find out what was on his mind.

He picked her up in their usual spot at the barn's entrance. With a polite smile, he offered his arm, which she hesitantly took, and they went to his car.

"Where are we going?" Julia asked as they maneuvered around the city in his large, black Chevy sedan.

"How's Italian?"

Julia hoped it wasn't Robbie's parents' old restaurant. She bit her lip as she wondered if she should mention it. There was no way she was going to set foot in that restaurant ever again.

"You don't like Italian?"

"Oh, it's okay. I just don't want to go to, um, this certain...place."

"Which one?"

"Used to be called La Traviata, but I don't know what it's called now."

"No, that's not where I had planned on going. I'll make sure I keep that in mind next time, though. I'll make sure we never go there. What happened? Bad food?"

Julia pressed her lips together. "No. Well...bad...memories, I guess."

Kenny knit his eyebrows for a split second as he turned his head toward her, but she wouldn't meet his gaze. She was peering out the side window, remembering her visits there with Robbie for free meals, since his family owned the restaurant.

They were silent for the rest of their ride, which wasn't long.

They forced small talk until they ordered and were waiting for their food. Once the waiter left them, Kenny gave her a weak smile and took a breath.

"Is everything okay?" Julia asked.

"Oh, yeah. Everything's great."

"You seem nervous about something."

Kenny chuckled. "You know me, I guess. Can't get anything by you."

"No." Julia straightened the napkin on her lap.

"Jules." He scooted his chair closer to the table and leaned in. "It's been three years."

Three years... She knew exactly what he was talking about. She knew exactly how long it had been. *Three years, four months, one week. And a day.* "Yes."

"I think it's time you moved on. You can't be alone for the rest of your life. You have two children and you need someone to help provide for them, someone to help you pay the bills, give you and the kids a comfortable life. You shouldn't have to work. You should be home with the kids."

And who do you think you are telling me what I should and shouldn't do? Her jaw dropped slightly, but she was too stunned to speak.

He must have seen the smoldering ember in her eyes and backpedaled. He held up one hand. "I mean, it's up to you. You can work if you want. I know you love your job. I'm not trying to dictate your life, Jules. I know you're an independent woman. That's one of the things I l...like so much about you. You're strong. You can take care of yourself. You just don't deserve the hard work. You deserve to do what you want."

"What if I want to be a groom? What if I want to work hard? What if I love my job enough that it doesn't matter how much money I make?"

"That's fine wi–"

"Wait a minute. What are you saying? Why are you telling me this?" She tried her hardest to maintain her manners and not let her anger show. No matter what her career path, hard work or not, her mother raised her to be a lady.

Kenny pressed his lips together for a few seconds, then took her hand. "Julia, will you –"

"No." She interrupted him as quickly as she could and ripped her hand from his.

Kenny froze with his jaw dropped.

Julia's breaths were coming quickly now, as she hated to hurt him, hated to risk their friendship, hated to do any of this in public. She glanced around the room, but thankfully, no one was watching. When he did not speak, she decided to fill the void of silence. "Kenny, I appreciate your concern. I know you're just trying to help, but I don't want a marriage of convenience. I can do fine on my own. Besides, I have my parents and they help me from time to time, as does Mr. Hanover. He's like a second father to me. I don't need a husband to help pay the bills or any of that. I'm sorry. I hope you understand."

"I um, actually, I hadn't totally thought of it as a convenience thing. I kinda thought..."

Julia covered her gaping mouth. "I'm sorry. Kenny, I'm so sorry."

Kenny sat back in his chair and looked away. "Hey, it's okay. I guess that's how you feel about me. I took a chance, right? Just didn't pay off, that's all."

He looked so hurt that she felt his pain inside her heart. "You know I'm not over losing him yet, Kenny. I'm still struggling. I'm not even ready to date, let alone get married again."

"How could you not be over him? It's been *three years*."

"I don't know. I just can't do it. I can't imagine being with someone else. It would hurt and only remind me of what I used to have." Her voice shook now as she fought to retain control. "He was..." Her emotions choked her. It took her several seconds to regain enough control to speak again. "He was everything to me. We were so in love. We were soul mates. I'll never find that again. I'm still in love with him and will never stop loving him. I can't let myself stop loving him. I couldn't do that to him."

"He's not here, though. He doesn't know."

"Yes, he does. He is here."

Kenny's eyes bugged.

"I'm not crazy. Don't look at me like that. You know when people die, they go to Heaven. They can still watch over us."

"He would want you to be happy. He would never want you to be alone for the rest of your life. I'm sure of it. No man would want that for his wife. If you were in love as strongly as you say, he would love you enough to let you go and let you live your life."

Robbie *had* told her it was okay to date again. Still, she wasn't sure about it. She wasn't sure whether it was his voice or hers conjuring up his voice telling her what she wanted to hear. Julia looked into Kenny's desperate eyes. "You're probably right about that, Kenny. But I'm still not ready."

Defeated, Kenny lowered his head and nodded.

"I'm sorry. I hope you're not upset with me. We still have to work together, you know." Julia tried to smile, but he faced the floor and did not see.

Kenny nodded with almost an indiscernible movement. "I'm going to leave town."

It was dead silent between them. Finally, Julia managed to speak. "What? Why?"

"You still don't see it, Jules? Don't you see?"

"See what?" Julia had her hands out with desperation, her eyebrows knit, and she shook her head.

"I suppose I could wait."

"Don't see what, Kenny? What are you talking about?"

He met her eyes and took a breath. "I'm in love with you, Jules."

Julia froze. Her heart nearly stopped. Her stomach twisted in knots. She almost vomited.

He could tell. "No. It's easier this way. I'm going to have to leave. That's all. Find a new track, new boss –"

"Kenny, no. Wait. You don't have to leave. That's a little drastic, don't you think? Giving up a good job? Potentially a chance at the head trainer position some day?"

"I've made up my mind. I can't stick around knowing you'll never feel the same way and having you know how I feel. It wouldn't be right."

"No, Kenny. I can't let that happen. Please, stay. It's for the best." She placed her hand on his arm against her better judgment.

He looked at her hand, which she withdrew, and took a breath. "No. Leaving is for the best. We can finish dinner if you like. But I can't stay in the barn."

"I'm so sorry." Julia's words came out in whispers.

ひひひ

True to his word, he was gone by morning. Julia couldn't help the pain in her heart and she fought tears all day. She felt awful for breaking his heart, but she also wondered if she had just thrown away her chance at a comfortable life, buying things like new clothes for the kids, a dishwasher, garbage disposal, maybe a new washing machine. What was more important, though? Happiness? Or things? Intrinsic happiness, for sure. But wouldn't she be happier if she had more things? Better things? If she wouldn't have to worry about her grocery store budget every week, being forced to choose between eggs and chicken? What would be best for the kids? Certainly, having Mommy at home, raising the children herself would be better. Julia felt awful that she rarely had the opportunity to see Billy anymore. She couldn't wait for him to be old enough to come to the track with Rachel. She wouldn't have to wait, though, if she had a husband again. Maybe it would make him happier to be with her and make her happier to be able to spend more time with the kids. It would work out well for both.

Regardless, he was gone, now, and did not leave a forwarding address. She blew it. She blew her chance at a comfortable life again.

ᏅᏅᏅ

"Robbie, please," she begged that night. "Please, I have to talk to you. I have to. Please be here for me. You said you would be here for me."

"I'm here, Jules."

"Robbie, did I ruin my chances? Was I supposed to say yes? I couldn't, though. I couldn't do that to you. I wasn't in love with him."

"You made the right decision, Jules, because you decided to wait for something better. You shouldn't settle for less than perfect."

Her tears dried up immediately. "You're right. I would have been miserable. Though, he would have provided for the children."

"You're providing for the children, Jules. You're doing just fine. And just think. There's an assistant trainer job open now."

ᏅᏅᏅ

"I'd like to apply for the open position for assistant trainer, Walter."

Walter narrowed his eyes and wrinkled his nose at her. "What?" He almost laughed but caught it in time.

"I'd like to apply for the open position for assistant trainer."

"You're serious." It was more a statement than question.

"Perfectly serious." Julia stood next to Walter's desk, wearing wide pants and a matching jacket over a white blouse. She had curled her hair and pinned it back in a professional 'do. Just a hint of mascara and lipstick decorated her thin and angled face. She didn't want to overdo it. She looked professional but casual enough to portray a hands-on trainer, which is what she would want to be if she were a trainer.

"They'd never approve the license."

"I've thought about that. Give me a man's name. I could practice under that, like a pen name. They would only look at the application, not at me. They won't know it's me."

"Until a race and you're standing next to the horse in a...a...suit," he said, waving his hand toward her clothes.

She thought for a few seconds. "I could wear my regular work clothes until they find out it's me. Eventually, they will, but until then I want the chance to prove myself. They'll see I'm a hard worker, I know horses, and I could practically run this barn."

"The other workers would never listen to you."

"I think they would, especially if you told them to. If they didn't, there would be consequences."

"What kind of consequences?"

"Docking pay. Perhaps fines. Suspensions. Firing."

"You could never fire one of them."

"If I had to, I could. I'm sure it would ultimately be your decision, though."

Walter shook his head as he considered her words. "I don't know about this, Jules. The stewards could find out and suspend *me*."

"They don't have to find out."

"Isn't that a bit unethical? I could refuse to hire you just for that alone."

"Walter, you seem to forget how much I've seen. The drugs? Milkshakes? The buzzers? Running horses that should not run?"

"You disagree with my methods? How do you expect to make any money for the Hanovers? For yourself? You can't pay salaries unless you win races, Julia."

"I know. I would never question your methods. I understand that some of it needs to be done." However, on the inside, she had big plans for this barn, which included honesty and doing things in the best interest of the horses. She knew they could win more money with healthier horses, not horses that were on their last leg. However, that was for later, much later. First, she had to get in. "I would follow your rules without question, just as I have always done. I've been affiliated with this barn for eight years now, Walter. You know I could do it. You're only afraid to try because I'm a woman."

"You haven't let that stop you yet," he muttered, leaning back in his chair, making it squeak under his weight.

"No, I haven't. I'm the kind of person who takes initiative. I am organized, dare I say, as a modern woman should be. If I had to be a housewife, I would be the most organized and best housewife I could possibly be. Here, as a groom, I've been the best I can be, and my reputation has been spotless over the years. As a secret exercise rider, I was good, especially for only holding that position two weeks. As a secret trainer, I will be even better."

"It's not just about training."

"I know. I know what Kenny did. He took care of the bookkeeping, paying the employees, making sure everybody was doing what they were supposed to be doing. He ran the workouts and races when you were out of town, too. I have been there for works and races. I know exactly what to do before and after a race. Just how many times have I been in the winner's circle with my horses? Hundreds of times? I promise you, every single time, I was watching everything, learning everything I could."

"You've been pushing for his position for years, I take it?"

Julia shrugged. "I had always hoped for a chance, but to be honest, I never thought I would actually get that chance. And no, I did not push Kenny to leave. He left of his own accord."

"I know why he left." Walter softened and rubbed his forehead.

Julia gulped slightly. "I couldn't marry someone I wasn't in love with. I couldn't do it. I did not want to settle."

Walter met her eyes again, impressed with her determination for perfection. And her work ethic was undeniably the strongest at the track, aside from his own.

"Jules, if it were completely up to me, I would take you on. I'm worried about losing my license, though, getting myself kicked off the track, fined, whatever. What would Hanover say, anyway?"

"I could ask him. We're very close."

Walter knew Hanover would side with Julia. He was highly tempted to try this. But the stewards. What would they say? He relented with a sigh. "I'll think about, okay? I promise, I will think about it. I have to consider all sides of this. The risks."

Julia stepped forward. "And the rewards. Walter, we could be the best team at Belmont Park. I know it. I know we could do it."

The sparkle in her eyes was addicting and began to hypnotize him. He had to resist her charms. Pressing his lips together, he stared at the ground in thought.

Julia thought she saw a slight nod, and her heart soared with hope. Nevertheless, she resisted showing her emotion. Now she would have to be especially careful not to let the men know she was anything but tough and resilient.

Julia watched as several men came and went for interviews over the next few days. Her competition was stiff, and as time dragged on, she doubted more and more that she would get the job. Trying to prove herself, she had been taking on more responsibilities, helping fill the shoes Kenny had left behind.

"I got it, Walter," she told him, taking the books from his arms. He was holding them and shouting orders at the same time. One thing after another had distracted him, and he hadn't been able to take care of the paychecks for the day. With a grunt, Walter relented and gladly let Julia take the books. She took them into the office and closed the door.

It took three hours to write out each check for the staff, after having to find tax information, who had what taken out of their checks, who had nothing taken out of their checks, and, of course, their wages. She wished she could have given all the grooms a raise, and she smirked as she thought about how happy they would be. But no, she had to be right on and accurate, down to the penny.

She opened the door to the office at five to find a group of sweat- and dirt-covered men standing there, waiting. "Hello, boys," she called. They stared at her oddly, some grunting in reply. One by one, she handed out the checks, each one in an envelope with their name on it. Finally, Julia found one check left in her hand. The envelope had Walter's name on it. He approached cautiously, a hesitant aura about him. Julia tried to smile to set his mind at ease but wobbled with doubt. "I took care of it, Walter."

He knit his eyebrows. "Payroll?"

Julia nodded and lifted her chin. "Want to double check the books?" She handed him his paycheck.

Walter sighed and shook his head, then went into his office and slumped into his desk chair. "I'm beat. I trust you."

"Thanks, Walter. That means a lot."

Walter looked up at her. Julia could see something was bothering him. "Well, you want to be an assistant. Assistants help make decisions. We have a decision to make."

"What's that?" She stepped forward, eager to prove herself again.

"This isn't gonna be pretty." Walter stood while keeping his eyes on Julia's. He watched as her eagerness darkened to confusion.

They walked to one of the horse's stalls. A dark bay colt was lying on his bed of straw, breathing heavily. "Oh no." Julia ran to him, and then fell to her knees next to his head.

"He's been suffering for several hours now and he's not getting better."

"You have to get him up and walking," she urged. Julia stood and tried to pull the horse to his feet, but he refused. Walter stood by watching as Julia tried in vain, over and over. "Come on, buddy. You have to get up. You have to walk. I know it hurts. You have to move."

"Vet was here earlier, and he thinks the colon's twisted."

It took everything in Julia's power not to burst into tears for the colt. He was just a baby, a sweet baby, cuddly and loveable, and had never nipped at anyone. He was always looking for attention with his big eyes peering over his stall door, his tongue hanging out for the next person to come along and pull it. "Surgery?" They'd had such high hopes for him. Would surgery ruin his gut? Would he be able to race again?

"He wouldn't make it to the hospital."

"What are you saying? Y-you think we sh-should put him down?"

Walter said nothing, but Julia knew that's exactly what he thought. Julia couldn't give up so easily. She went to the other side of the horse and pushed his back, his rear quarters, his neck. "Come on. Get up. You have to. Please." Walter rolled his eyes and turned away for several seconds. "Come on, baby. Show him you can do it. Come on. Up! Up!"

The horse groaned, whined, then lurched a few times as he tried to stand. "That's it, baby. Come on." Julia was back by his head again, coaxing, swiping his forelock out of his eyes. The pain on his face would have been apparent to anyone, but Julia knew she had to get him up, so he'd feel better. She tried again, pushing his hindquarters. Finally, he was able to get himself up and immediately, Julia grabbed his halter and shoved Walter aside. She led the colt out the door and started down the shedrow. His abdomen was distended, and it looked so very painful. The colt was reluctant and moved slowly with labored steps. It made Julia sick to her stomach as she empathized with him.

"Jules –" Walter started.

"Just give me a half hour."

"He's suffering."

Just then, the colt's groom walked into the barn and stood with his jaw dropped. "Black...Blackbird. You're up." Walter sighed loudly and turned away.

Julia touched Walter's arm before he could leave. "Wait, Walter. What about the vet? Is he coming back?"

"He's on his way but not to fix him."

"Tell him to get the tube. He can tube him. You know."

Walter shook his head as he thought.

"Please? It's worth a shot. We should try for him, right? If it doesn't work, then...then...we'll do it. But let's try this one last thing. Okay? Please?"

Walter stomped away muttering something about "damned broads." Julia closed her eyes with dread for a second, but kept her colt walking, though slowly. At least he wasn't trying to roll anymore. They had that.

Minutes ticked by as Julia and the colt's groom, Harry, walked him and observed his demeanor. He was clearly still in pain and they anxiously searched every few seconds for the vet. Finally, he came carrying a bucket, a large bag, and his smaller medical bag. With the stethoscope, the vet listened to Blackbird's belly.

"Worth a shot," he said, leaning over to open the larger bag containing a long black tube. "You're not gonna like this," he told the colt, then slathered Vaseline on one end of the tube. "Shh," he whispered, then put one end of the tube into his mouth and the other end into the colt's nose. Blackbird tossed his head back, but the vet was quick, and as the vet blew air into the hose, he managed to get the tube far inside within seconds. Julia and Harry tried their best to comfort the colt as the vet worked.

Walter appeared, thankfully, and began rubbing the horse's sides. "Come on," he said, encouraging the others to do the same. Blackbird wanted to drop down again, clearly wanting to give up. It broke Julia's heart as she willed the tube to go to the right place. Fortunately, the colt was too tired and sickly to fight. Finally, the vet took the tube out of his mouth and declared that it had gone to the stomach.

Julia's eyes opened wide as she looked at the vet with hope. The vet still looked concerned but kept the tube in place. He jiggled it a bit more, released some air, and then it stopped. Blackbird stood wide-eyed, panting, his head drooped.

The vet got out his pump, connected the hose, and began pumping water from the bucket. After most of it was gone, the vet poured what seemed like a gallon of mineral oil into the bucket. He pumped the mineral oil through the tube, followed by more water.

Once this procedure was done, he slid the tube from the horse's nose, slowly and carefully. Then he put on a very long glove that covered most of his arm. "If it's twisted or blocked, we'll know for sure now." Then he greased up his glove-covered arm, reached under the colt's tail, and slipped his hand inside the colt's body. The colt did not protest at all, which surprised Julia. She knew the colt had to be exhausted from all of this. The vet pulled out clumps of manure. He examined it and declared it to be too dry. Walter eyed the groom, who lowered his eyes.

With his clean hand, the vet scratched his head as he thought. After several stressful seconds, he looked at the mineral oil and made a determination. "I'm going to give him a small enema. Too much could kill him if his colon bursts, so I'm going to give him about eight ounces or so. Harry, go get some beet pulp and start soaking his hay. Only soaked hay until the manure comes out soft, not dry. You hear me?"

Harry nodded and sprinted from the stall.

The vet inserted the tube under Blackbird's tail and pumped a few pumps of mineral oil into him. "There. That should soften things up a bit. I hope. Keep a close eye on him. If he hasn't passed anything in say, an hour, let me know. We'll have to do, well, other options." He glanced at Julia, wanting to keep the bad news from her. Unfortunately, she understood what he meant.

After the vet left, they put some beet pulp in his feed bucket, and he took it. "Good job," Julia praised, hoping his appetite was a good sign.

"I'll take it from here, Ms. Julia. You can go home if you want."

"Well, okay. Guess you're his groom, right? I'll just... Walter, will you call me and keep me updated?"

"I'm leaving too. Harry can call you."

"Yes, ma'am. I'll call."

"Thank you."

ᘒᘒᘒ

Julia got a call at midnight that the colt was going to be okay. He had "pooped up a storm," according to Harry. Julia was never so happy to hear about excess poop in her life.

The next morning, the colt was happy and hungry, but they only fed him a little wet hay, took him out to graze, and then went for a walk. He'd had quite an ordeal the day before, and his insides were most likely sore.

Julia visited him, but resisted giving him a sugar cube, afraid it would hurt him. She rubbed his forehead until Walter found her.

"You're in the wrong stall, young lady."

"Sorry. Just checking on him. Poor thing. He is feeling better, though." In the back of her mind, she knew how close to death the colt was, and not just from the colic. Walter had almost put him down. It was a relatively easy fix, too. He didn't need surgery. His colon wasn't twisted. He didn't need to die. He almost did! Part of her was angry with Walter for giving up so easily.

He saw the disappointment in her eyes as she passed him on her way out of the stall. "Jules..."

When she did not answer, but kept walking, he followed. "Jules, come on. You must understand. I've seen this so many times. It looked bad. The track vet said he thought his gut was twisted. He would never have lived through surgery if Hanover even approved it. It wasn't like I was trying to get rid of him."

Julia stopped and turned, stopping him in his tracks. "I told you, Walter. I will back whatever decision you make, but I couldn't let him go without trying first. If he hadn't gotten up, if he hadn't been able to walk, I would have said let him go, too. But I saw it in his eyes. He was worn out but fighting it."

"You a horse whisperer now?"

"Yes."

Walter sighed loudly.

"You think I'm a typical woman. In some ways, I am. Women are much better at non-verbal communication, reading minds, and body language, if you will. Humans or animals. Women can pick up on things men could never come close to seeing. You're not the typical man, either, Walter. You are much more open minded than most men, especially the men around here. I know you can accept that I could greatly benefit this barn by adding a woman's perspective. The question is, are you brave enough to try it?"

He chuckled silently as he shook his head and ran his fingers through his thinning grey hair. He looked up and surveyed his domain, his barn. The men did their work to the best of their abilities, but not because they feared the boss. They were self-motivated and loved their jobs and their horses. Julia wouldn't have to crack a whip over them, but she could organize them and have them working in the most efficient way. He knew she could do that while taking care of the horses. She was right, too. He was open minded, much more than the other men around him in the other barns. Her last question was certainly a taunt if he had ever heard one. How could a real man resist that? He connected strongly with her unyielding gaze. Then he held out his hand.

CHAPTER SIX

"What's my name?" Julia asked as she sat down next to Walter's desk. She tried her hardest not to appear too excited. On the inside, she felt like a kid on Christmas.

"Bob?"

"Boring."

"Okay. Boring."

They laughed. "Walter!"

"Who's your favorite actor?"

"Marlon Brando."

"Marlon...what's your maiden name?"

"Whelon. Not sure I like Marlon, though. Doesn't go with Whelon, anyway."

Walter dropped his shoulders. "Okay. Name another actor."

"Jimmy Stewart."

"Jimmy Whelon."

"Sounds good."

"Jimmy Whelon it is."

Walter walked outside and caught the attention of several men. "Spread the word. Staff meeting in five."

With silent nods, they milled around the barn, telling each employee. They hoped to hear the word on the new assistant trainer today.

In five minutes, everyone had gathered in the middle aisle of the barn in a semi-circle around Walter, who stood on a bale of straw with his back against the wall. Julia stood right in front of him and nonchalantly glanced from man to man, wondering what their reactions would be. There were a few, she knew, who would not mind, as they knew she was organized and was a hard worker. To the others, though, it did not matter how good she was. She was a woman, and that was reason enough to keep her out of management.

"As you all know, Kenny had to leave suddenly. Some of you know why, and I'd like you to keep that information to yourselves. Though, I know you boys spread gossip faster than little old ladies in a small town in Kentucky." He paused while they chuckled knowingly at each other, not because they themselves spread gossip. It was, of course, the man next to them who talked the most. "Kenny was a good assistant trainer. He was organized and commanded authority. He knew his horses inside and out. He was a good businessman. It only seems right to replace him with someone with similar skills. I have hired someone with superior organization skills, confidence, has an in-depth knowledge of the sport, someone who will be a good leader, and who will always look out for the best interests of the workers here in Hanover's barn, and who will also look out for the best interests of the horses."

"Who is it?" one man shouted. The others slugged him and shushed him.

"This person is someone within our barn. This person knows the barn inside and out, knows every horse inside and out, knows every person inside and out. This person is a go-getter. Someone with initiative. A drive for perfection. Someone with the skills necessary to organize the books and office work, while at the same time organizing schedules and making sure we have enough help and are doing our jobs to the best of our abilities."

Walter paused and looked at Julia, who was doing her best to hold in an enormous smile and was trying her hardest not to look too eager. Now, she had to look tough. She was going to be the boss. Okay, assistant boss. But still, a boss. Her heart beat strongly, and her face flushed as Walter held out his hand. She took it and stood next to him as he stepped down. She turned and faced the men.

They were wide-eyed and slack-jawed in silence. Finally, a few shook their heads. Walter spoke again. "You will respect her knowledge and authority, or you will be fired. Just because she is a woman does not mean she is less capable. In fact, I honestly believe she will be even better for our stable than Kenny." Several men scoffed and shook their heads. Julia narrowed her eyes at them and pressed her lips together. Immediately, they hid their emotions, but Julia could still see the muscles under their cheeks contracting and relaxing as they clenched their teeth in anger. "I have interviewed many men for the job, and I feel I have chosen the best person for the job. To make things easier for you, because I know some of you will have trouble accepting orders from a woman, we have decided upon a new name for her. She will be referred to as Jimmy Whelon from now on."

A few men laughed out loud, unable to hold back. Julia smirked knowingly, then spoke. "I agree. It does seem silly, but it will be for the best. To avoid backlash from other workers and the fans, this is for the best."

"What about Hanover? What's he say about all of this?" shouted a man in back.

"He's happy with our decision and backs us one hundred percent."

One man scoffed and muttered something about sleeping with the boss. Another man snickered.

"Comments like that will get you fired, Joe," Walter shot out immediately. Joe's eyes popped open and he clamped his jaw closed.

"First things first," Julia started in hopes of moving on. "I have talked with many of you over the years, and I remember your complaints about conditions or things you need and haven't had access to. Now that I see our financial situation a little better, I know why we have had to do without certain things. Washing machine, for one. I have devised a plan to save for one, putting a bit of money aside with each win. Hanover has okayed this and is on board with us fixing up the place a bit, making it more comfortable for ourselves and the horses. We will be getting more stall fans right away, for example. I have a list compiled of things we need and things we want and have prioritized those lists. If anyone has any other suggestions or would like to talk to me about the lists, feel free."

Hearing that they might get the things they had been longing for, they perked up and were a bit more open to the idea. *A little bribery couldn't hurt*, Julia thought. After all, it worked with the kids. It would work with men, too.

Everyone went about their work while Julia got her feet wet in the management business. All day, the men tested her with their issues, and all day, she answered with quick decisions. She was confident, or at least did her best to appear that way, knowledgeable, and at the same time, maintained that she was looking out for the underdogs of the barn, since she had been one of them. By the end of the day, every groom and hotwalker was on board with having her as assistant trainer.

ᴗᴗᴗ

Walking home that night, the smile on her face could not be squelched any longer. This was the best day in many years, and she could have flown home. Her mother met Julia at the house with the kids.

"How'd it go, Jules?"

"Mom, you would not believe what a great day it was." Julia clapped her hands, then threw them into the air in triumph.

"What do you mean? Did you get the job?"

"I not only got the job, but I got the guys on my side. They're okay with me doing this, Mom. I can't believe it." Julia covered her cheeks with her hands, and then sat in her kitchen at the table.

"Oh, my, Jules. You've got a man's job? You'll be making more money now?"

Julia nodded. "Not much more, but it'll be more. If we win, I will get one percent of the purse. Walter gets ten, jockey gets ten, I get one. But that's okay. It will definitely amount to more than a groom's salary."

"Only one? That's not fair," her mother protested with her hands on her hips. "You should get equal pay."

"This is what assistant trainers get. Kenny only got one percent, too."

"Oh."

"Yeah, but it's okay. If I can get this barn in tiptop shape, we'll start winning more, and I'll make more money. I can't wait, Mom. I'm so excited."

"You will be very good at this job, Jules. I know it. You've always been organized and good at making decisions. You're very mature and I think you will do fine. Maybe one day, you'll be head trainer."

Julia chuckled doubtfully, but inside, she hoped for that position. One day. Her eyes sparkled as she imagined herself as head trainer. Dare she dream? She had scarcely dreamed of becoming an assistant trainer, with only a fleeting thought from time to time. In the past, those thoughts had been quickly shot down by the practical side of her mind as it reminded her that she   was   only   a   woman.   But   now...

CHAPTER SEVEN

York, Great Britain 1956

On the windy tree-lined roads of Northern England, a young couple took in the lush, green scenery while driving in their new car. Thick grass blanketed the hills, dotted with an occasional rock or two. There were hills in the distance decorated with ancient castles where wars had been fought centuries ago. Kings and Queens had used these roads, only recently paved with asphalt and tar, changing the scenery from the way it had been for thousands of years.

"Yes, indeed, honey, this was the best wedding present anyone could ever have." Paul picked up his new wife's hand and kissed it. With a dreamy stare, Melissa kept her eyes on him. Their wedding had been an elaborate mass and reception in a castle just outside of York. The trip from America and their honeymoon in England in an authentic castle had been paid for by Melissa's father, who worked for Her Majesty's Secret Service.

Melissa was never quite sure exactly what he did, and she did not see him much. Her father had tried to make up for it over the years by buying his only daughter everything her heart desired.

This included a stable full of race horses, some of which were kept in America, in New York. Melissa was the proud owner of seven horses in the U.S. and ten in England. One was even a gift from the Queen of England herself, a devout lover of the sport.

Melissa had met Paul in New York while she was visiting for the Saratoga meet one summer. Paul was her assistant trainer for a whole year, but she hadn't met him until that meet. It was love at first sight, and the two were inseparable after first laying eyes on each other. When it came time for her to go back home, she resisted, but knew her family was expecting her and anxious to see her again. It had been two months.

Her driver had come for her and she had stood by the car door, crying softly, unable to release Paul's gaze, unable to say goodbye.

Before she could get into the car, he took her hand and breathlessly bent down onto one knee. "Marry me, Missy. Please, don't go."

That's all it took. She stayed in New York from then on. They had eloped secretly while her mother planned a grand wedding for several hundred people in England. In New York, everyone knew to tell her parents they were living in separate apartments, though they were happily living together in a small apartment near Belmont Park.

Paul wasn't making much and wasn't able to afford the place on his own, but with Missy's allowance from her family, they were able to live comfortably.

The following summer, they traveled to England for the wedding. Their wedding present from the Queen was the car they were driving.

"Does it feel weird to drive on the opposite side of the road?"

"Yes, definitely. Why do you Brits always have to do everything backwards?" he joked. "I feel like I'm going to run head-on into another car at any moment."

"Oh, Lord, I hope not."

"What should we do first?"

"I say we consummate our marriage." She winked.

"I like that idea." He glanced at her but was careful to keep his eyes on the road. Thankfully, there wasn't much traffic.

"Then we'll stand out on the balcony and take in the clean and fresh air, clean out the smog that's been building up inside us over the past year."

"I like that idea, too."

"You're a very agreeable husband, my dear. This will be a happy marriage, I am sure."

"I definitely agree with those words." He glanced at her again. The near empty road was easy to navigate despite the twists and turns. All he had to do was stay to the right. *Or, left. Stay left!* He jerked the car back into his lane after having drifted a bit.

"Goodness. Want me to drive?" She was kidding, but he almost did want her to drive. The road was making him nervous. He had to do this, though. She hated driving and was horrible at it. Besides, he would have to learn to drive like this, anyway, because he was due to spend a lot more time in this country.

It was strange that their reception was over an hour ago, and they had driven off amid a shower of rice and bird seed, but they were staying in the very same castle tonight. It was a strange act of tradition to drive off with the top down like that, with ribbons and cans tinkering behind the car. They had stopped just a mile outside of the castle and removed it all, then put up the top so Melissa's hair remained somewhat put together. She was always very fussy about her hair. He loved that about her.

The stars in his eyes blinded him every time he looked at his gorgeous wife, so, again, he tried his best to keep his eyes on the road.

"Oh, Lord, look at that," she screeched as she pointed out her side of the car.

There, he saw two horses, one mounted over the other. Melissa covered her mouth and turned away as her cheeks blushed, and Paul laughed loudly at her. "Come on. You've seen that before, baby."

She gasped loudly as she covered her chest and he took a split second to glance at her. That gasp was drowned out by the sound of a truck horn, and then the sound of breaking glass and twisting metal.

ꙨꙨꙨ

Paul heard the steady beeping of a heart monitor, and a strange sound that reminded him of a balloon filling. Even stranger, the air never seemed to leave the balloon, making him wonder how big the balloon would get before it popped. It filled many, many times a day, more than he could count. Sometimes, he would fall asleep to the rhythmic whooshing, despite worrying about being hit by bits of broken balloon. Later, he would wake up and listen to the sound all over again and continue his worrying about that dreaded balloon. One of these days, it was bound to pop.

Finally, he heard something other than the balloon. It was a woman's voice. Then, a man's voice entered the room, but he couldn't understand the words. The man seemed to be speaking in high speed, as if someone had turned the record to the old seventy-eight instead of the normal thirty-three and a third. The woman's voice did the same thing the next time she came in. It scared him, and he tried in vain to open his eyes to see what was happening. Was the entire world moving quicker now? Or was he moving slower? Was he on the wrong speed? Was this some sort of strange new dimension? He kept trying to open his eyes, especially whenever he heard the voices, but his eyes failed him. His whole body failed him.

Finally, after what seemed like weeks, he saw a bit of light through his lids. He turned his head away from the light and tried again to open his eyes. This time, he heard no voices, but the light beckoned him, so he tried his best to see. See what? Anything. Anything was better than nothing, which is all he saw now.

He sucked in a giant breath of air, realizing now that he had lungs. He had a body. He was more than just a set of eyes and ears. After a few breaths, he managed to force his eyes open. Everything was blurry and warped, as if looking through a bottle of castor oil. He blinked, clearing his vision slightly. He saw a silver pole next to him with a clear bottle, upside down, attached to the top. As he blinked again, he could see a clear line going from the bottle to his arm. It went into his arm, under his skin.

What? He screamed at the top of his lungs. "Help! Help me! Get this thing out of my arm! Help!" He might have grabbed it and ripped it out, but it was taped to his arm and he could not find the end of the tape. He clawed at it until a nurse rushed in and smacked his hand away. "Ow!"

"Stop that! Leave it there!"

"Why? It's going into my arm."

"It's supposed to be there, sir. It's saving your life. If you want to live, you'll leave it there."

"Huh?" He stared at it with narrowed eyes, wondering how a tube and a bottle could possibly save his life.

The nurse picked up a clipboard from the foot of the bed, then took out a pen. "So. You're awake now." She scribbled something.

"Um, I guess?"

"Do you know where you are, Mr. Holton?"

"Holton? That's not...um, no. Where am I?"

"You're at York Hospital, sir. Do you remember the accident?"

"Accident? No. What accident? What happened?"

"You were in a car accident, sir."

"I was?" He tried to sit up in his bed, but the nurse rushed over and held him down.

"You should not sit up yet, sir. Your head has had quite a tough time of it."

"What?" he asked, narrowing his eyes.

"Your head. You have a head injury." The nurse sighed, rolled her eyes, and shook her head. "I'll get the doctor."

"Um, okay."

Once she was gone, he sat up despite the ache in his head. He remembered the balloon noise and looked around the room but did not see a balloon. There was a machine in one corner with a black tube and a large cylinder with what looked like bellows inside. What was that thing?

"Lie down, sir," the nurse screamed as she rushed back into the room. A tall man in a white lab coat followed closely behind.

"You need to keep a close watch on him, nurse," the tall man said.

"Yes, sir," she mumbled as she eyed him with hooded eyes.

"Good afternoon, sir. My name is Doctor Thornber. Do you remember your name, sir?" The doctor picked up the clipboard and began scribbling.

"Um...um..." He thought carefully but could not remember what the nurse had called him. The thought panicked him. Name? He had no name. "What's my name?" he cried, sitting up again. The nurse pushed him back down.

"Paul Holton, sir. Does that sound familiar?"

"No. How do you know that's my name?" Panic still rushed through his body, invigorating it, waking him up, but it still did not help him remember his name or this accident the nurse had spoken of earlier.

"You have an American driver's license. *New* York, apparently."

Paul shook his head. That didn't sound familiar at all. The nurse pursed her lips and glanced at the doctor.

"Well, it might take a few days to come back. You've had a head injury, but as it heals, your memory will probably come back. You're still quite swollen, you know."

"What do I do now? I don't know where I live or anything."

"Just wait, sir. As I said, once the swelling goes down in your head, you should remember everything. Don't worry. It will come back to you."

Paul fought panic with every second that ticked by, every minute, every hour. The nurse gave him a few books to read, but his head hurt, and he could not bring himself to read. All he could do was lie there and try to remember what had happened or wonder where to go once he recovered and was let go from the hospital.

Someone brought a radio in on a cart after the first day, and it made his wait for healing a bit more bearable. The station played a good variety of music, thankfully. The news wasn't particularly interesting to him because he had no idea what they were talking about. There were mentions of a queen and some other royals, a beauty pageant, a steel mill, nothing of interest to him.

Finally, days later, his head began to feel better, ache less, and he could think more clearly. Even with his radio he had been extremely bored, as no one had come to see him at all. No one helped him remember things, which he thought odd. Didn't he have family or friends? There was a woman, though. Beautiful, young, she had blue eyes and long blonde hair curled up on top of her head with stray locks framing her face, a perfect smile...but who was she?

He stared and stared at the wall as he tried to picture her. Maybe it was his wife? Though, he had no wedding ring or jewelry to speak of. Maybe it was a girlfriend. He wondered if she knew he was here. Most likely, no, since she never came to see him. Maybe they broke up, though. Maybe she didn't want to see him. He closed his eyes, but he couldn't picture her with him, couldn't see her doing anything. He could only see her face.

Well, she's happy, whoever she is.

Darkness finally came, ending the seemingly endless hours of the day. This was his chance to go to sleep and to escape for a few hours. However, tonight, even darkness could not help him escape. His mind worked feverishly despite his attempts at shutting it up.

Flashes in his mind formed into images, switching like a slide show where someone was turning the knob too quickly. He thought he saw a horse in a stall, but it turned into an old man with a fedora. A dirt floor, worn wooden shutters, buckets, other animals. Did he work at a zoo? There was another horse, then another. Now the flashes melded into a home movie. He walked down an endless row of horses, each poking their heads from their stalls to eye him curiously. Finally, he came to the end of the row where the last horse walked out of his stall and glared into his soul with hauntingly dark eyes. "How could you?" the horse asked him.

He woke up screaming as the nurse rushed in, fortunately, a nicer nurse than the one from the daytime.

"Are you okay? What happened? Nightmare?" She placed a hand on his arm.

Paul grabbed his chest as he caught his breath. "Yes. Sorry. Oh my, that was scary."

"What happened?" She helped him straighten the sheets that had become tangled in his legs.

"Um, well, there was this long row of horses, and one of them was mad at me for doing something. I don't know what."

The young nurse looked surprised for a split second, then immediately changed her expression. "Hm. Interesting dream."

"Yeah." With one eye half closed, he watched her. Occasionally, she glanced at him as she straightened his bedding again. She patted his foot.

"Looks like you're okay, though. Good night, Mr. Holton."

"Wait, nurse."

"Yes?" She stopped with her hand on the doorknob, but still opened the door.

"Do you know something?"

"No, sir. Good night." Before he could respond, she left and closed the door behind her.

"What the hell?" he almost shouted at the door. He was tired of sitting around in his bed day in and day out, for no apparent reason. His headache was gone, nothing else was broken. He was perfectly fine, other than being weak from not walking for God knows how long. No one would tell him. Every time he got up to go to the bathroom, he could feel how weak his legs were. It had to have been weeks. He was glad for the help of his cane, but that was just as wobbly as his legs. Sometimes he did not bother to use it.

This time, he decided to get up and look at his chart. After all, it was about him, and he should know everything the doctor says about him. It was his right. He supposed.

Carefully, he folded back the blanket and sheet at a perfect angle in case he had to hurry back into his bed. After turning his body and letting his feet touch the cold floor for a minute, he leaned over and placed his weight over his feet. His legs shook beneath his slight weight and he knew he shouldn't take too long. One step at a time, he walked to the foot of the bed and picked up the chart.

He could hardly read anything, but from what he could read of the doctor's ridiculously scratchy handwriting, the first date on the record was "12 Aug '55." The last date was "1 Sept '55." Almost three weeks? Wow. He could really only remember the last four days. This whole time, what had happened? Had his family and friends given up on him? Is that why they weren't here? Did they think he was dead? Why wouldn't the hospital tell them he was alive? He noted the name of the hospital. York Hospital. He wondered if that were anywhere near New York. *Must be the same place*, he thought.

He ran his fingers through his thick, light brown hair. *Greasy.* He smelled awful. He hadn't showered yet. That was next on the list. First, though, was to find out about his family. Flipping through the chart, he saw nothing about visitors or anything other than medical jargon. No mention of other people. He saw the words, "automobile" and "accident," but they had already told him that much. Frustrated, he hooked the clipboard back onto the foot of the bed and shuffled to the bathroom. Fortunately, there was a small shower stall inside.

He could only find a bar of soap, so he washed his hair with that, not willing to ask the nurse for shampoo. She would have stopped him from doing this. They were so ridiculous. He didn't understand why...

"Mr. Holton?" he heard. "Sir? Mr. Holton?" He felt slapping on his hands, then his face, and he opened his eyes. His wide eyes darted back and forth as he tried to figure out how he had ended up on the floor of the shower. "You're lucky I found you, Mr. Holton. Come on. Let's get you back to bed."

The water was off, but the floor was still wet and slippery. He had no clothes on and a tiny nurse was attempting to lift him. He had no clothes on! "Give me that towel," he bellowed as he shrugged off her hands. With a frustrated sigh, she let go, grabbed the towel, and handed it to him. "Turn around."

She rolled her eyes and turned away. "Mr. Holton, do you have any idea how many people I have seen unclothed? I've been a nurse for ten years and worked in hospitals as a candy striper before that. If I were you, I wouldn't worry what others think when your safety is in question. You need to be asking for my help, not pushing me away." Her foot tapped repeatedly as her arms crossed in front of her chest.

"You're too small to lift me." He tried his best to keep his voice under control and hide his anger and embarrassment.

"I'm perfectly capable, if you just give me a chance. Are you quite ready, sir?"

"Yes. I guess." He had tucked the towel around his hips, but knew it was bound to fall off as soon as he stood up. She faced him again, then bent her legs and reached under his shoulders, holding his arm over her shoulders.

"One, two..."

"Am I really that big?"

She giggled, then wiped away her grin. "Sorry. No, you're not too big, sir. Ready? One, two, three." She lifted as he attempted to help with one hand on the wall. As he straightened, his towel slipped to the ground. He muttered a curse word, but she ignored it and kept him moving toward his bed. She helped him sit, and he yanked the covers back over him. "I'll get your gown."

"Gown," he mumbled with distaste while she was in the bathroom. He didn't want to wear a gown. He wanted to wear clothes. He'd had enough of this hospital.

Without a word, she helped him dress again. "Okay, sir. Now you know why you weren't supposed to take a shower yet. Now, you'd better stay put or I'll be forced to lock you in the bed."

"What? What do you mean?" *Handcuffs? Straps?*

"We have a very modern system here. It's an invisible electric beam of energy that zaps you if you get out of the bed."

As he stared at her, trying to figure out if she was lying, if this thing was really something she could do, she straightened his room, his blanket, and then left the room. She had had no expression on her face. He could not read her at all. *How could that be? How could they do that? Was that even possible?*

Before he knew what was happening, it was morning. He must have fallen asleep without realizing it. He had also passed out without realizing it back in that shower. He didn't remember feeling faint or having any indication that he was going to pass out. Well, maybe it was for the best that he was still stuck here. Still, he was bored stiff. To keep himself occupied, he tried to remember more about his life.

His eyes drifted to the window, and he saw trees swaying in the breeze. The leaves were already turning. It seemed to be happening too early. Didn't that start in October when the weather started cooling off?

The nurse came in to bring him his breakfast. More dreadful food. At least, that's what they called it – *food*. It wasn't quite edible, though, another reason he wanted desperately to go home. Wherever home was.

"Nurse, what is the temperature outside?"

"Lovely day, isn't it? So sunny. I suspect it's about twelve or thirteen today. A little chilly."

"A little? That's below freezing."

After recovering from her laughter, she explained, "We use Celsius in England, sir."

His heart thumped in his chest. "England." He narrowed his eyes as he peered out the window again. "England," he repeated. "New York is in England?"

"No, sir. New York is in America. That is where you are from. You are in England now. Haven't you gathered that you speak with an American accent?"

"Me? No. You have an accent."

She laughed again and put her hands on her hips. "Well, sir, if you must know, if you're in Great Britain as an American, *you* are the one with the accent."

"What the hell am I doing in Great Britain?"

"Oh, um. I'm not supposed to tell you. Sorry." She adjusted his table for him and slid it near his bed. She was close now, and he grabbed her wrist. She gasped and tried to pull back.

"Listen. If you could just tell me something, maybe I'll remember it. Hasn't anyone ever thought of that?"

"But I might tell you the wrong thing, and I don't want to steer you in the wrong direction. I wouldn't want you to believe your name is Marvin Dinglebury or anything."

"What the hell are you talking about?" he asked, finally letting her go.

"I'm not allowed to tell you anything. Sorry."

"Just tell me where my family is. Why aren't they here? Why hasn't anybody come to visit me or take me home? Please, I have to know."

With her back to him, and almost to the door, she stopped, then looked over her shoulder at him. "Your family is in America, sir. You are across the pond in England."

"Can I go back to America? Maybe I could stay in a hospital there. Maybe it will help me remember things."

"I suspect it would help, Mr. Holton, but, unfortunately, you're not well enough to travel just yet. Maybe soon, though."

He was so relieved to hear a sliver about his life that it stunned him. As she left the room, he tried to thank her, but words would not form in his mouth. So, it wasn't that they didn't want to see him. They were too far away and couldn't get here. Did they know he was here, though? No cards? No flowers? That made no sense. Was he such an awful person that no one cared?

Throughout the day, he stared out the window, waiting for nighttime so he could sleep again. The radio was getting old. There was no television and only a few books, none of which interested him. They were insanely boring, and he could not get past the first few pages. At least his eyes weren't hurting as much as they were a few days ago.

If only he could remember. At some point in the afternoon, he fell asleep. He found himself dreaming of the beautiful woman again. Her blonde hair was flowing behind her in the breeze. Pinned into her hair was a wedding veil with tiny pearls woven in, and her spun gold hair glittered in the sunlight. They were in a car. She wasn't driving, but she was on that side of the car. Because they were in England. Yes! Now he remembered.

The grass and trees were green and lush; there were animals in pastures off in the distance. Two horses were...mating? What a strange dream. Then a horn, a crash, breaking glass. He woke with a scream. The events were still happening before his eyes even though he was awake. He was thrown from the car and hit the ground, rolling. After that, there was nothing. It was silent.

"Mr. Holton?" His nurse rushed in.

He was breathing heavily, sweating, making noises like whimpers. "Oh, God. Oh, God."

"What's wrong?" She placed one hand on his arm.

"I remember. I think. I was in a car accident."

"Yes."

"B-but you told me that, right? I mean, maybe it's like you said, and what you had already told me influenced me, and..."

"You were in a car accident, sir. You were thrown from the car."

"W-what happened to the woman? What happened to her? Is she okay? Was there a woman in the car with me? What happened to her?"

"I'm so sorry, sir. She didn't make it."

Before he could stop them, tears streamed down his face. She was his wife. He knew it now. She was wearing a wedding veil! It was their wedding day. The blood rushed from his head, so the nurse helped him lie down again. He curled into a fetal position, covered his head with his arms, and sobbed. The nurse stayed with him, seated on the bed, and patted his back as he cried. "I'm so sorry," she said. Her voice was strained, as if she was crying, too.

Several minutes passed before he regained some control of himself. "I missed her funeral?" His voice was pitiful.

"Yes," she answered softly. "I'm very sorry."

"Do her parents know I'm here? Why haven't they come to see me? We were married. They were my in-laws."

"They were quite upset, Mr. Holton. They could not come. I hope you understand."

"No, I don't. But I guess I don't have a choice, do I?" Paul sighed heavily. "I need to go home. I need to go back to New York."

"Once your head is healed, you will be able to handle the trip, but not until then. It could be dangerous for you to fly."

"I could take a boat."

"I suppose, but that is a long trip."

"Does my family in America know I'm here?"

"Yes, sir. They have been informed."

"Can I call them?"

"Unfortunately, we don't have the capabilities to make overseas phone calls."

"Then, how did you tell them?"

"Telegraph."

"I need to send a telegraph, then."

"What would you like to say?"

"Get me out of here."

She patted his leg. "You're not being held against your will, sir. But it really is for the best."

"I need to see my in-laws. I need to talk to them."

"Unfortunately, they have requested that you not contact them, sir. As I said, they are quite upset."

"Of course, they are. So am I. I just lost my wife, for God's sakes."

"Sir, they blame you for the accident. They said you were on the wrong side of the road."

His heart stopped, the blood rushed from his head again, and it felt like someone had knocked the wind out of him. Of course, it was his fault. He wasn't used to driving on that side of the road. It was all his fault. He closed his eyes as the realization blanketed over him like a black cloud.

There was nothing worth living for now. They were upset with him for the accident. They blamed him. It was all his fault. She was dead because of him. She was dead because he wasn't careful enough. They had been relaxed, laughing, having a good time. Then, in an instant, it was all over.

However, he was sure that he was on the correct side of the road. He remembered being extra careful about it, too. How could that happen? Obviously, it had happened without him realizing it. He wasn't careful enough.

This time, he was so distraught, he couldn't cry. A silent sob heaved his sickly body, but no tears fell as he gripped his sheet in his fists. He closed his eyes and hoped never to open them again.

Eventually, the nurse left. He hadn't said a word to her since she had informed him that the accident was his fault. He never wanted to speak again. He never wanted to breathe again. Melissa, he remembered her name now, would never breathe again because of him. He didn't deserve to breathe when she couldn't. He buried his head under his pillow hoping to suffocate himself. He fell asleep, but in doing so, he relaxed his arm and allowed air to seep in. When he woke up again, he beat his head with the pillow, hoping to cause a stroke or aneurysm. Something. Anything. The nurse came in to give him his medicine, but he left it in the cup. He would hide the pills, save them up, and then take them all at once.

It would have been a perfect plan, had the nurse not figured it out. Once she did, she always stayed in the room, watched him take the pills, then checked his mouth afterward.

"You're getting better, but you won't be able to leave this hospital if you don't stop this nonsense, Mr. Holton."

"Then kill me. Just put me out of my misery, would you? Please?" He tried to remain patient and not scream the request.

"You know I can't do that."

"Yes, you can. It's simple. Give me a shot of something. I don't care what."

"I took an oath, sir. I can't go back on that oath, no matter what."

"Would you put down a horse that was suffering? Huh? What if your horse had colic or a broken leg? What would you do then?"

"I'd call the vet. I'm sorry, Mr. Holton. I cannot oblige your request."

He scowled at her, so she left the room. She had said he wouldn't be able to leave the hospital unless he stopped begging to die. Well, then, he would stop begging, get the hell out of here, find a damned gun, and do it himself. With a sharp nod, he made the agreement with himself to end it as soon as he got home.

OOO

Later, the doctor paid him a visit and examined his head, reflexes, his eyes, and his walking. "You are improving nicely, Mr. Holton. I suspect you'd like to go home soon?"

"Yes, sir."

"There's one matter keeping you here, though. The nurses tell me you've been begging them to kill you."

"Not anymore. I've realized my mistake. That's silly. I know they could never do such a thing."

"But I can't let you out of the hospital knowing you'd hurt yourself."

"I'd never do that, sir. I don't have the guts to do it. I'm too scared." It hurt to say that to the doctor for two reasons: it hurt to admit his unmanly weakness, and it might be the truth.

The doctor studied Paul's eyes as Paul attempted to make them look as sincere as possible. Paul managed to lift the corners of his mouth.

"I think you're a smart man, Mr. Holton." The doctor patted Paul's leg as he stood at the foot of the bed. "We can arrange for you to leave on the next flight out. How does that sound?"

"Great! Thank you. I'm so happy." *It's killing me inside.* "I can't wait to get home," *so I can get myself a gun.* "We'll need to tell my parents, so they can meet me in New York." *Oh, shit. My parents...*

"Yes, sir. We will send a telegram to them straight away." With another pat, the doctor left.

Paul did his best to hold onto his fake grin until the door closed. He let his head fall back against the angled bed. It was going to be a long trip, but worth it. Part of him couldn't wait to see his parents again while the other part couldn't wait to end it all.

While no one was in his room, he cried non-stop for Missy. The love of his life was gone. The most beautiful girl in the world was gone. She was practically royalty around here. One nurse had shared a newspaper story with him, which was the front-page headline that day, the day after his wedding. The article mentioned that the car was a gift from the Queen and reported that Paul was driving and was not used to being on that side of the road. A truck had hit them from the opposite direction, and the driver of that truck lived to tell the story. He had said Paul was driving on the wrong side of the road as they came around a corner, and they slammed into one another. Paul could not believe it. He was sure he was on the left. He was sure of it, because every few seconds, he reminded himself to stay to the left. It was impossible for him to be on the wrong side. Still, that had to be the reason, if that's what the truck driver said.

Of course, it was most tragic to lose a beautiful young girl on her wedding day, especially the daughter of one of Her Majesty's staff. The whole country mourned her loss. The whole country blamed him.

Once released, wearing baggy donated clothes from the hospital, he carried his small bag and plane ticket as he walked through the airport. The taxi driver had driven him the entire hour without saying a word, even when Paul tried to make conversation. He knew right away how everyone else would act as well. He told himself not to bother talking to anyone. *Just get on the damned plane and get home.*

It killed him to see all the scowls and sneers shot his way. It seemed everyone knew. The hatred he felt was like a wave, constantly trying to knock him off his feet. But he was determined. He had to get out of this country.

Paul understood why everyone was mad at him, but did they not understand how he might feel about it? Why couldn't they see that it was killing him inside?

Finally, he made it to the airplane. He said a prayer for safety, but then questioned his intentions. It would be so wonderful if the plane crashed, and he died on the way home. It would all be over. But, what about the other people on the plane? He couldn't do that to them. *Dammit.*

Fortunately, the man next to him on the airplane did not seem to know about the accident. He had spoken with the flight attendant at some point, and Paul could tell the man was American. *What a relief.* They made some small talk, but it was silent for most of the ride home. That was fine, too. He wasn't in the mood to talk. Too much on his mind.

He watched the skyline coming into view from miles away, and it seemed to take an eternity to get the plane lined up and descending into the city. His head ached as the plane landed. What if his parents refused to speak to him, too? What if they decided they did not want to pick him up? Where would he go? His apartment in Elmont? No. He was never going to go back to that place again. He didn't have the key, anyway. All he had from that car accident was his wedding ring, which he refused to wear. It would only remind him of her.

As he stood up, a dizzy spell hit him, and he grabbed the seat back to stay upright.

"Whoa. Man, you okay?" someone with a British accent asked.

"Yeah. Fine. Thanks." He nodded and tried desperately to look under control. The last thing he needed was attention from the flight attendants or other passengers.

Finally, they were shuffled from the plane, and Paul made his way up the ramp and into the terminal. He kept his eyes on the ground, afraid to be disappointed if his parents had decided to disown him. Instead, he felt a tug on his arm, and he was swept to the side and into his mother's arms.

She moaned and shrieked as she grabbed at his clothes and wrapped her arms tighter and tighter around him. Paul's father stood next to them with his eyes filled with tears and his hand on Paul's back. Paul was sad but could not cry. Crying wasn't nearly enough to express the pain he felt.

"My baby," his mother cried repeatedly.

"Let's get you home," his father finally said with a pat. Paul nodded and allowed his parents to lead him to their sky-blue Oldsmobile 98.

His mother turned to him in the back seat and took his hand. Paul tried to avoid her gaze, but she was relentless, and insisted he look up at her. "Paul, you will go through a tough time. But it won't always be this tough."

Sure, it won't. I'll be dead in less than twenty-four hours if I can find Dad's pistol. He nodded and then dropped his eyes again to the black upholstered floor.

ᘓᘓᘓ

"We took the liberty of bringing your things back home. I hope that's okay."

Honestly, he didn't want anything from his and Missy's apartment anywhere near him. His shoulders dropped, and he closed his eyes as he realized he was only steps away from those things. He made it to the doorway of his old bedroom where they had put some boxes but turned around and went back to the living room.

"Are you hungry?"

Paul shook his head in reply to his mother's question and let himself fall onto the sofa. Scanning the room, he saw that not much had changed. Then again, he had only been gone about a month. He and Missy had visited his parents to say goodbye before the wedding and then had flown out the next morning. The last time he was here, he had sat right here on this sofa with his girl in his arms. After dropping his head into his hands, he gathered the strength to stand up again and move to the chair nearby. He told himself never to sit on that sofa again.

His father came in and sat in the matching chair next to him, then packed his pipe with tobacco. He lit it, puffing it a few times, releasing the sweet-smelling smoke to form a cloud above their heads. He leaned back and set his eyes on his son. "I know it's hard, Son. We've all lost someone in our lives. The older you get, the more people you lose. Unfortunately, it's a part of life. You're going to have to learn to deal with it."

Paul nodded. He wouldn't have to deal with it for long. He was silent for the rest of the evening but was so tired, he finally relented and went to his old bedroom. He decided to leave the lights off, so he wouldn't see any of the boxes or things from his apartment. He collapsed onto the bed face down and instantly fell asleep.

He awoke at some point during the next day, stiff and sore. His head ached, of course. As he rubbed his fingers through his hair, he moaned and sat up. Unfortunately, the sunlight lit up the room and everything in it. His mother had tried to put things in some sort of order, so it wasn't a complete disaster, but the room was still full of boxes and clothes. God only knew what was in those boxes, but that was okay. He did not want to know. He would never look.

His mother, he assumed, had brought in a pitcher and glass of water. A slight warmth passed over his heart, then disappeared again as he appreciated his mother's gesture. No one had been so kind since, well, since Missy. His beautiful wife was the most kind and gentle soul on earth. She didn't deserve to die such a violent death. Again, for the hundredth time, he saw her face just before the crash. She was laughing, smiling, and happy. He desperately hoped she hadn't suffered. He hoped it had ended quickly for her.

It hadn't ended quickly for him, that was for sure. He wondered if he would even be successful in taking his own life with the gun. Knowing his luck, the gun would jam, and he wouldn't be able to fire it. Or maybe it would blow off half his head and leave him alive with only half a face for the rest of his life. Maybe this was his punishment – to live out the rest of his days in complete misery.

Flopping his exhausted body back onto his bed, he decided to stay there and sleep for a little while longer. He felt like an eighty-year-old man.

It was dark when he woke up again. This time, his mother had come in and covered him with a blanket. He groaned as he wondered how she would react to his death. She would most likely be devastated. His cousin had died several years ago after falling while skiing in the Poconos, and he remembered his aunt's reaction. She was distraught beyond explanation. That's exactly how he felt right now. There were no words to describe how much it hurt. How could he do that to his mother? Especially after she had been told he had lived through the accident, and then had come home?

"Damn it," he mumbled as he pounded his fist into his bed. The only way would be to try to explain it to Mom, but he knew she would beg him not to do it. He imagined her kneeling at his grave, crying her eyes out over losing him, her only son. He shook his head. He would rather suffer all the days of his life than to do that to his mother. Life was going to be miserable from here on out.

ꙨꙨꙨ

Finally, over dinner, *because that's the perfect place to talk about things like this*, his mother asked him the question he dreaded the most.

"Were you really on the wrong side of the road?"

First, he could not believe she had the nerve to bring it up. He'd been there four days, and no one had mentioned anything about the accident, which was the easy way. Suddenly, here she was asking? Second, he really didn't want to talk about it. But, if he knew his mom, she would ask until she found out one way or the other.

"I don't know. I don't think so. But, I have to assume I was on the wrong side because the truck driver said I was. I'm American and I'm used to driving on the right. Maybe I drifted. I don't know."

"How could you not know?" his dad asked, putting down his fork.

Paul glanced at his father's plate. He had shoveled most of it away already, while Paul's plate was still full. So far, his days here had been spent pretending to eat, shoving food one way or the other to make it look like he'd taken a few bites. If his mother watched closely enough, he forced himself to take a bite. The food never had any taste, though. His mother was a great cook; he simply couldn't taste anymore. Missy would never taste food again. He didn't deserve to, either. Really, he should be dead. He felt like he was supposed to be dead. In some ways, he felt dead.

He forced himself to come up with an answer for his father, who normally might not have bothered him if it had not been for Mom bringing up the subject. "We were looking at horses in the field."

He saw her face once again, smiling, beautiful, perfect, with the horses in the background in the field. There was a truck's horn blaring, and then the crash that should have killed him. The truck probably swerved and hit her side of the car, smashing it into her beautiful face, breaking glass all over her porcelain skin and designer wedding dress. Desperately, he hoped it was over before she realized what had happened. For her to experience only a second of pain was too much for him to bear. The thought of what she might have gone through nearly killed him all over again. "Nearly" wasn't good enough, though.

Without another word, he jumped up from the table and ran down the hall to his father's closet. He would have to do it before thinking about it.

Just do it! Just do it! I will see Missy again! Who cares what Mom thinks? Just do it! Tossing his father's belongings from side to side and onto the floor near the closet, he frantically searched for the case with the pistol. His father had hidden the gun from him, but he always knew where it was, anyway. Even as a child.

Finally, there it was. He yanked the case by the handle, knocking over another small box. The box fell to the ground and opened, spilling its contents onto the green carpet. There, at his feet, was a pacifier, a rattle, a tiny baby sized t-shirt, a few small toys, and a photo. He picked up the black and white photo with one hand while the other clenched the handle of the gun case. The picture was of his mother, dressed in a cloche hat and low-waisted dress, holding him as a baby. She was kissing his cheek, smashing her lips into the side of his chubby face. Even as a baby, he looked annoyed, and for some reason, Paul let out a chuckle. He knew his father was probably taking the picture. He loved that camera and had taken seemingly millions of photos over the years.

Standing in his parents' bedroom, he turned his head inch by inch, taking in his surroundings. He was between his parents' queen-sized bed and their closet. Their tall dresser was against the wall between the closet and the door to the bathroom. A longer dresser with a mirror spanned almost the entire length of the wall to his right. A chair and tiny table decorated another corner of the room. On the bed lay a white, lacey, knitted blanket, folded nicely at the foot of the bed. They never used it; it was only for decoration. His grandmother had made that for them as an anniversary present one year, and his mother cherished that blanket even more now that Grandma was gone.

The most horrible thing imaginable was for him to blow his brains out all over her bed and that blanket. It would kill her in so many ways. His eyes drifted back to the photo still in his hand. His father would get over it. But his mother, no. He couldn't do it to her.

He would have to suffer.

Just as he bent down to pick up the spilled baby items, his father rushed into the room. He snagged the gun case from where Paul had set it on the floor next to him. Paul looked up at his father while his father looked down with disappointment. He didn't say a word as he glared. Paul froze. His mother peeked around his father.

"What are you...Oh my!" Her hands flew to her face for a second, and then she rushed over to help pick up the baby items. Paul let his mother put the box back together, and he stood up, finally able to separate his eyes from his father's. His head drooped with shame, and he could still feel the fire burning from his father's gaze into the top of his head.

Once his mother had packed up the box and had set it on the shelf in the closet again, she stopped and crossed her arms over her chest. *Great.* Now she was mad.

"Sorry," Paul tried, and then ducked to one side of his father, attempting to slip between his father and the bed. His father reached out one strong arm and stopped him.

"Martha, I'd like to speak to our son alone, please."

His mother glanced from Paul to his father, then, without a word, left the room.

"What the hell do you think you're doing with this?" his father growled between clenched teeth.

As if you don't know.

"Do you really think this will help? You selfish prick. You'd kill your mother if you did that. Me too. Don't ever think about doing this ever again, you understand? If I have to, I'll lock you in a padded cell and make you do shock treatments. You're not taking your own life and taking yourself away from your mother. She would not be able to handle it."

"I know, Dad. I wasn't going to do it."

"Good. Well, let's make sure nothing like this happens again, or I will follow through on my threat. Understood?"

"Yes, sir."

"I hope no one robs the house because I'm going to have to hide this thing somewhere else." Frustrated, he tossed the box onto the bed.

"It's locked."

"I suppose you know where the key is?"

Shaking, Paul pointed to a jewelry box on his father's dresser.

"I thought so. Well, I'll just have to hide that, too." Finally calming down, his father sat on the bed and placed the gun case on his lap. He let out a huge breath of air and rubbed his face with one hand, making sure not to let go of the gun case with the other. Paul glanced at him, worried about upsetting his father in this way. He thought he saw his father's eyes moisten, but the tough, aging man hid his eyes before Paul could see. "Go to your room."

"I'm not twelve, Dad."

"Get out of here."

His father's voice was choked, and he knew why he was trying to get rid of him now. Mercifully, he left his father alone and went to his room.

There, he saw the boxes again, and wondered if any of Missy's things had been packed along with his. In an instant, he had gone from not wanting anything of hers to now wanting everything, so he could have part of her with him again. Rushing over to the pile of boxes, he ripped open the three boxes on top and looked inside the first one. He shuffled through but only saw his clothes. He tossed that box onto the bed, spilling shirts and sweaters from it. In the next box, he found photo albums. For a fleeting second, he wanted to look at the photos, but the pain he would experience in doing so would be too much for now. He closed that box and set it aside.

The third box had a few small framed photos that had been on their dresser, a mirrored tray, and a hairbrush. His heart nearly stopped when he saw her blonde hair again. This was really her. It was part of her. Cradling the brush, he brought it to his bed and lay down. He set the brush next to him, on what would have been her side of the bed. Gently, he let his fingers drift over the hair hanging over the side of the brush. It was so soft that he could barely feel it. But he was touching her again, and it was such a relief that he laughed.

Tears mingled with laughter and spilled onto his pillow until he fell asleep.

"Darling..."

Paul's eyes shot open. His wife's brush still lay beside him. Did he just hear her voice?

"Darling, please hear me."

The voice wasn't coming from the brush. It was coming from the room behind him. As soon as he realized this, he spun around, hoping to see her. Of course, she wasn't there. *Oh, no. I really do need shock treatments.*

He very nearly called for his father to call the paddy wagon when he heard her again.

"Can you hear me?"

"Yes," he answered, surprising himself. He shook his head in denial. "I'm going crazy. Oh, my God. I'm going crazy." His breathing quickened as his eyes darted back and forth in search of his wife.

"No, you're not crazy, love."

Taking deep breaths, he tried to calm himself and think rationally. *This is impossible.* "I'm making this up in my head."

"No, love. I'm really here. I need to talk to you."

"About what?"

"The accident."

"D-did you, um, did you suffer?" He couldn't stop the tears; they came on like a rushing wave.

"No, I didn't. Please don't worry about me. I'm fine."

"Well, I'm not."

"I know, love. That's why I'm here. I need to tell you something."

"What?" He shook his head in disbelief. This couldn't be happening.

"It wasn't your fault. I don't want you to blame yourself. It wasn't your fault. The truck driver was out of control. He was going too fast, and *he* was on the wrong side of the road. It wasn't your fault, baby."

With wide eyes and his lips pressed together, he wondered if this was all in his head, if some part of him wanted so badly not to be at fault that he had made her voice say that.

"I promise you, it wasn't your fault. Please don't blame yourself any longer."

"Really?" A slight chuckle of relief escaped. "But, how do I know this is real, and I'm not just dreaming this or making it up in my head?"

"I don't know. I guess you'll have to trust me, darling."

"Are you okay?"

"I'm fine."

"Not in pain? You didn't suffer?"

"No, I didn't realize what had happened until later."

"You didn't realize...what? That you're dead? Oh, and here I am talking to a dead person. This makes loads of sense. I need shock therapy."

"No, honey, you don't need shock therapy." She giggled, and the sound of her laughter went straight to his heart. It burned, though, as he reminded himself that she wasn't really there. "I can't stay long, honey. But I really needed you to know that. I hope you believe me."

"Of course, I believe you, baby."

"Good. I will try to visit again soon, okay?"

"Wait. Why do you have to go? Just stay and talk to me. I haven't talked to you in months. Can you stay?"

"No, honey. I don't have the strength. I'll be back another time."

"Strength? What do you mean?"

"I love you."

"I love you, too, baby. Please explain this to me. Can you just try for me, please? I miss you so..." The words burned. When she didn't reply, he turned back to her brush and touched her hair again. "Please come back. Please."

He sat back up and slammed his head into his hands. "This is ridiculous. My God, I'm really, truly crazy now. I can't believe this. I'm losing it." He reached behind him and picked up the brush. "Am I going crazy because I lost you?" he asked the brush. "Yes, I'm going crazy. I'm talking to a damned brush!" He lifted it as if to throw it, but then thought better of it and set it back down on the bed next to him.

It was the middle of the night now, so he changed into his pajamas and climbed into bed, making sure to carefully place the brush on the bed beside him again in case it would make her return to him. Not that he really believed it could happen, but even if his crazy mind were making this up, it was okay, because it was almost like being with her again. The feeling was so real that he didn't care if it was real or not. He only wanted to feel her presence again.

ᴕᴕᴕ

That slight and entirely too short conversation with his wife made him feel as though an enormous weight had been lifted from his shoulders.

Even though he knew Missy's family would never believe him, at least he knew it wasn't his fault. Better yet, she hadn't suffered. The best part was that he had an opportunity to talk to her again and to hear her voice. He had actually heard it. He was excited about that, despite the cold, hard truth that she wasn't physically here. It was better than nothing.

If only it were real.

He found himself believing it happened without a shadow of a doubt. Every time he tried to talk himself into believing that he was losing his mind and making it all up, that notion disappeared from his head. A war waged inside his mind as he told himself it wasn't true, time and time again, but that part lost out to the bigger part of his mind that believed it *was* true. He *did* hear her voice and she *did* tell him it wasn't his fault. He was sure of it. Mostly.

She did not come to him again for several days, days full of hope that she would fulfill her promise of coming back. Every night, he went to bed with her brush at his side, though he knew it was silly. However, that brush had to have been what called her to him, so he had to keep it next to him. It was like a security blanket, but he didn't care. It meant being close to her again.

"Darling."

"Missy?" Was he asleep? Or dreaming? Did it matter? There she was. He could see her this time. He took her hand. She was still wearing her wedding dress, and it was in perfect shape, which was exactly how he had remembered her. His body ached as he longed to pull her in for a hug, but he was afraid it wouldn't work, or it would make her disappear. Holding her hand was good enough for now. "You're so beautiful."

She smiled. "You believe me, I know it."

"That it wasn't my fault?"

"Yes."

"Yes, I believe you. Part of me wonders if this is real, but part of me wants to shut that part up." They stood wordlessly gazing into each other's eyes for what seemed like an eternity, though it was still too short a time for Paul. "Baby, stay with me all the time. Can you?"

"No, I'm sorry."

"But, baby, you're an angel now. You're my angel for real. Right?"

"Yes, and I will look out for you and try to talk to you when I can. But it does take energy for me to talk to you, and I don't have an unlimited supply."

"How come I can see you?"

"You're asleep."

"I am?"

With a grin and a suppressed giggle, she nodded. "Yes, darling."

"So, you will be back other times, too."

"Yes. I came this time to tell you that I think you should go back to work. You should get back to the track. They gave your job to someone else, but I'm sure you'll be able to get another job easily. I think it will help cheer you up and get you back on track to becoming a head trainer. You can't sit in this room with that brush forever, honey."

His cheeks flushed with embarrassment. It was sort of silly, sleeping with a brush. "But your hair. I can touch it. Part of you is there with me."

"It's okay, baby. I understand. I'd probably do the same thing. You still need to get out of the house and go back to work. It will make you feel so much better."

"But you won't be there. I'll be at the track without you, and that will just make things worse for me."

"Trust me. You will not feel that way for long."

He wondered if she could tell the future in her state. Or was she only saying that to get him out of the house?

"Trust me. Please. You need to be at work and with the horses. You need to check on my horses, too, you know."

"Oh. I forgot."

"I understand."

"But they hired someone to replace me?"

"Yes. I'm sorry. You were gone an awfully long time. They'll be glad to talk to you, though. So will the horses. It will do you good, darling."

Paul dropped his gaze for a second as he wondered if it would be something good for him, or something bad that would remind him of his loss and make memories come back to him in a flood as they had at times. "I suppose I could try it."

"Don't worry. It won't upset you too much."

"You're just saying that so I won't go completely mad once I'm there."

She giggled. "No, I trust you will be fine. Remember, I will try to be with you whenever I can. You're never alone."

"Are you leaving me again?"

"Not forever. I promise I'll be back whenever I can."

"Okay. I love you, baby. I miss you so much."

"I love you, too. And I miss you."

He stood in his spot, one with no surroundings, for several minutes, wishing she hadn't vanished from before his eyes. He wished none of this had happened. He wished this was all a giant nightmare. Maybe he was still in the coma in the hospital in York and she was really visiting his bedside.

His eyes opened, and he found his hand on the brush handle, tightly gripping, afraid to let go. She had laughed at his silliness, but that was okay, as long as she was laughing again. He would do anything to make her happy. He picked up the brush and spoke to it. "Listen here, Missy. You'd better be a good girl, or I'll be forced to spank you."

Oh, no. He shouldn't have said that. That only brought back memories of him chasing her around the apartment with no clothes on, and him cornering her in the kitchen and spanking her. Seconds later, he had bent her over the table. An image of her from behind bothered him in so many ways. Physically, mentally, each in their own way, it was painful to know he would never know the intense feeling of their connection again.

Gently, he placed the brush on his nightstand, keeping his eyes on it the entire time. He touched the golden hair hanging from the brush one more time, and then stood up. It was the middle of the night, but he knew the track would be bustling with activity already. After dressing, he left a note for his parents and headed to the subway.

ᛣᚸᛣ

"Hey! Look who it is."

"Hey there, Denny."

"Good to see you again. Sorry about...you know."

"Yeah. Thanks." The instant those words came out of Denny's mouth Paul realized that he was probably going to hear those same words many times today. *Great.* He debated going back home to avoid all the apologies. "Just here to visit. Check on the horses. How are things?"

"Good. But, they hired someone for your position, Paul. I don't –"

"I know, Denny. It's fine. I'm not here to work. Just making sure everything's okay. Missy would want me to check."

"Right. That, she would. Well, everything's fine and dandy. Ribling won his first stakes race the other day. Uh, Peaches had colic, but she's okay now. Was a close one, that one. Then, uh, Bartles. He won an allowance race. Oh, we lost Marish in a claimer. Boss is gonna try and get her back, though. How are you? I heard you were in a coma."

"Yeah. Guess so. They had me on a breathing machine."

"You mean it breathes for you?"

"Yes, it has this thing like bellows for a fireplace; it goes up and down, pushed air into my lungs. Anyway, it worked. Here I am."

"Here you are. Have any hot nurses there in England? Huh?" he asked with an elbow to Paul's ribs.

"I didn't really notice." He'd never notice another woman as long as he lived, just as he had promised on his wedding day. That line, "...'til death do us part," meant nothing now that even death could not separate him from the love of his life.

"Sorry, Paul, I..." His voice trailed off.

"It's okay. Let me go say hello to this fellow." Paul made his way to the nearest horse peeking over his stall door.

It was a tough morning as he shuffled from one barn to the next in search of a job. Unfortunately, all he could find was a groom's position. *Gone for two months and I go from almost head trainer to lowest man on the totem pole again.* Swallowing his pride, he took the position to get his foot in the door. It also afforded him the luxury of having something to keep him busy for a change.

As he walked to his car, he watched Julia walking in with her little girl, Rachel. *Probably just picked her up from school.* He remembered that she had lost her husband in an accident here at the track last year. She was terribly distraught, he had heard. While he had never met the woman, he understood now how she felt. Or feels? He wasn't sure which stage of grief she would be in, or what she was feeling. He wanted to ask her about what she was going through. At the same time, he did not want to bother her about it by bringing it up. Maybe she had forgotten or had been able to put it out of her mind most of the time by now. In addition, talking to her about it would upset him as well, and he didn't want to cry in front of a woman. Better to stay well away from her. He hoped his friends would not try to set them up because of the horrible tragedy they had in common. A few of the guys were dumb enough to try it.

ひひひ

Paul managed to work his way out of the grooming position to "gallop boy" in a few short months. It had been a long time since he had ridden a horse, but his first day back in the saddle was exhilarating. Between horses and during breaks, he often hung around the barn attempting to help in any way he could, to prove himself. While he loved working horses, he wanted to be a trainer, and he could not lose sight of his goal. Every move he made was with that goal in mind.

Finally, it paid off, and he found a position in another barn as assistant trainer. Nine months after coming back to the track, he was back to where he started. With each step, he told his wife, and she was always excited for him. He kept her up on every detail every night. Sometimes she answered, sometimes not. He wasn't sure if she could hear him, but he talked anyway, just in case. She had mentioned something about using energy to speak to him, but he did not understand it.

It was okay, though, as long as he could maintain contact with her.

"I said hello to your horses for you, like you asked. They send their best."

Missy giggled. Her voice was faint, but he was able to make out her words and giggles. Every time she laughed, it healed his heart a bit more. "They're talking to you, too, now? You might want to call that psychiatrist."

Paul actually had thought about calling a psychiatrist, thinking his head injury had made it so he could talk to his wife. But he was too afraid the psychiatrist would make him unable to hear her voice anymore, or might do shock treatments on him, or drug him and toss him in a padded cell in a mental institution. The notion that his life could be ruined over admitting that he talked to his dead wife kept him quiet about it. He told no one, not even his parents. Especially not his parents. They would call that paddy wagon before he could blink an eye.

CHAPTER EIGHT

Elmont, New York, September 1968

It was still warm for September, but Julia didn't mind. The afternoon sun warmed her thin frame, which she appreciated greatly because she knew what would happen soon. The weather would chill, then grow bone-chillingly cold, and she would spend the entire winter shivering and trying to keep from freezing to death. She wasn't about to gain weight, though. Not that it mattered what she looked like because she most definitely wasn't on the market. She simply wouldn't feel comfortable in a layer of fat. Besides, thin was *in* these days.

Rachel's friend, Candy, was so thin you could almost see through the poor girl. It wasn't on purpose; she never ate much because of her money troubles. Rachel had told her mother that Candy's brother kept stealing her money to buy drugs, leaving nothing for food. Julia and Rachel would try their best to give her food or money to buy lunch, but many times, she refused out of pride. The girl's pride was going to kill her one of these days.

Julia slouched in her chair and leaned her head against the bare metal back, getting as much sun on her face as she possibly could before it disappeared again behind a cloud. The sun was so comforting and cozy, like being enveloped in a warm bath that never got cold. She almost moaned, as it felt so good.

"You know, we've worked at the same track for at least ten, twelve years and have never met?"

Julia opened her eyes with a start. "Um..."

"Sorry to wake you. Were you sleeping?"

"No. Just resting my eyes between works." Julia sat up.

"I'm Paul Holton." He held out his hand for her and she accepted.

"Julia McMahon, but it sounds like you know that already." She narrowed her eyes as she slipped her hand from his.

Paul chuckled slightly. "And you've never seen me around town?"

Julia shrugged one shoulder. "Well..."

"I knew it. And why would we not have met?"

"We work in separate barns?"

Paul shook his head and relaxed into the seat next to her. He faced the track and took in a deep breath, fully appreciating the still warm fall air laced with a hint of manure.

"No?"

"No." He glanced her way, slightly more serious now.

Twisting in her seat to face him, she asked, "So, what is your theory?"

"They've wanted to set us up for at least ten years." He was perfectly serious but did not meet her gaze. He could see out of the corner of his eye the surprise on her face. It disappeared, and she faced the track again, settling into her seat. She was silent. "But don't worry. I'm not here to ask you out."

She was almost insulted as she turned back to him again but was still unsure of what to say or how to react. A nervous, "Ha," escaped as she turned away from him and crossed her arms over her chest. Finally, she found words. "So, why are you here?"

"Someone dared me to ask you on a date. Said I was chicken if I didn't. I didn't want to be chicken. So, here I am. But it's okay. I know you never go out with anyone. At least with men from the track, anyway. And, it's the same for me, by the way. I mean, women. I mean, I don't date women. From the track. Or anywhere. I don't date," he reiterated.

Julia bit the inside of her lip. She wasn't sure whether to scream at him or laugh. Either way, she still could not look at him.

"So, the answer's no, I take it?"

Finally, she looked at him, though incredulously, with her mouth in an O. One chuckle from Julia answered his question. Paul nodded and frowned at the same time, then stood up, looked at her one more time, waved, then walked away.

Julia blinked. That was certainly the strangest conversation she had ever had. As he walked away in his well-fitted suit, she looked for the so-called friends who had dared him to talk to her. *That's ridiculous. It sounds like something they would do in Rachel's school. High school behavior, that's for sure.* Just as she expected, she saw no one, though he did disappear around a corner.

Well, this was certainly bad news. It showed that people talked about her. She had never thought about that before. Why would any of the self-absorbed men working here discuss her dating or social life? *Or lack thereof.* Honestly, she had no life other than life at the track. She hadn't been on a date since the kids were toddlers. Julia wondered if the men of the track had been talking about her all along. She didn't care about their dating lives, and never even considered that they might wonder about hers.

She had noticed Paul before, of course from afar. Apparently, he had noticed her too, but was doing exactly what she was doing and avoiding the opposite sex. They had very similar circumstances, but that didn't mean they would be right for each other. Besides, no one else would ever be right for her, and the same applied to Paul, she was sure. Obviously, his wife was the one and only woman for him. No one else would measure up.

That didn't mean they couldn't be friends, though. Why not? What was stopping them? Rumors. Gossip. They were both avoiding rumors that might develop if they were seen together.

Julia found it strange, also, that they had run horses in the same races, had passed each other on the track, but had never acknowledged each other. Suddenly she realized how rude that was. She couldn't allow that to happen again. If she was anything, she was polite, even to the men who treated her poorly. She figured it would make them feel guilty at some point for being mean to her. So far, though, most men hadn't shown one bit of concern for her feelings.

Paul, too. That was rude of him to talk to her that way. Well, he could keep his distance for all she cared. She was better off, and for many reasons.

ʊʊʊ

"Hey, Mom," Rachel called as she entered the barn through the side door. She had just walked from her high school across the street.

"Hi."

Rachel began talking about something as she set her backpack on the ground by the door. *Probably talking about school,* figured Julia. *Maybe boys.* She hated the fact that she had also been thinking about boys, or men, lately. It wasn't something she should be thinking about at her age.

"...and then she said she wanted to go with him..."

Then again, she was only thirty-five. What was she going to do with the rest of her life? Sure, be a trainer. She had been the head trainer for a few years now, and that was great. She was the second female trainer ever licensed in New York. Great. But was she doomed to be alone for the rest of her life? Her kids were teenagers now and might be grown and out of the house soon. Rachel had just turned seventeen. Billy was almost fourteen. It wouldn't be long for them.

"...but I said she was crazy for thinking..."

Julia patiently took a breath and pretended to listen to her daughter. She had too much on her mind to concentrate, though. All she could see was herself, just like her mother, sitting in a chair, knitting, and sitting amongst ten cats. *Spinster.* That was the word for her. Was she doomed to become a spinster? Well, did she have any choice? If she couldn't have Robbie, she couldn't have anyone. There was no one else.

Rachel always talked about the "guys" at school. Julia wished she had someone to talk to, as well. It hit her that she had no girl friends. She had male friends in very shallow relationships. They'd see each other in the grandstand in the morning and maybe talk for a few minutes, then would go about their day.

It was her own fault for being so distant. She had done it on purpose, too, to make sure they all knew she was not on the market. Goodness, what must they think of her? Do they think she's some sort of evil or crazy woman plotting ways to beat men at their own game?

"Mom?"

They must hate her. Maybe they only tolerate her, enjoying the novelty of having women on the track until the fun wears off and she goes back home to the kitchen where she belongs. They should know better by now. It's been twenty years here at Belmont. One of her first dates with Robbie was watching the 1948 Belmont Stakes, with Citation stumbling out of the gate, then going on to win the Triple Crown. That was twenty years ago. Julia shook her head. *Twenty years.*

"Mom?"

"Huh?" Julia jumped.

"What's wrong?"

"Nothing, honey. Everything's fine." Standard answer. Mom's always okay. Mom never has any problems.

"No, it's not, Mom." Rachel came closer and touched her arm. Julia wondered if perhaps her daughter were old enough now to have heart-to-heart talks that included something about herself as well as Rachel's life. Their talks were always about Rachel, never about Mom. It's not that Rachel hadn't tried, though. She had always been very empathetic and sensitive to others' feelings. Teens these days are egocentric, and think they are the most important person on the earth. No one else's needs matter. However, Rachel had always been good at noticing that other people have feelings, too. Julia was proud of her daughter for that personality trait. Despite Rachel's attempts in the past to get her mother to open up about her own troubles, she never had. Could she now?

As she gazed into her daughter's beautiful green eyes, the ones she had inherited from her father, she hoped Rachel would have a better life than she had had. Without a word, she wrapped one arm around Rachel's shoulders and led her to the grandstand.

"Let's sit by the winner's circle," Julia suggested as they climbed the stairs.

"Okay. So, you don't need me to muck stalls?" Rachel asked with narrowed eyes.

"No. The others are taking care of it. I want you to watch a race with me." *Maybe we'll talk.*

"Oh, okay. Why? Are we going to claim one of them?"

Julia glanced at her program. The fifth race was a claiming race. *Perfect.* "Yeah, possibly that number four, Angelic."

Rachel leaned over the arm rest toward the program her mother was holding. Julia handed it to her but kept her eyes on the post parade. Rachel looked at the tote board. *Fourth race.* She flipped the program back one page. Number four was named Silvery Moon. Not Angelic. And it wasn't a claiming race. "Mom, you know this is the fourth race, right?"

"Yup."

"And it's a maiden special weight, not claiming."

"Huh?" Julia's eyes flashed to the tote board. As soon as she realized it was only the fourth race, she chuckled at herself. "Oh. Well, I guess we have a bit of a wait, then." Julia's cheeks flushed.

"Let's go back to the barn, then. We have another half hour or so."

"No, let's just stay here and wait."

Rachel couldn't believe her mom had said that. Normally, she would have tried to use every minute wisely, not sitting around in the stands waiting for a race. There had to be something else, some other reason. It didn't take long for her to figure it out.

Rachel turned her head toward her mother, and immediately, Julia turned her head to the track. What had she been looking at? Rachel followed the previous line of sight and saw a man sitting even closer to the winner's circle. He was several rows in front of them, wearing a tailored suit, leaning back against his seat with his legs up on the railing in front of him. Another man sat a few seats down, and they appeared to be having a conversation.

Once the man in the suit turned his head, Rachel could see his face. She knew that face, of course. It was Paul, the poor man who had lost his wife in a car accident many years ago. People around the track had always joked about setting him up with Julia, but it never happened. In fact, the two of them had always gone well out of their way to avoid each other. Rachel knew why. Mom resisted and wanted nothing to do with dating someone. It was sad to Rachel. Just the few months she had been without a boyfriend had been lonely. She couldn't imagine going thirteen years without so much as a date.

"There's that guy, Paul, Mom."

"Mm hm." Julia kept her eyes firmly on the track now, though the horses were in the gate.

Soon, the horses were released from the gate. Julia sat patiently next to Rachel during the race. As the horses closed in on the finish line, Julia sat up, leaned forward, and held her breath. Rachel could tell her mother wanted a particular horse to win. And when that horse crossed the wire in first place, her mother clapped and smiled. Rachel didn't have to check her program to see why. Paul stood up in front of them, cheering and patting the man next to him on the back. They both went to the winner's circle to have their picture taken with their horse. Rachel folded in her lips to avoid the grin desperately trying to take over her face.

Dare she ask? Oh, she wanted to so badly it almost hurt. It was killing her not to ask her mother about this. Of course, she would deny it. *Do you have a thing for Paul, Mom? Oh, geez. Come on. Just say it, already. Let it out. Come on.*

Julia turned her head toward her daughter as she realized Rachel was staring at her. "What?" she asked.

"Do you ha..." She couldn't do it. She stopped herself and shook her head.

"Do I have what?"

With her top teeth firmly holding her bottom lip, Rachel glanced up at her mother. "Um..."

Julia could see it on Rachel's face. She always looked like that when she talked about boys. Rachel had already figured it out. Julia sighed and slumped into the back of her metal chair. "He did something weird today, that's all. I can't figure it out."

Rachel couldn't stop her eyes from opening wide. She was stunned but had to say something. Mom was actually talking to her about a man. She couldn't believe it. "What'd he do?" Rachel wiggled closer.

Julia winced slightly, as if it were painful to even think about. "He um, he um, he sat next to me."

"Okay..." *Did he ask you on a date? Oh, please, oh please.*

"He said that somebody dared him to ask me to go out with him."

Rachel jumped as she sucked in air. Her eyes lit up like the sun as she continued to bounce in her seat.

It was at that point that Julia realized she was acting immature by talking about it. This wasn't her anymore, talking and giggling about boys or men or being asked out. She wasn't even asked out. Julia shook her head and faced the ground in defeat.

"Mom," Rachel prodded loudly. "Come on, please? Tell me. Are you going out with him?"

Julia chuckled with only one corner of her mouth raising slightly. "He didn't ask me out."

"What?"

"You heard me," she answered, then laughed.

"What are you talking about? You just said –"

"He said it was a dare. He didn't really want to ask me out. He just didn't want to look like a chicken. He probably got five bucks for it. I don't know." Julia waved dismissively.

"What?" Rachel shouted, then shot a dirty look towards Paul. He was headed back to his seat.

Julia shrugged. "He said he knew I would say no anyway. And that he knew I didn't date, and he wanted to make sure I knew that he didn't date either."

"But, Mom, why not? Why don't you? Come on, Mom. It's been plenty long enough." Rachel pled with her eyes as much as her words. The big, green puppy dog eyes always got Rachel whatever she wanted. Not this time.

"I'm not interested in him, anyway. Doesn't matter."

"Aw, come on, Mom. You don't even know him. How can you judge unless you actually go out with him?"

"I can't go out with him, anyway, because he made it clear that he would never ask me out. So that's it." Julia threw up her hands and then slapped them to her jeans. "Let's go." She stood up.

"But, what about the claimer?"

"Changed my mind." Julia walked away, and Rachel jumped up to follow as they walked well clear of Paul.

That was about as far as she wanted to go with the heart-to-heart with her daughter on the subject of her own feelings. She wasn't used to this. Nobody ever asked about how she was doing unless it was in respect to horse racing. "How are you?" always meant, "How are the horses?" Of course, it was probably her own fault for always answering with information about her horses and not herself. Somehow, it had developed that way over time.

Maybe self-talk had done it to her. In other words, it was her own fault for telling herself no one really cared about how she was doing, that they only cared about her horses. After all, this was a race track, where the horses' needs came above everyone else's. In many of the male trainers' minds, their horses' needs came above their own, certainly, and many times above their family's needs. Even their wives.' They never even went on vacations. It's a wonder many of them stayed married over the years. Usually, the ones that stayed married had wives involved in the care of the horses, too, or they were content to stay home and be kept.

So, why shouldn't she believe that people only cared about her horses and not her?

Of course, Rachel cared. Billy, too. Somewhat. He was a pimple-faced teenager now, just starting puberty. His voice would be changing soon, too. Billy had much more important things to worry about than his mother's well-being. Rachel, as the most empathetic person she'd ever met, cared, but Julia was still uncomfortable talking to her about her own life. Besides, she had to maintain herself in authority. If she suddenly became Rachel's friend, she'd never be able to discipline the girl. Not that she ever needed it. Other than allowing the horses to run too fast during their workouts, Rachel hadn't been too much trouble over the years. It seemed Rachel's only goal in life was to ride horses as fast as possible...and to get her jockey's license, which Julia did not want to happen.

There was a woman in Maryland who had been attempting to sue the Maryland Racing Commission to force them to give her a jockey's license. So far, she'd been turned down after every request, but Julia had heard that the woman, a jump rider in the Olympics, was determined to appeal every decision until they gave in and gave her the license. Inside, Julia was pumping her fist, excited for the possibility of advancement in women's rights. But she had to hide that excitement because if this woman were ever granted a license, Rachel would be all over the New York Racing Association to push for the same.

Julia did her best to downplay the effect it would have on the racing world, but she knew inside that this would be the biggest decision in the history of the sport – the decision to allow women to become jockeys. Every morning, Rachel went right to the *Daily Racing Form* to search for any progress in the case. Then she would fill Julia in on the news. Julia tried to seem as though she wasn't excited about it, so Rachel would calm down, but it didn't appear to be working. Rachel had enough excitement for the entire state of New York.

ᴕᴕᴕ

That night over dinner, Julia could tell Rachel wanted to talk about something. Rachel kept glancing at her mother as she ate, and any minute now, Julia expected her to say something. It surprised Julia that Rachel had kept quiet through most of dinner. Finally, it came, but only once Billy took his plate into the kitchen.

"Mom, why haven't you dated anyone? Ever?"

Julia closed her eyes for a second and dropped her shoulders. She really did not want to discuss this. Well, she did, but not with Rachel. Unfortunately, Rachel wasn't going to let it go, though, and she knew it was hopeless to resist. "I can't see myself with any other man than your father. He was a good man, and I have not met anyone who could even come close to him. I won't settle, either. So, until I meet someone better, I won't do it." Surely, Rachel couldn't argue with that answer. Julia hoped that was the end of that topic. "What's the latest with Kathy Kusner and her battle for her license?" *That'll do it. Rachel would certainly take the bait.*

"I just think you need to go out and have fun once in a while. Okay, so the men at the track are old fuddy-duddies. Paul might be off limits. But then again, he might just be teasing you."

"Huh?" Julia set down her fork and wished she could jump from the table and run away. Her heart beat strongly, though it felt like half the blood left her face.

"He may be playing hard to get, Mom. Has it really been that long? You don't notice these things anymore?"

"No."

"He was just saying that to make you think." Rachel leaned forward. "And it worked, Mom."

"It has not. You're talking about it more than I am." She picked up her fork again and pushed her rice around her plate.

"Only because you never talk about anything but your horses. Mom, I'm not a kid anymore. You've been on your own since you were twenty-two, only a few years older than I am right now. It's been thirteen years. And I see now that thirty-five isn't that old. You still have a lot of life left to live. Why spend it alone?"

Julia was becoming annoyed with her inquisition and wished she could end the conversation politely and without coming across as angry toward Rachel. After all, she was only trying to help. She meant well. Julia blew out a breath of air and adjusted her seat. "One reason for staying single is because I didn't want to upset you or your brother by bringing another man into our house. I didn't want anyone to replace your father." Julia sat up straighter and cleared her throat as she did her best to keep her emotions in check. "Also, I couldn't be a good mom if all I thought about was dating or men. I wanted to focus on being a good mom first. Then, maybe later, I'll date. I'm just not ready yet. You're almost grown, sure, but Billy still has several years to go. After he's out of the house, I'll think about it. Until then, that's not my focus. You and Billy are my focus." *Maybe this time she won't argue?*

"He's old enough to realize now that people date. He was even talking about a girl at school the other day. He'll be dating soon. Then he'll wonder why you've never been out with anyone."

"And I'll tell him what I told you. I'm not ready, and I'd rather be a mom than distract myself by trying to go out on dates. Besides, where am I supposed to meet men anyway? A bar? I'm not going out to some bar and picking up some disgusting drunk. No way."

"You work in an environment with thousands of men. Plenty of them are single, including Paul. Look, I don't want to bother you about it." Rachel stood up with her plate. "I just want to let you know, if you want to go out with him, do it. It's not going to make any difference to Billy or me. You know you don't have to watch over us every second. We're not toddlers anymore. Look, Billy's already in his room doing his homework. I'm about to do mine." Rachel shrugged. "It wouldn't hurt us one bit, Mom."

Julia could not think of a response fast enough, and Rachel was gone by the time something came to her. It wouldn't hurt the kids, of course. That was an excuse, and she knew it. So did Rachel. So, what was the real reason?

That night as she lay in bed trying to fall asleep, she wondered if Robbie would talk to her. "Robbie?" she asked softly, though she knew he would not answer her. Maybe in her dream, though. She hoped. She hadn't talked to him much lately. Why was that? Was she falling out of love with him? Could be, though she didn't want that to happen at all. But, how can you stay in love with a dead man? Someone who could not be here in real life? Someone who may have been a figment of her imagination all these years? She wondered if she needed to see a psychiatrist. Here she was wondering again, for the millionth time. With a sigh, she turned over and hugged her pillow, trying to get comfortable. One of these days she was going to have to talk to a doctor, not just think about it.

People would think she was crazy, though. If they ever found out why she had gone to the psychiatrist, it would be all over the Belmont backside like wildfire. Rumors spread faster there than anywhere else in the world, it seemed. It might even be in the backstretch newsletter. Besides, Julia couldn't take the time off to go to the doctor anyway. Too many responsibilities. Unless she went after morning workouts. No, then there would be gossip. Once her kids figured it out, it would all be over for her.

"You could go to the library, check out a book if you want."

Oh no. He read my mind again. "Oh, Robbie, no, it's okay. I believe you're real."

"Jules, honey, it's okay. I'm sure I would be wondering the same thing. Just go read about it and then decide."

"Decide what? If you're real or a figment of my imagination?"

"Yes."

She giggled. "Which one?"

"Why, both!"

"How can you not be mad at me for doubting you?"

"First of all, I've never been mad at you for anything." He chuckled. "Second, I completely understand. Like I said, I would probably feel the same way. But, I would suggest reading more than one book. Don't just listen to the psychiatrists. Read other books too."

"Like what?"

"Look up paranormal activity."

"Oh, come on. Really?"

"Face it. I'm a ghost. So, you should read books about ghosts."

"Now I know I'm going crazy."

"You're not crazy, Jules."

"How do you know?"

"Because crazy people don't know they're crazy."

Julia rolled her eyes and chuckled. "You always say that."

"One of these days you'll believe me."

"Okay. Tomorrow, I will go to the library during the break."

"Good. And, for the record, if he asks, you should go out with him."

Julia dropped her jaw. "Robbie, I can't believe you just said that. You want me to go out with another man?"

"Yes."

Julia thought about it for a moment. "I'm almost insulted."

Robbie chuckled. "You know I still love you. That's why I want what's best for you. Face it, Jules. You're lonely."

Now, she really was insulted and lowered her gaze. He always knew exactly what she was thinking. It was almost scary. Not almost. It *was* scary. She didn't have a private thought for herself. Ever.

"Baby, it's been thirteen years. No one goes this long after losing a spouse. Your mother's even considering dating again."

Julia wrinkled her nose in his direction, or at least where the direction of his voice was coming from. She couldn't see him. He had explained before that if he wanted to talk to her for a longer time, he had to only talk and not appear visibly. She had decided she would rather talk longer than see him. "At her age?"

"Yes. And your father only died a year ago. Besides, she could live another twenty, thirty years. That's a very long time to be alone. Why not find someone else? How many more years will you live? At least fifty? Can you imagine? You would have been alone for over sixty years at that point. That's as long as your mother has been alive. Think about that."

First, Julia had to get past the thought of her mother going out on a date while she sat at home being the spinster. Then, she had to imagine herself with another man. She even tried to see herself standing next to Paul but couldn't. She couldn't imagine being with anybody besides Robbie.

"Keep trying, Jules. I want what's best for you. And it's best for you to have companionship again. Think of it this way: you've accomplished every goal you've set for yourself. You've proven over and over again that you don't need a man to take care of you. You don't *need* a man, but it's okay to *want* a man. A real man. Someone who can be there for you, if you know what I mean."

"Oh my God, Robbie. I can't bring another man into my bed," she whispered loudly, in case one of the kids was listening.

Robbie chuckled. "Yes, you can. I promise not to watch. All the time." He burst out in loud laughter as Julia picked up a pillow, threatening to throw it at him.

"Oh, my goodness, I cannot believe you just said that," she said, then laughed heartily with Robbie. She thumped the pillow into her lap, still laughing.

ॐॐॐ

The next morning, workouts were done, the kids were in school, and it was the perfect time to go to the library. She decided to go to the science section and browse, but a librarian interrupted her search.

"May I help you find something, ma'am?"

"Oh, um, I um, I don't think so. Thank you, though." Julia tried turning toward the shelf again, but the librarian insisted.

"I see you're in non-fiction. Are you doing research for something?"

"Oh. Um, yes. Research. For my mom." Julia tried turning away again.

"That's very nice of you. What does your mom need?"

She finally relented and faced the woman. "She needs help dealing with the loss of her husband. My father. She's seeing things, hearing things. I think she may be going crazy."

"Like what? What kinds of things?"

"She says she hears his voice. And she sees him. But only in her dreams."

The librarian smiled knowingly. "That happens all the time. It's perfectly normal."

"It does?" Julia tilted her head towards the librarian, who nodded.

"Oh yes."

"Is it real?"

The young librarian thought for several seconds. "Good question. And that's why you're here, I take it? To see if he's real?"

"Yes. I guess so."

With a nod, the librarian checked the shelf. "The book I'm thinking of isn't here. Someone checked it out the other day. But in the meantime, let's go over here." They walked to another section, one Julia wasn't familiar with, one she had never been to. The covers of the books were spooky and dark, with bare trees silhouetted by the moon, werewolves howling. Julia almost rolled her eyes.

"I don't know about this," Julia tried as she glanced around to see if anybody had seen her here.

"Give it a shot. Here." The librarian chose a few books for her and piled them in Julia's arms. "This ought to get you started while you wait for that other book."

"What's that book called?"

"It's simply called, 'How to Grieve.'"

"Okay. That sounds more like what I want."

"Like I said, once it's back, you can check it out. Until then, read these. It will give you another point of view."

Well, Robbie *had* said to read things like this. She couldn't go against her husband's wishes. "When is it due back?"

"Wednesday."

"Will you set it aside for me and I'll come get it Thursday?"

"Yes, ma'am. Certainly." Julia gave the librarian her name and phone number, and then left with her books. She shook her head at the pile on the passenger seat of her new Oldsmobile. Robbie had helped her decide to take the big step to purchase this new car. He had also helped her move up from groom to the head trainer. He had helped her along the way with so many things. Could he help with this, too? Even if it meant never speaking to him again?

Oh, God. I can't do that. I can't get rid of him forever. I just can't.

As she drove home, she further convinced herself that Robbie was real, and that she could not live without talking to him from time to time. It would kill her inside. She couldn't do that to him, either. It would hurt his feelings, even if he said it didn't.

∪∪∪

It was a week later, two days after the book had been due back at the library, but it hadn't been returned. Julia waited with bated breath, calling each day to check for it. She had read two of the other books and found them to be silly and unbelievable because they were a bunch of ghost stories, people claiming to have seen this or that. Though, she did read both books with wide eyes and was unable to put either one down. She had been up too late, reading, ever since that day she went to the library. While reading, she did believe the stories, but after putting them down, common sense told her it wasn't true. It couldn't be.

Julia went to the track kitchen for lunch. Strangely, she saw Paul sitting at a table by himself, reading a book. *Wouldn't it be funny if that was the book I'm waiting for?* He glanced up at her for only a second and she quickly turned away. She ordered her food and sat at the counter while she waited. As time ticked by, people came and went, waitresses carried food by her, her curiosity grew. She had to see the title of that book. He was holding it low and sort of under the table, so the title was hidden. She had to think of something, some way to see that book title. Hmm. If she dropped something and got down on her knees...no, that would be too obvious.

A man walked up to Paul and they shook hands in greeting. The man sat down at the table with him. Paul closed his book and set it on the table faced down. Well, if she couldn't see the front, maybe she could see the side. Nonchalantly, with her face downturned, slipping her hair behind her right ear, she looked to her left and tried to read it. Suddenly, he spun the book around so that the binding was on the other side. Julia pursed her lips. Did he know what she was doing? *He couldn't. Could he?* The waitress brought her a sandwich and chips. Suddenly, it came to her.

"Excuse me," Julia said quietly, leaning over the counter.

The waitress leaned in as well. "Yes?"

"Could you go ask that man, Paul, I think his name is, right?"

"Yes, ma'am."

"Ask him if he needs anything, and then try to get the title of that book he's reading."

"Isn't that an invasion of his privacy?"

Julia pulled out a dollar bill and slid it across the counter under her palm. "It's kind of important."

Biting her lip, the waitress glanced at Paul. He wasn't looking, so she took the money and shoved it in her apron. Then she nodded at Julia, who smiled in reply.

It didn't take long for the waitress to find out the title. Julia wondered if the girl had experience spying on people and chuckled to herself as the waitress came back. She wrote something on a napkin, glanced at Paul again, and then slipped the napkin to Julia.

It read, "How to Grieve."

Julia shook her head in amazement, completely dumbfounded. She thanked the waitress and ate her lunch. Julia balled up the napkin and made sure to use it to wipe her hands after eating the greasy potato chips. She finished her food, then left, making sure to keep her eyes diverted from Paul. And the book.

The second she was gone, Paul leapt out of his chair and to the counter. The waitress dove just as he did, but he snatched the balled-up napkin before she reached it. "Hey!" she tried, but it was no use. He had the napkin now. He went to his table, picked up his book, and said goodbye to his friend. As he walked out the door, he opened the napkin. Just outside of the glass door of the track kitchen, knowing the waitress could see him, he stopped to read the scribbled words. He knit his eyebrows at it, then turned and gave a puzzled look to the waitress, who was biting a corner of her lip.

He went back inside. The waitress tried to duck into the kitchen. "Wait a minute, Marta. Come back here."

Marta closed her eyes and turned around, then looked up at him as he reached the counter. "Yes?"

"Why did she want to know the title of the book I'm reading?"

"She said it was important. That's all she said."

"Important?" Paul narrowed his eyes as he tried to figure it out. Why? Why would it be important to her what he was reading?

CHAPTER NINE

"Hey, Julia," Paul called down the shedrow of barn eighteen. "Julia!"

Julia stepped out of a stall with an incredulous look on her face. When she saw him, she turned white. *That napkin.*

He spoke as he approached her. "You know what I'm going to ask."

"He'll be in a five-thousand-dollar claiming race next week." Julia tried to walk away but he followed. After a few steps, she realized she'd never get rid of him, so she stopped.

"That's not what I was going to ask."

Julia crossed her arms over her chest. "Okay. I give. What is it?"

He wasn't fooled by her fake confidence. "Why is it so important you know what book I was reading?"

Julia uncrossed her arms and turned away again. She found a bucket and picked it up. "It's none of your business," she tried, though she knew it wouldn't work. However, it bought her more time to think of something better.

He tried to duck into her line of sight. "It's also none of your business what book I'm reading."

She couldn't think of anything, so she decided to tell him the truth, and she looked up directly into his hazel eyes. He was tall, she noticed, and looked really good in a suit. She shrugged off her thoughts. "It was due last Wednesday but you didn't return it. I've been waiting for that book, too. Okay?" She put the bucket back down and walked away, but he followed.

"Why didn't you say so? I'm almost done with it. But I guess I could just tell you what the book says, and you wouldn't have to read it."

Julia froze from the inside out. "I'm perfectly capable of reading –"

Paul laughed. "I know that, Julia. Just saying that it would save you some time. That's all."

She crossed her arms again. "You must be a slow reader. Can't even read a whole book in a week?"

Paul chuckled again and pointed at her. "You didn't answer the question, Julia."

"What question was that?"

"Would you like for me to tell you what the book says so you won't have to bother checking it out?"

"No, thank you. I'd like to read it myself. Thank you, though."

"Give me two more days and it'll be back at the library."

"Need some help paying those overdue fees?" she asked, surprising herself. She bit the inside of her lip to keep from laughing.

Fortunately, he wasn't angry. He smiled, waved, and left the barn.

"Oh, my God," Julia mumbled as she ducked back into the stall to hide. With her stomach in knots, she couldn't believe what she had just done. That was the closest she had come to flirting in twenty years.

OOO

Paul shook his head as he left Julia's barn, then peeked back. She was gone. That was certainly the strangest interaction he had ever had with a woman in his lifetime. Of all the books in the world, they were reading, or trying to read, the same book at the same time. This after losing their spouses so long ago, too.

A friend had suggested that book after Paul had had a few too many drinks and let it slip that he had been talking to his dead wife ever since her death. The book had several chapters about how people often conjure up the people they lose in dreams because it makes it less painful to lose them. The book also said that in doing this, it does not allow you to grieve properly. You were supposed to be sad, move on, then get used to life without them. Paul certainly did not like that idea. It meant he would never get to talk to Missy again. What was he supposed to do? Tell her to go away? Leave him alone? There was no way he could do that. Impossible.

But what if she were not actually real? What if all of this was his imagination? What if this was his way of feeling less guilty about getting her killed in that accident?

"You're going to ask me about that book, aren't you?" Missy asked. Paul could tell she wasn't happy about it.

"Yes, baby. It says that you're not real, and that I made you up to avoid grieving."

"You grieved my death, love. Remember? I didn't talk to you for a month after the accident. I let you grieve and I talked to you when I knew you were ready."

"Maybe I made you up so I wouldn't feel guilty about the accident."

"It wasn't your fault. You know that."

"Maybe I only know that because I've been telling myself that for so many years."

"Don't push me away, please, honey? I told you it was okay to date other women. But I want to be here with you, too."

"I can't be with you if I'm with another woman. It wouldn't be right. She would probably put me in an insane asylum, for one. And I can't give my heart to another woman if my heart is still with you."

"Are you saying you want me to go away?"

"No, I don't want you to go away, baby." His heart ached at the thought of losing her all over again. "Please don't go."

"Then, how will you manage to have a relationship with somebody else? You said you couldn't do that with me around. The way I see it, I have to leave."

"No," he bellowed, and then dropped his head into his hands. "I just...I won't see anyone, that's all. I told you before. I won't see anyone, so we can be together."

"Yet you don't believe I'm real."

"I do, baby. I do believe you're real. Please believe me."

"I suppose I do believe you, but I also love you enough to want you to be happy. I love you enough to want what's best for you. Maybe it is best if I step out of the way, so you can be with a real woman."

Paul was enamored with the way she often talked in circles like this. Though, it was confusing for him. He never knew what to say. He knew one thing, though. He didn't want to lose her. "But this is fine, baby. It's fine this way. As long as I can see you or talk to you once in a while, I'll be okay. I don't need anybody else."

"Yes, you do."

"No," he started, but then stopped. He knew she could tell what he was thinking. He had wanted to date again. He had thought about asking Julia for a date. She was pretty and very strong. She was confident, mature, smart, very smart, organized, a good person. Although that little stunt paying off the waitress to spy on his book was a little unethical. Though, when he confronted her, she eventually told him the truth. It had to have been embarrassing for her to admit that she wanted that book, too. He was also embarrassed to be reading it, which was why he was hiding it.

"You should go to the bookstore and buy the book for her."

Paul's eyes shot open. "What?"

"Buy it for her."

"Why is it you can read my mind, but I can't read yours? How is that fair?"

"I'm the one who's dead, remember?"

Paul pursed his lips. "There's that."

"Do it, Paul. But I must warn you, she is even more resistant to the idea of dating than you are."

"How do you know this?"

"Trust me. You trust me, don't you?"

"Of course."

"She will probably turn you down a hundred times if you only ask her to go out. I suggest becoming her friend first."

"My dead wife is giving me dating advice."

Missy giggled. "Yes, I suppose so. But you'll listen, right?"

"I don't know if I can ask her out."

"Why not?"

Paul dropped his shoulders in defeat. "I told you, baby. I can't say goodbye to you. I can't do it. I'd much rather have you in my dreams than have her or any other woman in real life."

"I might have to leave you for your own good," she answered after a long pause.

"No, please, baby. I can't do that. I can't live without you in my life in some way. You've gotten me through the past twelve years. Without you, I couldn't go on. You know how I was after I lost you. Do you want me to be like that again?"

"You're manipulating me. Don't you see? You're threatening to hurt yourself if I leave you."

"No, I'm not. I would never do that."

"You would. But who would take care of your parents if you die?"

"Once they're gone, what have I got to live for, anyway? You're gone, they'll be gone soon. There is no one else. Why not just blow my head off?"

"Please don't do that. It won't turn out well for you, I promise. You can't do that."

"What do you mean by that? What's that mean?"

Panic set into her voice. "Just don't do it. Trust me."

"What? What do you mean? What will happen?"

Silence. Finally, after a long pause, she spoke. "We won't be allowed to be together."

"Why not?"

"It's cheating."

"Oh, come on. You're just trying to scare me, that's all." Paul chuckled.

"Please trust me. Don't do it. Please? Promise me?" She sounded desperate. So desperate, he couldn't help but appease her.

"Fine."

She breathed a sigh of relief. "Thank you, love. Listen. For now, just be her friend. Nothing more. Don't try to go out with her. Just be a friend. Can you do that? This way, you won't be romantically involved with her and you won't feel pressured to get rid of me."

"Okay. I guess I can do that."

"Hey, uh, Julia, right?" Paul stood over her, blocking the sun from her eyes so she could see him.

Julia looked up at him from her chair in the grandstand with a look that said, *Are you serious?* She couldn't help but chuckle, and also couldn't help the slight grin. She felt like a teenager trying to hide the fact that she had a crush on a boy. Only she didn't have a crush on him. "Have a seat. Paul? Is it?"

Paul grinned at her, pushed the seat down, and sat down before it sprang back up. Then he handed her a package wrapped in what looked to be grocery bag paper. She looked at it oddly, and then took it.

"Thank you. Wow. I'm honored. A gift. How...thoughtful." Julia inspected the package on all sides, as if expecting something to happen any second. *Will those bouncy snakes pop out? Will it suddenly disintegrate in my hand? Hell, it looks as though nothing could make it out of this package.* It was almost completely covered in Scotch tape. Holding in a grin, she searched for a way to open it, but she couldn't fit her finger, or even a fingernail into any crease or fold. Everything was taped down.

"Oh. Sorry. I guess I overdid the wrapping."

Julia suddenly couldn't hold it in any longer and burst out laughing. A man seated several rows in front of them turned to look at her. Julia smothered the laughter with her hand. "How am I supposed to open this? Blowtorch?"

Paul grinned, pulled out a pocketknife, and handed it to her. Without flinching, she took it, flipped it open, and carefully carved an opening through the tape. She closed the knife and handed it back to him. Slack-jawed, he froze.

Julia pointed at the knife to redirect his attention. "Thank you. Good thing you brought that."

"Good thing." Impressed, he put it back in his pocket.

She reached inside and pulled out a book – "How to Grieve." With wide eyes and her smile now vanished, she eyed the book, then him. "Thanks," she finally managed to say.

"My wife told me to buy that for you." Paul sat back in his seat and grinned, waiting for her response. She would never want to be his friend now that it was obvious how crazy he was.

"Your...wife." She didn't know he was married again. That was strange. She checked his finger. No ring. She narrowed her eyes at him.

"Yup." He rubbed his chin, and then continued. "The book says I have not grieved my wife's death because I keep seeing her in my dreams. I...talk to her."

Julia's eyes widened, but she was silent. Her cheeks flushed pink as she wondered if he somehow knew the same had happened to her.

"I see on your face that you experience the same thing."

Still wide-eyed, Julia nodded slowly.

"The book says it's not real."

"B-but, you th-think it is?"

"Yes."

Julia nodded again. "Um, that librarian gave me a few paranormal books. They're kind of just ghost stories. They lead me to believe that there is a chance it could all be real. Not in my head. Our heads."

"Really?" Paul leaned his elbows on his knees.

"Yeah. I know it seems silly. It's the kind of thing you don't tell people, you know? I can't believe you told me that."

"Only because I kind of figured you were going through the same thing with your husband, since you wanted that book. How long have you seen him?"

"Since right after the accident. You?"

"Same. Well, a month later. She said she waited because I wasn't ready."

"Wow." Julia was floored, and her eyes were still wide and curious. It was as if suddenly she wanted to read every book in the world that had to do with this subject. She wanted to talk to Paul more about this, too. "What else does she say?" She was curious what he and his wife talked about. Though, she knew it was personal. "Does she know what you're thinking?"

"Yes, but I wonder if that's because I'm making her up in my head. How else would she know?"

"Telepathy?"

"I honestly don't know what to believe anymore. I'm so confused."

For a man to admit that was really something, Julia thought. She'd never heard those words uttered by a man before. "I am too."

"I guess that's why we were at the library, huh? Funny we were after the same book."

"At the same time."

Paul nodded and chuckled silently. "I have to get back to my condition books. Anyway, there you go. You don't have to worry about going to the library now."

"Thank you." She smiled up at him as he stood again. Just as he started to walk away, she called him. "Paul?"

"Yeah?"

"Talk about this later? Not a date. Just talk. I mean, I'm curious about your experience."

"You'll tell me about yours?"

"Of course."

"Sounds good. We'll talk later. But it's not a date," he added with his finger pointed her way.

Julia's lips curved into a knowing smile as she nodded.

OOO

For the next few days, Julia waited for a chance to sit down and talk with Paul, but they were both so busy, they could not find the time. It was apparent they would have to schedule a time to talk. She wasn't about to ask, though. It wasn't right for her to ask him. It would be too much like asking him to go out. However, they would have to schedule something, at this point, to make sure they fit it into their schedules. Julia couldn't get past the weirdness of it all. To schedule a meeting like this would technically be a date. Not the kind where you dress up, though. She wouldn't have that happen. If he ever asked her, and if they ever were able to sit down together, she would make sure to dress as she normally dressed day to day.

She waited. And waited. Several more days went by. Still, they hadn't talked. She had started to read the book and skipped to the chapters that had to do with making up the deceased person in one's head. Of course, it said exactly what Paul had said. It wasn't real. Something inside her could not believe she had made it all up, though. She believed whole-heartedly that Robbie really visited her from time to time in her dreams. She'd even heard his voice audibly before. Just a few times. Those were the times when she really thought she was losing it. She was hallucinating sounds. It meant she was crazy. Maybe that's why Robbie didn't talk to her often this way. He didn't want her to feel crazy.

She ran her fingers through her mousy brown hair. *I am over-thinking here. Gotta think about other things, not analyze everything to death.* She cursed her mind that noticed everything, analyzed it, categorized it, wanted to fix it, change it to make it better. Everything, every situation was important in its own way because it could be a learning experience. Knowledge is power, but that's not what she was hungry for. She was hungry for more information and to learn as much as she could about whatever subject she was interested in at the time. Sometimes, she realized, she got on these kicks, or obsessions, as her kids would joke, where she did all she could to learn everything related to that subject. Then she would preach to her children that knowledge was important and that they should do the same. Of course, the only thing they were ever interested in were their horses.

As she made her way to the paddock for a race, someone tapped her shoulder. She turned but didn't see anyone. She felt it on her other shoulder, so she turned to the other side. No one was there. She stopped in her tracks and spun around to find Paul there with a silly grin on his face. *How old are you*, she wanted to ask. Instead, she shook her head at him. "What are you doing?"

"Headed to the paddock. You?"

"You've got a horse in this race?"

"Yup."

"Oh. I didn't notice." Actually, she had.

"I thought you were more observant than that."

"Not always."

"So, uh, we never did get together to talk about that book. And, well, you know."

"Not yet."

"What are you doing Thursday night?"

"Um, nothing." Panic set in, but she stopped it by looking around at the sights. They were walking side by side along the tree-lined path toward the saddling paddock. Last night had been chilly, as were a few nights before that, which made it feel more like fall. Julia could see just a hint of red in the leaves of the oak trees. Birds chirped from their perches, horses whinnied, talking fans lined the fences around the walking ring, ivy reached halfway up the back of the brick grandstand. She wondered if the ivy would ever cover the building completely.

"How's six? I hope you don't mind, I took the liberty of checking to see when your last race was that day."

"Oh yeah?" Julia giggled, and then shut herself up as she realized she sounded like a child. "When's my last race?"

"Fourth."

Julia nodded. "Then, I guess I'm free."

"Okay. Not many places around here private enough to discuss something like that. I think we should go off the grounds. What do you think?"

"Makes sense to me." Logically, yes, that made perfect sense. And she especially didn't want her kids to see her with him or overhear anything they talked about. After all these years, she hadn't mentioned to either one of them that she talked to their dead father.

They agreed on a local restaurant and Paul made sure to point out that it wasn't a date. Again. Julia agreed. "Okay, let's just agree that anything from here on out is not a date."

Paul agreed with that statement.

OOO

"So. The book."

"Yes. The book."

"What do you think?"

"About what, specifically?"

"Does it make you think your husband is made up in your head? Or do you still think he's real?"

Julia thought for a few seconds and relented to tell the truth. "I guess I still believe he's real, despite what the book says. You?"

He nodded. "Same. I just can't say she's not here. She's too...real. I mean, the conversations we have, the things she says, it's her. It couldn't be me."

"Well the book says we'd stored their personalities in a tiny box in our minds, and we bring it out whenever we need it. I guess to a certain extent, that's true. He always comes around whenever I need to talk to him."

"Missy, too. Yeah, I remember reading that. That was one point I was conflicted on." Paul took a breath and blew it out. "So, you've been talking to him since the accident?"

Julia nodded but did not elaborate.

He leaned closer to her. "Did you ever consider trying to go..." He stopped himself with a shake of his head. "Never mind."

She knew immediately what he meant. Of course, she had considered that. "Yes."

He peered intently at her. "You did?"

"Only for a second. I had two small children, and I couldn't do that to them. Or my parents."

"I didn't have kids but had the parents."

"Are they still alive?"

"Barely. They're both in a nursing home."

"Oh. I'm sorry."

"Fact of life, I guess."

Julia nodded. "I'm fortunate my mother is not in that condition yet. She's only sixty-one. Still as healthy as a horse."

"Your father?"

"Heart attack last year."

"I'm sorry."

Julia shrugged. "I wasn't nearly as upset to lose him as I was Robbie, of course. I mean, I was sad, definitely, but we were never very close. He was the dad who went to work, came home, wanted peace and quiet, and then went to bed."

"My parents knew I was thinking about...you know...trying to be with her, and they got mad at me. My father's reaction surprised me. He was a bit like your father, but to see his reaction was very hard for me. It made me realize how much it would hurt him if I...died. I bet your father had more feelings than he let on."

Julia pressed her lips together. Funny. She had often wondered if her father loved her. He never said it. Never really showed it in any way. "I guess they were from the generation of men that hid their emotions."

"It was a tougher generation, for sure. They had some really hard times. So did we when we were kids. But for them, it had to have been much harder."

"Did you grow up around here?"

Paul nodded. "Long Island, born and raised. You?"

"Same."

"Funny how we never met before this."

Julia nodded. *Getting too personal.* "Back to the book, what did you think about their theory on hearing audible sounds? Did you ever hear anything?"

"I thought I did."

"Robbie, I think, doesn't talk out loud because it's easier to talk while I'm asleep for some reason."

"Energy."

"Yes, energy. That's what he said. Is that what Missy said?"

"Yeah. See? Now, there's a reason to believe they're real. They both mentioned this thing about using energy. I know there had to be more things you could never have known that they brought up. I bet if we compared story for story, there would be similarities and things we didn't know before, things we both couldn't have made up off the top of our heads."

"It's not completely ridiculous, though. We might have thought that up to explain how they appear to us because we couldn't come up with any other explanation."

"Are you leaning towards not believing in him? After all this time?"

"No. I couldn't say goodbye to him, regardless. Real or not, I would fall apart if I couldn't talk to him anymore."

"Same."

Both saddened by their thoughts of losing their spouses again, they sat in silence with long faces and frowns.

"Did you read past that point in the book?" Paul asked her.

"Not yet. Kind of didn't want to. But I might."

"It offers some suggestions on how to stop this whole thing from happening."

"Like how?"

"If you ever hear him, in a dream or awake, you should repeat to yourself, 'He's not there. He's not there.' Personally, if I were dreaming, I don't think I would remember to do that."

"You might. I mean, have you ever gone to bed and asked her to visit you? And then, she does?"

"Yes. I guess so."

"What else does it say?"

"It says to do an exercise where you write over and over that it's not real. Kind of like writing on the chalkboard in school when they punished us. It reminds us of the rule, over and over."

"I don't know if I want to do that."

"Why not?"

"Well, you said yourself you don't want to get rid of her. That you'd mourn the loss of her all over again. It would be too hard."

"But, then again, isn't that what everybody does? Are we living in the past? Are we holding on to things that cannot be?"

Julia sat back and thought. She felt like an idiot, believing in all this paranormal stuff. It couldn't be true. She was too smart for this. Too practical. How could she get herself into this mess? She stared at the bar, where their waitress was flirting with the bartender. Julia's throat was suddenly parched, She needed more water, but her glass was empty.

Adjusting the straw in her glass, she managed to produce another few drops of water and drank it. She coughed and touched her throat.

"You okay?"

"Oh," she chuckled. "Yeah. Just thirsty."

Paul turned around to try to catch the waitress's eye, but she was too focused on her bartender. He groaned. "I'll get you some water." He stood as Julia thanked him, and then marched over to the waitress. Julia was impressed that Paul didn't show his anger or frustration and stayed in control. It was obvious he wasn't trying to prove himself to Julia. Other men might have loudly scolded the waitress for ignoring them or called her names to make themselves look more manly and tough. As if that's supposed to impress a woman. *Men can be so ridiculous.*

It didn't take long, and he came back as the waitress followed closely.

"I'm so sorry. I've been busy," the waitress said casually as she picked up Julia's glass.

Julia couldn't help her laugh. It slipped out before she could stop it, and the waitress eyed her strangely as she left. Paul laughed just then and touched Julia's arm. "Oh boy, she might put something in your water for that." He withdrew his hand and fixed his napkin on his lap.

Julia's eyes bugged. "Oh no, I hope not." She giggled like a child, then stopped herself again by shaking her head. Paul turned in his seat, still smiling, and kept an eye on the waitress to make sure she didn't slip something in Julia's drink. "Oh, come now. You don't really think –"

"Oh, I know they do. They'll spit in it or toss something in."

"But it's water. Surely, I'd see it."

Paul shrugged. "Never know." The whole while, he kept an eye on the waitress until she finally brought the glass back to their table.

"Here you go," she said with spurious joy to her voice.

"Thank you," Julia answered, and as the waitress walked away, Julia inspected her drink. Paul laughed at her. "Are you pulling my leg?" she asked as she slammed one hand onto her hip.

Paul laughed louder. "No. I'm serious."

"How do you know? Have you had it happen?"

"No. But some of my guys in the barn have worked in restaurants and you should hear some of the stories." Paul shook his head. "Woo-ee. You wouldn't believe."

"Like what?" Julia asked, leaning forward. Gingerly, she took a sip of her water, though it looked harmless.

"This one guy was absolutely horrible. I'm really glad he doesn't work in a kitchen anymore."

"Wait," Julia interrupted with her hand up. "Where did he work?"

"Um, La...LaMancha something? Mexican place. You know."

"Oh, okay." Julia was relieved, having never been there. "Go on."

"If someone complained about a dish, he would spit in it, most of the time. Sometimes, for variety, he'd stick a hair in it."

Julia made a face.

"Try to imagine the worst *kind* of hair you'd want in your food."

Julia's face was neutral for a few seconds, then it hit her, and she was immediately filled with disgust. "No," she groaned and made a face.

"Yes," Paul said, laughing. "And if that weren't bad enough, he'd toss it on the floor, then put it back on the plate."

Julia covered her mouth and very nearly turned green. Paul laughed at her face and she slapped his arm for laughing at her. "That's...Oh no. I'm gonna be sick. You'd better stop."

Paul shook his head. "Yeah, and if you think that's bad –"

"No," she interrupted with one hand up and the other over her mouth. He laughed at her again.

They changed the subject, mostly because Julia was getting queasy at the thought of what could be in her food. They had ordered some appetizers and when they arrived, she inspected them closely as Paul laughed at her. She was too hungry to say no to the food, though, and decided to chance it.

An hour later, they realized the time and Julia felt awful about leaving her kids at home alone. Her mother sometimes came over to cook for them, but Julia didn't think she would be there tonight. Rachel and Billy would have to fend for themselves, and that was a bit scary. Rachel was a horrible cook. As she drove home, Julia hoped the house was still there and not burned down.

Fortunately, it was still there, but as she walked inside, Julia could smell the remnants of burnt grilled cheese sandwiches. The bread bag was still open, bits of cheese scattered on the counter, the butter was sitting open without its yellow ceramic cover. Julia checked to make sure the burner was off. Fortunately, they had remembered to turn it off. As she packed up the bread and butter, Rachel came into the kitchen.

She failed to notice that her mother was cleaning up after her. Julia scolded herself for not teaching her daughter these things. She'd never had the time. They were always at the track.

"So, how'd it go?" Rachel asked eagerly, plopping into a kitchen chair. At that point, she noticed that her mother was cleaning up after her and hopped up to help. By then, it was almost clean. Rachel wiped crumbs from the counter and threw them into the sink.

"How'd what go?"

"Mom. Come on. Your date. How'd it go?"

"It wasn't a date."

Rachel raised an eyebrow. "What was it?"

"Business meeting." She kept her face hidden from her perceptive daughter.

Rachel chuckled. "Okay. How'd this...*business meeting* go?" She added air quotes around the term.

Julia pursed her lips at Rachel's emphasis on those words but decided to let it go. Arguing about it would have only lessened her position. It wasn't a date. It wasn't a business meeting either. What was it? "Fine."

"Was it about racing?"

"Somewhat, yes." They had talked about their horses, some.

"What else?"

Julia huffed and turned to Rachel. "None of your business," she said frankly, and then waltzed right by Rachel with her head held high. Out of the corner of her eye, she saw Rachel's grin growing. She couldn't get anything past that girl.

That night, she sat in bed, staring at the book they had been talking about. Julia wondered if she was harming Robbie by not letting him go. The problem was that no one knew for sure what happened on the "other side" because no one on this other side ever gave them any answers. *Must be a rule. Once they arrive, the first thing they're told is, "Don't tell them a thing."*

She asked Robbie to meet her anyway in her sleep, and then went to bed.

He didn't come. It was the first time in recent memory that he had not come when she asked.

"Oh my. What have I done?" she whined the next morning. Was it her doubt? Was it that she met with Paul? "Robbie, please forgive me."

∞∞∞

Since Billy was in school, she had to take down the times of the horses' works herself. She had to focus, but it wasn't easy. She wanted desperately to talk to Paul about this. What did it mean? Did it mean anything? It had to. It had never happened before. He always came when she asked for him. He promised to be there whenever she needed him, too. Where was he?

Finally, it was break time, and she sneaked away to Paul's barn. With quick steps, she searched outside, inside, other side, his office, and finally found him near a manure pit. She hurried over to him and waited for him to finish a conversation with an exercise rider. He turned to greet her.

"Hello, Julia. How are you?" he asked politely. It caught her off guard considering how casual they had been the night before, laughing and joking around. He had called her Jules, too, but that was last night. Did something change overnight? Did he...oh. He wanted to make sure she knew he wasn't interested. Well, that was fine. She wasn't interested either.

"Paul, please, I have to talk to you about something."

The look on his face scared her. She tried to read it. Was he worried she was suddenly in love with him? Julia hoped not. But she didn't have time to worry about that. "Can we...here. Let's go over here." Julia led him to a nearby picnic table and out of earshot of Paul's employees.

"What's the matter?" He seemed more concerned now, less afraid.

"Well, last night, I asked Robbie to come to me and talk to me, but he didn't. It was the first time he...well...he ignored me. He didn't come." It hurt her deep down inside to say that, but she was used to hiding her emotions, and made sure it stayed there. "I wonder if he was mad at me for doubting. Oh, I can't believe he didn't come."

"It was the first time..." Paul repeated, gazing into the distance.

"You think he's mad? Did you talk to Missy last night?"

Paul shook his head. "Didn't ask, though."

"Tonight, ask her to come. See if she comes. What if they both know we're doubting their existence and they're mad?"

"Oh, no. They wouldn't be mad at us. You said yourself Robbie had never been mad at you for anything."

"True, but maybe they're hurt. Like hurt feelings."

Paul took in a large breath and blew it out. "Maybe he was busy."

Julia huffed. "Busy?"

"Well, I don't know. How am I supposed to know these things?"

"You're right, Paul. I'm sorry. I'm just scared. I don't want to hurt him."

"Maybe we should read more about this. Maybe there are more books with more information on what goes on with them on the other side."

"Want to go to the library after work?"

"Okay. Let's do that."

Julia nodded, and they agreed to meet at the library. Later that day, she realized she had forgotten about the kids again. She scolded herself for being so thoughtless. What were they going to eat for dinner? Well, she could ask her mother to come cook for them. She felt awful doing that, though. *See, this is exactly why I didn't want to date. I knew I would be distracted and my kids would suffer.* She considered canceling her plans with Paul but decided to talk to her mother first since she was desperate to know more about "the other side." She dialed her mother's number and waited while it rang.

"Hi, Mom."

"Jules? Everything okay?"

"Yeah, Mom. Everything's fine. I was wondering if you could come make dinner tonight for the kids. I have to go...somewhere. After work. I have a meeting. A business meeting."

"A business meeting," she repeated. *She doesn't believe me.* "You've never had a business meeting after work before." Julia could practically see the smile growing on her mother's face.

"Well, I do now."

"Celebrating a big win?"

"No."

"A date?"

Julia's heart thumped, and she swallowed. She was glad her mother couldn't see her through the phone. "No."

Her mother was silent. She knew. Julia shook her head at herself. She couldn't hide anything from her mother. The woman had the ability to mind-read over the phone. It was ridiculous.

"Okay, okay. I'm meeting someone, but we're just going to the library to do some research."

Julia thought she heard a gasp. "Research? On what?"

"Colic." That was the first word that came to mind.

"You know everything about colic. What else is there to know?"

"That's why we're going to the library. To find out."

Her mother chuckled, but it was obvious she was giving up and letting Julia off the hook. "Okay, I'll be over at six. What time will they be home?"

"Six thirty or seven. Thanks, Mom."

Julia was glad to finally hang up and be free from the inquisition. If she'd stayed on the line another minute, her mother surely would have figured everything out by then. Not that it was a date. It wasn't a date.

ᴜᴜᴜ

"I feel kinda silly about this."

"Why?" Paul answered as he thumbed through the card catalog. He pointed to a number and Julia wrote it down.

"I don't know. I guess there must be a good reason for him not to show up. What could he have been doing? You won't forget to ask Missy to come tonight?"

"I won't forget."

"Okay. Just to see. You know."

"Of course."

They found several books and went to a corner of the library with couches for reading. They sat on two different vinyl couches, one orange and one green. A carpet with multi-colored swirls sprawled on the floor and a large round table was centered on top of that.

Paul came across something he wanted to show Julia and looked up at her. He couldn't very well show her from his couch. After a few seconds, he realized he would have to sit next to her. So, he stood, paused, then mustered up the courage to move to her couch. She glanced up at him as he approached. Paul thought he saw a warning in her eyes, so he made sure to sit a good distance from her.

"Look. Check out this part." With enough room between them for a large person, a very large person, he handed the book to her with his arm nearly fully extended.

"Which part?"

He leaned in to point, and then sat back up again, making sure to keep his distance. She kept her eyes in the book, fortunately, and began reading.

"'...not uncommon for the grieving spouse to hear voices or even have full conversations with their dead husband or wife. In such cases, we must remember that it is not real. While it can be comforting for the person left behind, we cannot allow this to go on for very long or else they will become so attached to this imaginary person that they will eventually become unable to give up the thought of them.'" Julia looked up at Paul with wide eyes, then back to her book as she read aloud softly. "'We must gently coax patients to focus on the living and not the dead.'" Julia kept the place with her finger. "Paul, we've gone too far with this, haven't we?"

"Certainly seems that way. That's a reputable textbook from a Harvard psychology professor. He ought to know."

"I guess so." Julia's shoulders sagged, and she blinked. "We need to focus on the living. Not the dead. How? I focus on the living. I focus on my kids and my work. My horses. I don't neglect them." *Except tonight. And last night. Oh, Lord.*

"It means we should not waste our time with things that are not real." Julia heard a deep hurt in his voice. She felt awful for him, especially knowing exactly what he was feeling, for she felt the same way. "Maybe it's time."

"Let's just read another book." Julia searched through the pile and found a book on angels. "This one," she started as she thumbed through several pages. "says we should believe they are angels for us, like guardian angels. They're here to watch over us. What's so wrong about believing that? And look. Testimonies from people who have seen them."

"I guess it's not wrong. But if it's not true, we shouldn't believe it."

"But what if it *is* true? We will never know until we die, and at that point, it's too late."

Paul closed his eyes for a second, and then turned away.

Julia put the book on the coffee table. "We don't really know and neither do these authors."

"Then, what are we doing here?" he asked, standing. Julia was stunned, hoping he wouldn't leave angry. She looked up at him and he held out his hand. "Let's go. We'll believe whatever we want to believe. Naturally, we'll only believe the books that only prove our beliefs."

"But I'm willing to..."

"No, you're not. Don't you see? You argue both sides, but I know what you really believe."

She took his hand. He pulled, and she was standing, then let go immediately. They left the books on the table and walked out of the library together.

"I'm nervous," she admitted as they stood outside. It was chilly, and she rubbed her arms. Paul took off his suit jacket and put it over her shoulders. "Thanks."

"Nervous about what?"

"I don't really know," Julia admitted. She shivered and pulled the jacket tighter around her body. The warmth from his body heat left over inside the coat felt like a warm bath. She caught a whiff of faint musky cologne, but she couldn't let it distract her. "Maybe that Robbie will be upset with me and never come back."

"I highly doubt that. What would *you* do if you were in his place? Would you give him another chance?"

"Of course."

"I'm sure he would give you another chance. Maybe he was just trying to help you learn to be independent."

"You're right. Maybe that's it. He was trying not to interfere."

"Right."

CHAPTER TEN

"Missy, baby?"

"Yes, love."

"Can you tell me something?"

"Anything, love."

He knew that wasn't true. She couldn't really tell him *anything*. But it was worth a shot. "Are you real?"

Missy giggled. "Of course, I'm real."

"You know this new friend of mine..."

"Julia. Yes."

"Do you approve?"

"Of course, love. I told you that you should date again."

"But we don't go on dates. We're just friends, like you said we should do. We agreed that we're not dating."

"I see."

"I want you to be okay with me having a friend that's female."

"Of course, I am, love. I told you to pursue her. As a friend."

"Question. Do you ever see her husband, Robbie? Can you see other people there?"

"Yes."

"Which question did you answer?"

"Both."

"Oh. So, have you talked to him about my seeing Julia?"

"Yes."

"What do you two think about it?"

"We both feel the same way. We feel you should move on. If you're ready to date again, that's wonderful. He feels the same way about her. He wants her to date again. He wants her to be happy."

"She's not happy?"

"She is managing, but she could be happier. So could you."

"I told you. I'm happy with the ability to talk to you whenever I want."

"Baby, you know there's more to a relationship than that."

"Yes, but that, I can live without."

"Do you have any idea what you're missing? You and I were so close. We were so intimate. We would look into each other's eyes as we made love. Don't you miss that?"

"Of course."

"You could have that again."

"I don't need it. I still have you."

Missy was quiet.

"Missy?"

"Yes."

"I know what you're thinking. You might abandon me and force me to move on. Don't do it, please. I couldn't go on. Don't you realize how hard it would be for me?"

"Yes, I do, but you do need to move on. It may help if I don't come back."

"No! Don't do that. I can't live without you, baby. I can't." Paul felt stinging in his eyes and nose and he took a breath to quell the waters. "Please."

Missy sighed softly, relenting. "I could never hurt you, but I want what's best for you. I only wish you could move on without drastic measures."

"I don't want to."

"There's the problem, hon. You don't want to move on. You won't move on until you're ready. I suppose after all these years, you're still not ready."

"No one else goes this long, do they?"

"No, love. They move on much sooner. You've been dwelling in the past and trying to live there. It's hard, but somehow, you've managed to do it. That doesn't mean it's right, though."

Paul's heart ached as he realized she was right.

ʊʊʊ

"Robbie? You're not ignoring me, are you?"

"Why would I do that?"

"For my own good?"

"It would be good for me to ignore you?"

"You know what I mean. Trying to teach me a lesson."

"No, honey, I wasn't ignoring you."

"Where were you?"

"Well, maybe I was. I wanted you to think for yourself."

"Oh, great." Julia rolled her eyes.

Robbie laughed. "I know you can think for yourself, but I can't tell you everything, you know. You need to learn to stand on your own."

"What do you call the last fifteen years? I've raised two kids and kept the house. I've worked. I think that qualifies."

"Yes, honey, I know. You are strong, and smart, too, but, you know how kids are sometimes. You can't tell them everything. Sometimes they need to learn things on their own. Am I right?"

"Yes. Of course."

"You went to the library today." Robbie was obviously changing the subject.

"I guess, but we didn't learn anything."

"Yes, you did. You realized something."

"What's that?"

"You're ready to let me go."

Julia burst into tears at the thought. There would be no controlling her emotions this time. She sobbed as she bent over her knees. She wanted to bring the covers over her head, too. She wanted to hide forever, maybe bring him with her, and stay there forever with him. A memory flashed before her of their first dance in his backyard during the party. Her heart ached as she wanted so badly to go back to that moment. "I don't want to lose you. I can't imagine my life without you."

"We can compromise, you know."

"How?" Julia sat up and wiped her face with her sheet.

"Try not to call on me so much. I'll still be here, but I want you to feel more independent and open to trying new things."

"Like what?"

"Like spending more time with your new...*friend*."

"Why do you say it like that? You're not okay with this? Should I –"

"No, baby. You should spend more time with him. I was teasing you, that's all. You know damned well what's going to happen."

"Huh?" Julia's eyes nearly fell from their sockets. Did he mean...?

"But only if you let it."

"I don't want to!"

"Then maybe you're not ready. But when you are, go ahead and take the opportunity."

"You and Missy set us up, didn't you? Is that what's going on?"

Robbie laughed. "You think we're matchmaking?"

"Yes." Julia couldn't help a stray sob.

"No, baby. We're doing no such thing."

"So, you've talked, then."

"Yes."

"And?"

"And, what?"

"What do you two talk about?"

"You."

"She knows me?" Julia was so confused. Was she making this up in her head? How could this be? A stray tear fell in her attempts at understanding everything that was happening. She could lose Robbie, but she didn't want to. Yet, she still felt drawn to Paul for some strange reason.

"Yes."

"You two think Paul and I are having trouble letting go."

"Pretty much, yes."

Julia's shoulders slumped, and she sighed loudly. "Well, you're right."

ᴗᴗᴗ

The next morning, in the clocker's section of the stands, Julia stood with her arms crossed as she watched Rachel work a horse. The girl certainly loved riding. She loved it enough to ride two or three horses before school, go to school smelling like a horse, then come back in the afternoon and ride more, ponying horses in post parades. Julia knew Rachel would get her jockey's license eventually. The thought petrified her. Billy also wanted to get his license, but something told her that he would turn out too big to be a jockey. At fourteen, he weighed one hundred fifteen pounds already and was still growing like a weed. In the past six months, he'd grown at least two inches. If he grew anymore, there'd be no way he could be a jockey. For that, she was grateful. One less kid to worry about.

Not that accidents didn't happen during workouts. She'd witnessed her kids falling and getting back up several times. Rachel had broken her arm once but had otherwise escaped anything too serious. Watching that fall had scared her to death. Julia remembered running to the track as the outrider went to catch her horse. She was torn between screaming and looking like a hysterical female and not reacting at all. She chose not to react at all, which seemed to confuse other people. They wondered why she wasn't more concerned about Rachel's spill. Their wondering was better than having them witness her acting hysterically. She'd never live that one down. Better to have no emotion.

It wasn't easy but she had done it.

"Hey," Paul said from beside her. He had settled in with his arms crossed just like Julia's.

Julia fought the urge to smile. Again, fighting emotion. Story of her life. "Hey."

"How'd it go last night?"

Julia took a breath. "He says he doesn't think I'm ready to move on yet. But that I should. What about you?"

"Same. She said the same." Paul looked down at his suit jacket and adjusted his lapel.

"They have talked, you know."

"She told me," Paul said with a short laugh. "You think they're trying to set us up?"

"Robbie said no, they weren't."

"Missy said the same."

Julia glanced at him and finally smiled. "Sounds like we had the same conversation."

"Pretty much."

"But I'm still not ready." The smile disappeared in an instant.

"Neither am I."

Good. Julia nodded as she stared out over the near empty track.

Paul stood next to her, staring out at the grass in the infield, and wondering   if   he   would   ever   be   ready.

CHAPTER ELEVEN

Paul was short an exercise rider this morning. He knew Rachel was busy with her mother's horses, but it was a Saturday, and maybe she'd have more time since she didn't have school. He set out for their barn, hoping it would work out and she'd have time to ride a horse or two for him. It was strange on a Saturday not to have enough help, but it did happen from time to time.

"Hey, Rach," he called. She was on a horse, heading out, when he stopped her.

She pulled her horse to a stop from his slow walk. "What's up?"

"I was wondering if you could work a horse or two for me this morning. I'm running short on riders."

"Sure. I have three more here, though. Can they wait?"

"Yeah, I'll wait. Come on by when you're done."

"Okay, great." Rachel set off again for the track and Paul turned to walk back to his barn. He saw Julia on horseback, watching. The slight smile on her face, he thought, was cute. She tried to be so tough, but he knew underneath that leather exterior, there was a woman in there. He mirrored her smile and waved, then kept walking. He couldn't appear interested. He had to keep his distance. It wasn't hard, considering she was doing the same.

Strangest friendship ever, he thought. *Well, men and women aren't good at being friends.* There was always that sexual expectation hovering over them, so it was easier to stay away. They could wave from afar, maybe exchange tiny smiles from time to time, like this morning. That would be good enough.

Though, occasionally, it was good to have someone to talk to. Over the last month, they'd stood around here or there, discussing business. Very rarely, they would ask how their dead spouse was, but that was always an awkward conversation. Paul chuckled as he remembered her face the first time he asked, "So, how's Robbie doing?" Her face was very expressive despite her attempts at looking tough.

One of these days, he figured he would ask her about why she always had to keep a wall up, although, he could guess. It was probably to avoid teasing. She was trying to be hard-hearted, the way she saw men. Most men, anyway. He hoped she didn't see him that way. Not that it mattered what she thought.

Rachel arrived after an hour or so, surprising him.

"I didn't expect to see you so soon. Did you ride all three?"

"Yup. We churn 'em out over there." She adjusted her saddle on her coat-clad arm. "Who am I riding today?"

"Bell. She's over here." Paul led her to a stall where a grey filly stood, munching on her hay net.

Rachel smiled. "Hey, girl," she said, and then offered a mint. The filly eyed Rachel, sniffed the mint, and then swiped it from her hand. She disappeared into her stall to chew it, as if she thought someone would take it from her. They went inside and tacked up the filly. Paul boosted her into the saddle.

"Two-minute lick today, go a mile like that."

"No problem."

"Your mother tells me you've got a good clock in your head."

"I try," Rachel answered, winking as she slipped her toes into the stirrups.

Paul handed her and the filly off to a rider on a stable pony. The rider grinned as he looked at Rachel. He greeted her and kept his eyes on her. Paul shouted after them. "Keep your attention on your horse, boy!" The rider widened his eyes and faced front again. Paul shook his head. This is why he didn't hire girls. They were a distraction. While he knew Rachel knew what she was doing, he didn't like having his employees ogling her or any other girl for that matter. There were a few other girls around the track, too, that worked horses in the mornings. They were good with the horses. There was something to be said about girls and their horses, but it was too much of a distraction for the men.

He walked to the stands to watch and saw Julia a few rows up. She waved. Well, now he figured he would have to go up and talk to her because if he didn't, he'd come across as rude. He didn't want that. He jogged up and stood beside her. "I thought your horses were done."

"One more," she answered, pointing to a quickly moving horse on the rail. She clicked her stopwatch as he passed the finish pole, and then wrote down his time. "All done."

He heard himself ask, "Grab lunch later? Around eleven?"

Julia couldn't help the look of surprise, though he knew she was trying not to look it. "Okay. Meet you there."

Paul nodded, and Julia walked away clutching her yellow legal pad, pen, and stopwatch. As she walked away, he discovered his eyes had drifted down to her hips, and he noted their shape. She had a nice figure, not too thin, not too fat. Small waist, round hips, his favorite combination. He wondered if having two children meant she had that little tummy bulge in front, but he was unable to tell. She always wore pants that were a little baggy.

He sucked in a quick breath of air as he snapped his head to face the track again. What was he doing looking at another woman like that? He swallowed. No, he couldn't let this happen.

♘♘♘

At the track kitchen, Julia sat down, and Paul sat in the seat across from her. He avoided her eyes, hoping she wouldn't see what he was thinking earlier. The way Missy and Robbie talked and could read their minds, Julia would probably find out anyway. In his head, he told Missy to keep her trap shut. He pictured her giggling.

"Rachel enjoyed riding for another stable for a change," Julia started. He finally caught her gaze. She looked almost as nervous as he felt.

"It was great having her. She's a good rider. Just wish the boys wouldn't stare at her."

Julia laughed and nodded. "Yeah, I have trouble with that, too. That's why you see Billy leading her most of the time."

Paul nodded slowly and pointed upward. "Ah, I see now."

"Gotta beat 'em off with a stick sometimes."

"Does she have a boyfriend?"

"Believe it or not, no. Not right now. She went on a date a few weeks ago, but I guess it didn't work out. She never talked about him again."

"You don't talk girl-talk about boys and stuff with her?"

Julia suppressed a grin. "No. We don't. I don't want to be her friend. I want to be her mother."

"Good thinking."

Julia nodded.

"You're a good mom."

She didn't try to hide her smile this time. "Thank you."

"They're good kids. Always have been. People expected them to be brats, running around getting in trouble, but all they ever want to do is help."

Julia beamed. This obviously made her the happiest – talking about her kids. "That's them. They love working here. Always have. I guess I brainwashed 'em pretty good, huh?"

"Seems so. They've been here since the beginning, haven't they?"

"Yup."

"I remember seeing Rachel ride her pony around and wondered what kind of trouble she was getting into. I mean, I remember being that age. I was no angel. But, I guess Rachel never really did anything bad, huh?"

"Well, she wasn't completely perfect. I can't complain, really. She used to run off without me, pretending she was a jockey. She wanted to ride thoroughbreds from the time she was...well, forever. When I got her the pony, she was happy, but still had that inkling to ride the horses. Every year on her birthday, she'd ask, 'Am I old enough now?'"

"She's eager, all right. Billy the same way?"

"Yeah, guess so. Not quite as bad. I mean, as eager. He sort of stays in the background, quietly wishing for his chance. He's the quiet one."

"More like his mom."

"I'm not quiet."

Paul tilted his head.

"What? I'm not," she shouted, then laughed as her face tinted pink and she hunched her shoulders to hide.

Paul laughed. "Okay, let's put it this way, then. He looks more like you, so I assume he acts like you, too."

"Hm." She nodded thoughtfully. "Interesting deduction there. Partially true. I wasn't as shy as a child. But we do have a lot of similarities."

"I'm curious about something."

"What's that?"

"Is Rachel's personality a lot like her father? I mean, she must look like him, because while she looks a little like you, she has completely different hair and eyes."

Julia bit the inside of her lip as she thought about it. To tell the truth, she couldn't remember all that well. The conversations she'd had with Robbie were just conversations. It's not the same as being with someone. She tried to analyze the way he talked, and the way Rachel talked. They were different. Julia's eyes darted back and forth as she searched for the answer to that question. "I don't know," she finally said. "I, um, I think she's like her father with her desire to ride. She's a lot like me, too, though. She has drive. You know? She wants to succeed. Wants to get ahead in life. She wants to be a part of 'women's lib' and do something about it, not just hold a sign. She wants to be a part of the change."

Paul's eyes widened. "Wow. Color me impressed."

"I like that quality in her, but now that I think about it, that's the way I am, too." She lowered her head. "I sound conceited."

"No, you don't. You're definitely not conceited. You're a woman who knows what she wants, and you go get it."

Julia nodded. "I guess I do." Julia wondered if he thought she was pursuing him. Did she want him? Did she even know what she wanted?

The fear was back, and he knew why. He didn't mean to focus it back on him or their possible relationship. That look told him everything, though. She was still scared. But, so was he.

CHAPTER TWELVE

Paul heard shouting and ran toward the commotion. "What's going on?"

"We're looking for Rachel. She's missing."

"What? What do you mean?"

"Julia said she didn't come home last night."

"Where's Julia?"

"She's out driving around looking for her."

"Oh, no," Paul muttered. He looked around. He'd never find her. She could be anywhere. "Where was Rachel last night?"

"With Candy, in Queens. They went to the movies, but Rachel never came back."

Paul sprinted for his car. A fleeting thought about the workouts this morning passed through his mind, but he let it go, promising himself he'd get back to it soon. First, he had to find Julia or Rachel, or both. Hopefully, both.

His car roared to life and Paul was glad it was still warm. He turned on the heat, and then set off for Queens.

⳪⳪⳪

Julia crept along the streets of Queens. It was daylight now, easier to see, and she hoped and prayed not to find her daughter in an alley. She'd much rather this be some sort of misunderstanding where Rachel was okay, maybe at Candy's. Julia tried to remember where Candy lived. She thought she knew but wasn't sure. She'd try anyway. On the way, at each alleyway, she parked, got out, searched, and then got back in the car, empty-handed. Finally, she thought she found Candy's house, but no one was there. Or, at least, no one answered. She'd even opened the door, but didn't see anyone, and she didn't want to walk in uninvited. She had a feeling Rachel wasn't there, anyway.

She knew her daughter was still alive. She could tell. So, she had to keep looking. She was sure the police weren't looking yet, which made her nauseated. Why wouldn't they try to find her as soon as possible and before she got too far? What if someone kidnapped her and took her on a drive across the country? She could be anywhere. Unfortunately, the police were dealing with a large number of runaways, hippies, and transients. To the police, Rachel was merely another number. Julia stopped along the curb as she realized she couldn't see through the ocean of tears.

"Robbie, please find her," she begged. At this point, she couldn't stand to consider the possibility Robbie wasn't really there. He *had* to be. He *had* to be there for Rachel now. It was one time when she hoped she didn't hear from Robbie. She wanted him to be with their daughter. Her shoulders bounced as she sobbed over the steering wheel.

"Julia!" she heard from outside. Her face filled with confusion. *Paul?* She rolled down the window as quickly as she could, but he headed for the passenger side and hopped in. She rolled up the window again, and then looked at him.

"What are you –"

"Jules, you're a mess. You should let me drive. Please? Come get in my car, we'll drive around and look for her."

With her lips parted, her breathing slightly heavy with exhaustion and worry, tears running down her face, she nodded. They turned off her car, locked it, and left it on the side of the road. Paul noted the location of the car, so they'd be able to come back and get it later.

"How long have you been out here?"

"I don't know," she said as she stared out the window. "I can't believe this, Paul. I can't believe it. This can't be happening."

"We'll find her, Jules. Everyone at the track is looking."

Through her tears, she turned to him, smiled weakly, and nodded. "Maybe she's out with Candy somewhere. Maybe they're okay. Maybe they just spent the night at someone's house and overslept."

"Yeah."

"Maybe some boy convinced her... Oh God, no."

"No, don't think like that, Jules. Stay positive."

She whined as she looked outside again. "This is one of those times I wish Robbie would speak out loud to me, so I could hear him, but he won't."

"Maybe he's looking for her, too."

"I hope so," she whispered.

They drove for another two hours before finally giving up. They decided to go back to the track and call the police again to beg for help. "They said they had to wait twenty-four hours, though."

"Call a press conference, Jules."

"Good idea."

"Offer a reward."

"I don't have anything to offer."

"We could take up a collection."

Julia's stomach burned at the thought of something else to pile on top of her 'to do' list. She was already full. She shook her head and closed her eyes. "I can't. I just can't handle it."

"I'll take care of it. And the press conference. Okay? Don't worry about that. I'll take care of it."

She smothered a sob and thanked him as they drove through the Belmont backside gate. "See her, Pete?" Julia asked. Her bloodshot eyes were so swollen, she could barely see straight, but she could tell from Pete's face, he hadn't seen her there, either. With his face sagging, Pete shook his head, and they drove through.

"My car." Julia sniffed and turned to look out the back window.

"I'll get someone to pick it up. Give me the keys. We'll go get it. You stay here, okay?"

"What about your horses? Are they okay?"

"I'll check on them then go get your car. I'll bring someone from my barn, and I'll get the press conference rolling."

"Okay," she answered in a small voice. Paul saw then a broken woman, not the same strong and successful woman he had come to know. She was almost childlike. She was exhausted already, and the day had only just begun. He helped her into her barn, then went to his own.

A few men came to him. "What can we do to help?"

"We're going to start a collection for a reward. Get together whatever you can. Ask owners, trainers, grooms, hotwalkers, everybody. Stewards, too. Maybe track management could contribute. How are workouts going?"

"They're going. We had to guess on what a few needed, but I think they'll be okay."

"We take care of the horses first, then everything else. I need someone to go with me to pick up Julia's car from Queens. We had to leave it there."

He took one man and left again to bring Julia's car home.

∾∾∾

Billy paced the house as he waited for the phone to ring. Every hour or so, someone would call and ask if she came back yet. "No, not yet," he had to tell them time and time again. He had asked his mom if he could come to the track, too, but she said he had to stay home and keep watch for Rachel. Just in case. Maybe she was walking home and would be there soon.

Julia had feared Rachel had been mugged on the way from the subway, so she and another track worker searched the area between their house and the station but found nothing. Someone else asked subway workers if they'd seen her. No, they hadn't.

Finally, by noon, police called Julia and said that they had picked up the search. By that time, the press conference was scheduled, and Julia stood outside her barn with Paul at her side. With several television cameras in her face, microphones all around her from every direction, she began speaking.

Her voice quivered as she spoke, but she did her best to project her voice for the cameras and microphones. Paul brushed his hand up and down her back in an attempt to relax her. She hardly noticed it.

"My name is Julia McMahon. I'm a trainer at Belmont Park. If you've been to the races, you've seen my name in the program and probably have bet on my horses. My daughter, Rachel, plays a big part in helping prepare those horses you bet on. She lives for her job. She loves her job. But now, something has happened to her. She didn't come home last night." Julia stopped and clenched her jaw tightly until she was in control again. "I need help finding her. Here is a picture of her, and I am told her picture will also be shown on television. She's small, about five feet tall, beautiful green eyes, long, curly, brown hair. She weighs about a hundred pounds. She was last seen last night in Queens with her friend on the way home from the movie theater on Fresh Meadow Lane. She had on a blue coat, mittens, jeans, and a green blouse. We're offering a reward for any information leading us to her. At this point, we've been able to obtain about two thousand dollars for that reward but hope to increase that number soon. I'm begging for help from the people of New York, especially those who are racing fans."

Julia quivered as she suffocated her emotions as much as she could. Paul's hand was still on her back as the cameras turned off and away from her. Fortunately, they did not ask questions. She wouldn't have been able to handle talking about it any more than she already had.

"Jules, we need to get you something to eat."

She shook her head. "I can't."

"You have to keep up your strength, so you can look for her or be here for her when she comes back."

She kept her eyes on the ground, sniffed, and then nodded. She let him lead her to the track kitchen where he sat her down at a table. He didn't ask what she wanted to eat but tried to remember what she had ordered the last time they ate lunch together. She had ordered a ham and cheese melt. He ordered another one for her. The waitress glanced at Julia, then gave Paul a sympathetic frown. Everybody at the track knew by now.

Julia was already crying heavily by the time he came back. Tears dribbled from her face onto her lap and she made no attempt at hiding them. She didn't care anymore. She felt like the worst mother in the world, letting her daughter walk around the city at night. She remembered the time Rachel had taken off on her pony. Rachel wound up out of control and had fallen off. Of course, there were plenty of other times Rachel had gotten hurt. She had even allowed Rachel to exercise horses two full years before she was allowed to by the track's rules. Julia felt like the worst mom, ever.

"Aw, Jules. We will find her. Stay strong."

"Trying," was all she could muster.

It took her a half hour to eat her sandwich, but she could not force herself to eat one of the normally delicious homemade potato chips next to it on the plate. Paul watched her eat without looking like he was watching. He'd never seen anything so sad in his life. He wondered if he had looked this bad after Missy died, or if she had looked like this after Robbie died.

By late afternoon, she looked as though she would collapse at any moment. She had scratched all her horses' races for the day and had someone take them out to work them instead.

"I'm out of tears," she said by six that night. "I'm numb. I can't feel anything anymore."

"We need to get you back home," Paul offered, and she merely nodded in reply. Her car was in the lot at Belmont now, but they lived close enough to walk. It was cold, so Paul drove her. Once they were at her house, she found her key in her purse and opened the door.

Billy was there with an expectant face. He had been there most of the day by himself, until Grandma had come over in the middle of the afternoon to keep him company, and to keep herself occupied, as she was equally as worried. When Billy didn't see Rachel, but instead saw Paul, the disappointment was unmistakable. He very nearly burst into tears but ran to his room instead.

"Oh, my God," Julia mumbled, and then ran down the hall after him.

Grandma was in her favorite chair in the living room, knitting. She stood to greet him. Paul noticed her eyes were red, too. "How do you do?" she asked. "I'm Margaret Whelon, Julia's mother. You are?"

"Paul Holton. Uh, I work with Julia at the track. Fellow trainer."

"Come in, please." She offered him a seat in the living room.

Julia had disappeared into Billy's room and Paul wasn't sure if he should stay or go. His eyes darted around as he tried to decide. He wanted to stay, but did she want him to stay? "Um, I just came to drop her off. I'm not sure if..."

"She would want to say goodbye, at least. I'm sure she'll be back out soon. Billy's been a wreck today, as you can imagine." She blotted her face with a tissue. "We all have."

"I can imagine." Finally, he relented and sat down on the couch. Grandma turned the television on for him. The news was just starting. Paul hoped their story would be the leading story. He wanted everyone in the city to see it.

Sure enough, they talked about it. Paul jumped up and went to Billy's door. "Julia? Billy? The story is on the news. Do you want to see?"

"Yeah."

Paul waited until Julia opened the door. She held Billy's hand and they walked to the living room together. They sat together on the couch with Paul as Julia began speaking on the black and white television. They showed Rachel's picture and included a phone number to call for police. Billy was crying again but tried not to look like he was. He was silently clenching his fists, shaking, and breathing heavily, but listening closely. After his mother's speech, he nodded.

"That's good, Mom." Billy's voice squeaked, partly because of his voice changing and partly from his emotions. He cleared his throat and wiped his cheek.

"I said enough?" she asked him needlessly. She had asked everybody at the track the same question all afternoon. She merely wanted him to feel included. Paul admired her for considering his feelings, too.

"It was good, Mom."

Julia nodded and patted her son's knee.

"Want me to come get you in the morning?" Paul asked. He narrowed his eyes, almost flinching as he awaited her answer, although, he wasn't sure why. He wanted to be there for her, he knew she needed him, needed a friend, though he didn't want to overdo it. He couldn't just sit around, though. "After all, I need to do something to help, too."

"Oh, Paul, you've been such a big help to me all day today. Thank you so much."

"Don't mention it. I'll be here at five. Okay?"

"Well, you don't have to."

"I do. I need to do this. Help me feel useful, Jules." He winked, and he thought he saw a slight smile on her face. She nodded, so he stood, patted her shoulder, then left. Grandma jumped up to see him out, as it was the proper thing to do. Paul knew then where Julia got her propensity for sticking to the rules and routines at the track.

∪∪∪

Eventually, Julia went to bed without eating, and collapsed without changing. She hoped desperately to fall asleep soon and to see or hear Robbie tonight. This was one time when he was going to have to answer her about things on his side. She had to know if he could watch over Rachel somehow, or even get her out of that mess, whatever it was. Maybe he could tell her if Rachel was still alive. Then again, she knew in her heart that Rachel was still alive. She even felt that Rachel was in the city somewhere. Thus, she hoped that the news story would help convince people to keep an eye out for her.

She woke up at four, with her alarm blaring and moving across the nightstand by itself. She slapped it to shut it off then sat up and rubbed her aching head.

Robbie hadn't come last night.

∪∪∪

Julia watched as her horses worked and tried her best to stay busy while keeping Billy busy as well.

Billy worked the horses Rachel normally worked, which was hard for him. He told himself he would make sure the horses were well taken care of while she was gone. She would want it that way.

Everyone stared as Julia sat in the stands. Her eyes were still swollen, as she occasionally burst into tears. Some tried to console her while knowing it was impossible. Clouds blanketed the sky over the city, partially hiding the barely visible Empire State building in the distance. A cold wind brought the smog from Manhattan and chilled everyone to the bone.

Breathing warm air into his gloves, Paul approached and sat next to her. She glanced at him, seemingly unfazed by the chill in the air. "Hi."

Paul was encouraged by her greeting because she hadn't been able to say goodbye last night. "Hi," he answered. "What do you want to do today? Drive around again? I was thinking we could get the track to print out some fliers for us to post around town."

The light from the overhead lamps twinkled a reflection in her tears. "Yeah."

"Whenever you're ready, let's head over to the office and ask."

"Think they'd do it?"

"Absolutely."

"Okay. I need another hour or so with the workouts, though."

"Are you watching? Really?"

She lifted her yellow legal pad and let it fall onto her lap again. "Keeping time."

"You could get someone else to do that for you. We could go now."

Julia looked around. "Who?"

"I could get one of my guys."

She agreed, so Paul went back to the barn and picked up one of his assistants. They left him there with her legal pad and stopwatch, and then went to the track office.

The print shop agreed to print one hundred fliers for them, and Julia burst into tears as she thanked them. "This will be so helpful. Thank you."

"Anything you need, Julia."

Julia was glad for something to keep her busy. She, Paul, and a few others they had gathered and posted signs on telephone poles with staple guns. After two hours of stapling, Paul heard Julia's stomach growl. It surprised him.

"Lunchtime," he announced. "Let's go to the diner across from the track."

"Yes. Rachel goes there. Maybe they have seen her, or maybe we could put up fliers there."

"Good idea, Jules."

Paul bought Julia and the others lunch for helping. As they ate, one of Rachel's friends approached.

"Dawn, right?" Julia asked the tearful girl standing next to their booth.

"Yes, ma'am. I heard about Rachel." Dawn's body shook as she suppressed her emotions, so she could continue. "If there's anything I can do..."

"We have fliers. Could you post some for me? Maybe at school."

"Or my church. They would help, I'm sure."

"Good idea, Dawn. Thank you so much."

Dawn took several fliers for the school and her church and left.

ᴗᴗᴗ

Julia finally got the call she had been hoping for – Candy. Finally, the chance to get more information on what had happened that night.

"Candy, where...are you okay? Where's Rachel?" Julia could not get her words out fast enough once she realized who was on the other end of the line.

Candy sniffed and spoke through tears. "I don't know where she is. We walked to my house, and then she was on her way to the subway. That was the last I saw her. I should have walked with her, Julia. I'm so sorry. It's all my fault."

"No, honey. No, it's not your fault. She's walked that way plenty of times. How could you have known?"

"It's only a block."

"I know. I know."

"I looked." Candy sucked in a stuttering breath. "I tried. I looked in every alley in Queens."

"Me too."

"I'm so sorry."

"Honey, it's not your fault. Nobody can fault you. I don't."

"Thank you."

"You're welcome. Are you coming to work tomorrow?"

"I don't know if I can."

"I could use all the help I could get, Candy."

"I know."

"Will I see you there?"

Candy paused. "I guess."

"See you tomorrow, then."

That night, again, she wanted to talk to Robbie, but then again, she did not. When he didn't visit her in her dreams, Julia told herself that Robbie was probably with their daughter, and she was slightly encouraged.

ʊʊʊ

Paul and Julia sat together in the stands again, watching morning workouts. It was silent between them, but that was okay. Paul knew she needed someone to be here with her. Being alone would only make it worse.

Candy hadn't shown up at all since Rachel's disappearance. Julia had a feeling it was because she would only be reminded of Rachel's absence. However, since she didn't have a phone in her house, they couldn't call her. Julia figured Candy had to have called the other night from a payphone or someone else's house.

Julia told reporters the next morning everything Candy had told her, which wasn't much. Police had been getting tips and trying to follow up on them, but many of them were false – people trying to take a stab at the reward money. Julia shook her head in disgust. Didn't they care that her innocent little girl was out there somewhere suffering? Did they only care about themselves and the money? The reward had risen to five thousand dollars, which was about half of what Julia made in a year, and Julia considered dropping it. The police told her not to, that they would follow all leads, false or not. Julia thanked them.

Paul stayed with her as much as he could for support, whenever she needed something, even just to talk. Julia was so grateful for his help. They sat together near the winner's circle as they awaited a race. They still had to make to run races and make money. The horses needed to run, too. Race horses are geared up for a race and if they don't run it, they have pent up energy that boils over and causes behavior issues or even health issues.

Julia took a stuttering breath and smiled up at him for the first time in days. "I appreciate everything you're doing for me, Paul. Really."

"No problem at all. What are friends for?" he asked, smiling and leaning toward her slightly.

Without thinking, she let her head rest on his shoulder for just a second, then sat up again. He grinned at her as she tried to distract herself by looking in her program. He found it cute the way she pretended not to be flustered by what she had just done. It didn't have to mean anything. After all, friends sometimes hugged one another. He put his arm around her shoulders and squeezed. She tried to smile at him again, but it was weak. Her face was overflowing with pain.

"Come here," he said, opening his arms. She became an instant puddle of tears and sobs as she fell into his chest. He held her tightly, rubbed her back, and offered the handkerchief from his pocket.

"Sorry," she said after a minute or two, as she realized there were people around, probably watching her every move. She'd been on the news every night with updates, or lack thereof, and people knew who she was now by her face, not just by her name in a racing program.

"It's okay, Jules." He handed her his handkerchief from his coat pocket.

Julia glanced back and forth as she dried her eyes. She hadn't worn make up for days, knowing she would cry it all away anyway.

"People aren't looking," Paul tried.

Julia tilted her head at him and he chuckled.

"Okay, maybe they are, but they expect you to be sad. It's perfectly okay."

"I guess." She sniffed and blew out a breath of air as she regained her composure.

Each day became harder and harder as she hadn't heard from Robbie and had come up with no good leads on Rachel. She thought she would lose her mind any second. If Paul hadn't been there for her, she might have. She'd cried on his shoulder so many times now, she had lost count. He was so warm and supportive, and she thanked God she had him. He picked up the slack she left in her barn, as she had been unable to keep up with everything. Her employees did their jobs to the best of their abilities, but sometimes had to guess on how a horse should be worked based on his other workouts in the past. Paul picked up the pieces and put together workout charts for them. The task had been too much for Julia to handle.

Billy refused to go to school for the first week and wanted to go out and search for his sister, but Julia wouldn't let him out of her sight. On the third night, Billy had said, "We've lost half our family," and that statement nearly killed Julia. She couldn't keep her composure in front of her son after that and broke down in front of him.

"Oh no, Mom. I'm sorry. I shouldn't have said that."

"It's okay, Billy," Julia had answered, then took a few deep breaths. She looked into her son's hazel eyes. "I'd had the same thought myself."

Where was her little girl?

◟◞◟

Another week went by with no word on Rachel or Robbie. What was he doing? Was he helping? Why was it taking so long? Julia had become a zombie, unable to sleep, unable to stay awake, unable to take care of her barn the way she needed.

Her stable's main owner, Mr. Hanover, sent someone from the farm down to help, which Julia greatly appreciated. She sat in her office and considered calling him again one morning to thank him again and to let him know the latest, which was really nothing.

Her phone rang before she could make that call.

"Hello," she answered without emotion. "Hanover."

"Mrs. McMahon, we've found her. She's at Mercy."

Julia stood up. "Is she okay?" she shrieked, and people came running. They stood anxiously at the door and waited for news.

"She's not doing well. She's lost a lot of blood, she's dehydrated, and we need permission to do surgery."

"Surgery? Why?"

"She's been raped. It's bad. We need to perform a hysterectomy. I'm sorry."

"Oh, my God!" she screamed as she fell into her seat. Paul came in just then and held her arm to keep her steady.

"Do we have your permission? She could bleed –"

"Yes! Do it! Fix her! I'll be right there!"

She hung up the phone and looked up at Paul, then at the people gathered at the door, all with expectant looks on their faces. "I have to get to the hospital. She's not doing well. They have to do surgery. I have to get there. Now."

"I'll take you." Paul helped her up, then through the crowd of people.

On the way, Julia shook and shivered and could not decide how or what to feel. She was overjoyed that Rachel was alive but scared to death she could lose her again before they got there, or even after they got there. "If she needs blood, I'll make sure they take it from me. We have the same blood type."

"Good thinking."

"Paul, they said she'd been raped. Bad enough to have to have a hysterectomy."

"What's that?"

"That's where...well, she won't be able to have children." Julia covered her mouth with her quivering hands.

"Oh, no." Paul shook his head sadly and glanced at Julia. Her eyes were more open now and she was more awake and aware than she had been in days, despite the possible horrors of what Rachel had been through. At least she had her daughter back. Almost.

They parked and ran inside from the garage. Julia ran right in to the help desk. "Rachel McMahon. They just brought her in. She was missing –"

"ER, down the hall, through those doors."

"Thank you." Julia and Paul set off running. Julia was glad then for the attention from the media because the nurse at the desk had known immediately who she was talking about. They hadn't had to waste time trying to find out where she was. They barreled through the doors and went right to the nurse's station.

"My daughter. Rachel McMahon. She's here?"

"She's in surgery. Come, have a seat. I'm sorry, but you'll have to wait."

"At least I know they're fixing her. She's still alive. Right?"

The nurse nodded, but the look on her face worried Julia and Paul.

"Did you see her?"

"Yes, ma'am, I did."

"What's wrong?"

"Doctors couldn't believe she was even alive. She's missing so much blood. She has a broken leg and scratches all over her body. She was bleeding..." the nurse glanced at Paul and lowered her voice. "between her legs. She had bruises. She was so thin." The nurse sighed. "She's still in critical condition, Mrs. McMahon. But we're all praying for her to make it."

Paul put his arm around Julia, who felt her body sag as she lost a bit of hope. It was even worse than the doctor on the phone had led her to believe. Paul led her to the chairs nearby to wait. Julia shivered, and occasionally bounced one leg or both legs. She bit her lips, chewed on her fingernails, things she had never done before this. The chair was black, hard, plastic, the floor was tiled with gray and white specked tiles, a typewriter clacked incessantly in the distance, a voice over the loudspeaker spoke, "Doctor Bennett to ICU please. Doctor Bennett to ICU." Julia heard or felt nothing, only thought about Rachel. She wanted so badly to see her and hold her hand again. She was so close, yet so far.

"We're supposed to get more snow."

Julia grunted.

"Yeah, it's going to be a big storm coming from the north east. Nor'easter, it's called."

"Yeah, I know..."

"We might not get as much as say, Maine or Vermont, but we'll get something to add onto what we already have."

Julia nodded politely.

"Gonna make it interesting for working the horses."

"I'll have to get Billy from school."

"Huh?"

"Billy. I'll have to get him from school so he can see her. If she's okay." Julia shivered and bent down over her knees. Paul rubbed her back, then hugged her shoulders.

"She'll be fine, Jules," he said into her ear. "Some of the best doctors in the world practice here. They'll take good care of her."

It took two hours for the surgery, and finally, the doctors came to get them. They took them to a different part of the hospital, the ICU.

"I'll stay out here, okay?" Paul offered as he spotted a small waiting area nearby.

"No, please. I need you. Please?" Julia asked with her hand out. He took her hand. It was ice cold. Their shuffling steps echoed in the hallway, and several heart monitors beeped evenly in the background as they entered the large space of the ICU. A nurse pulled back a curtain enough for them to walk through. There, they saw a slight figure and curly brown hair amongst white pillows and covers. Rachel was hooked up to an IV but was thankfully breathing on her own.

Julia could not believe this was her daughter. She looked nothing like the Rachel that had left home that Friday night two weeks ago. As the nurse had said, there were bruises scattered on her face and she was so thin, her bones sharply stuck out. A wide scrape on one cheekbone made it look like she had maybe hurt it on pavement.

A nurse approached and checked her pulse. Julia saw more scratches on Rachel's arm just then.

"Do you know how she got here? Did she walk? Did someone bring her?"

"Two men found her, wrapped her in a coat, brought her in, and left. They didn't give their names or any other information. They left before we could get anything out of them. They said they found her in an alley and that was it. When the nurse tried to ask more questions, they turned and left."

"Maybe they were the ones who took her."

"Doubtful, ma'am. They wouldn't have brought her in and let us see their faces if that were the case."

"You're right. I'm not thinking..."

Julia reached under the blanket and found Rachel's bony hand. It was ice cold. Julia tried to warm it for her but her own hands were ice cold. She shivered, and Paul rubbed her arms for her. She took a breath, and then tried to wake Rachel. "Rach? Honey?"

A tiny cry for help came from Rachel's lips, though she did not move.

"You're in the hospital now, baby. You're safe." Julia's body wretched with pity for the helpless girl in front of her, but she shoved it aside and stayed strong for her.

When Rachel didn't say another word, they hoped that it meant she was relaxing and knew that she was safe. Julia stayed with Rachel and finally convinced Paul to go back to the track and take care of telling everyone the news. He promised to check on her later, and to take her home. Julia said she would not go home until Rachel did. She wasn't letting her out of her sight ever again.

CHAPTER THIRTEEN

"She doesn't even look like Rachel. She's in bad shape," Paul told the people gathered in front of him. Hoping not to embarrass Rachel, he only mentioned her broken leg, bruises, and scratches. "Two men brought her in but didn't give any information other than the fact that they found her in an alley."

"Wasn't very nice of them," one man replied.

"At least they brought her in," another answered.

"I guess so."

"She's probably going to be in the hospital for a while, and Julia said she's not leaving until Rachel leaves."

"Understandable, but what about her barn?"

"I'll do what I can. I could use some extra help, though."

"We're in."

Paul thanked the men and gave them instructions. Paul vowed not to bother Julia, but to stay here and do what he could to take over for her until she could come back. Adding another twenty horses full time to his load would not be easy, but he would be able to do it, since everyone around him was also eager to help.

Rachel woke up screaming. Again. They had put her in her own room because she kept scaring the other ICU patients. Julia sat on Rachel's bed and held her hand for as long as she could. Once Rachel began to drift off again, Julia, still holding Rachel's hand, reached for the chair, and pulled it closer. She slipped into the chair, leaned back, adjusted the blanket to cover Rachel's arm, and fell asleep.

When the phone rang in the morning, Julia was still holding Rachel's hand, and they had slept two hours in a row. It was a miracle. Julia knew it was probably the pain medicine keeping her out. Julia answered the phone. It hadn't woken Rachel at all.

"Jules, we've got everything taken care of here. I don't want you to think about work at all, okay? Just stay there with Rachel."

"No, I have to come back some time to check on them." Julia sat up and checked the clock. It was six.

"Well, when you feel like you can leave her, then you can come back. I don't want you to feel pressured. I'm taking care of everything."

"Oh, Paul. It's so much."

"No, it's not as bad as you might think. Your assistant has been a big help. I just have to figure out a few more workouts, make sure everybody's doing their jobs, that's it. But everybody's doing well here, taking over anything extra, doing whatever is needed. Don't you worry about a thing."

Tears welled in her eyes as she leaned down to keep her voice quiet. "You're the best, Paul. I appreciate everything. You don't need to do all of this, you know."

"But I'll do it anyway."

Julia chuckled.

"How is she?"

Julia sighed. "She's been having nightmares. Bad ones."

"Has she woken up? Told anybody what happened?"

"A police officer was able to get a little bit out of her. She said something about a smelly man and a black van. The officer asked if she had been in the van the whole time and she said no, in a bed. That was all we could get before she passed out again."

"Wow. She's so lucky to be alive."

"Tell me about it."

"Have you heard from Robbie yet?"

"No. I think maybe because I've been too tired to dream. Have you heard from Missy?"

"Nope. Nothing. Really strange how they both disappeared like that when we needed them most."

"Maybe they were with Rachel."

"I hope so. Well, call me if you need me for anything. I'll be at my barn or yours. Don't you worry about a thing. Everything is going smoothly."

"I'm lucky to have you, Paul."

"Likewise."

Once they hung up, she checked on Rachel, who was finally sleeping quietly. She had already torn her hysterectomy scar open and they'd had to redo the surgery because of her nightmares. She had been thrashing around the bed so violently that they had no choice but to strap her in the bed. Two wide straps held her down, though all it seemed to do was make Rachel feel even more trapped.

Likewise. What did that mean? How was he lucky to have her around? All she did lately was cry. Well, men love to protect women. It had to be that fact. He felt useful, helpful, needed. Maybe he needed that, too. With everything that had been happening, she had noticed herself needing him more and more. Whenever he wasn't around, she was lonely, sad, and hopeless. Whenever he came to her with his positive attitude and his helpful actions, she always felt so much better. She couldn't imagine what she would be like if he hadn't been there for her this whole time.

She wished she could ask Robbie about what was happening, but she hadn't been sleeping well. She would sleep on and off in that chair, but it was uncomfortable, and it seemed every time she fell asleep, Rachel would have another nightmare and wake up screaming. Julia wondered if it would ever end.

Rachel still wasn't coherent after several days. Although, she did seem to be aware that her mother was there now, which was encouraging. Despite that fact, the fear in her eyes never diminished. Julia knew she would have these mental scars for the rest of her life. Everything was going to change now.

UUU

Paul came to visit, and when he saw Julia, his eyes bugged. She looked absolutely awful. She had taken a shower in the hospital room shower but had worn the same clothes for four days now. "Julia, please go home and rest. Do you want me to stay with her?"

"No, I can't leave her. What if she wakes up and needs me?"

"She'll have to learn to get through it, Julia. Maybe your mother could come? Billy? Anybody else? Jules, you need sleep. You need to change your clothes. You have to sleep, or you will not make it through this. Remember what I said about keeping your strength up, so you can be here for her? You'll be no good to her this way."

"Maybe just one night."

"It's a start." Paul hoped to convince her to stay home every night, eventually.

Julia couldn't muster up the courage to ask her mother to stay with Rachel. The chair would be too uncomfortable for her mother, and she wouldn't be able to sleep. Julia talked to the nurses, who promised to keep a close watch. She let Paul take her home.

He helped her into the house and Billy came running toward her. He grabbed his mother. "Mom!"

"Oh, Billy, I'm so sorry, I haven't been here."

"It's okay, Mom. I understand. Is she okay?"

"Still the same." They had talked on the phone several times while Julia was away.

"I want to go see her."

"Billy, I'm not sure you want to see her in that condition."

"It's that bad?"

"It is, honey. I think it would scare you."

"Mom, I'm old enough to take it. Look at me. I'm almost as tall as you now."

As if height equaled maturity. Julia couldn't help but chuckle as she looked straight ahead and into his eyes. She couldn't believe how tall he had gotten lately. His voice was changing, too, and she had been missing it all the last few weeks. A pang of guilt stabbed her in the stomach. She went to him and pulled him in for a hug. "I'll take you soon. I need to sleep first, okay?"

"Sure, Mom."

Paul watched Julia stumble down the hall. She turned and looked at him. "Thank you, Paul. Again. For everything."

"Any time, Jules." Paul turned to Billy. "Hopefully, we can get you in there tomorrow."

"Thanks. Is she awake at all?"

"Not really. She might be aware of her mother's presence, but I wonder if she understands what's going on. Her mind seems to be somewhere else. It's a little scary. I want you to be prepared. She may not recognize you."

Billy's eyes opened wide with horror.

"Just trying to prepare you, okay? I'm telling you this because you're old enough now to be able to deal with things like this. It's a very adult situation."

Billy nodded and squared his shoulders. "I still want to see her."

Paul nodded and patted Billy's arm. "You're just as brave as your sister and mother, Billy. I admire that. I'll see you tomorrow. Tell your mother to call me for a ride, okay?"

Billy bit his lip and nodded as his eyes misted. Paul left, gently closing the door behind him, and then forced himself to walk to his car. What he really wanted was to run into Julia's bedroom, lie down next to her, and hold her for as long as she needed.

COC

In her room, Julia collapsed in her bed and sobbed. "Robbie, please," she begged quietly so no one would hear outside her room. "Please, Robbie," she repeated over and over until she finally fell asleep.

"Jules."

"Robbie! Oh, thank God. Where have you been?"

"Trying to keep her alive, Jules."

"Where was she?"

"Honestly, I don't know where exactly it was, I'm sorry."

"Can you tell me what happened?"

"She was walking from Candy's to the train. A man in a black van chased her down, picked her up, and threw her in the van." Julia gasped but tried to stay quiet. "He took her to his house, drugged her with something, tied her to the bed, and...raped her."

"Oh, my God," she cried. "You couldn't stop it from happening?"

"No, unfortunately, I can't interfere with things. All Missy and I could do was try to convince him to give her water every once in a while. We tried with food, but he wasn't giving. I think he felt guilty about not feeding her, but he was more worried about feeding himself, and he didn't have much money."

"Asshole. So, Missy was there, too?"

"Yes. She did her best to convince him, but it's not easy to do that with someone who is insane. We couldn't just make things happen, either. It's not like we're magic or anything. Jules, he had killed other women. It's a miracle Rachel is still with us. He's a serial killer."

Julia whimpered. "Oh, God. How did she get away?"

"Rachel seemed to be listening to us after a while. She started to become used to the drug, I think, and was more aware. He was leaving her untied because she was too weak to get up. So, I convinced her to try and get to the bathroom for water, at least, and try to find a way out. He found her in the hall, but she talked him into letting her take a shower. She was able to get some water that way, and to rinse the blood off her."

"Oh, my God."

"Yeah, it was bad, Jules. I can't tell you what a helpless feeling it was for me, and how painful to see her like... Anyway, that night, it was trash night and the truck would be coming down the alley behind the house. Missy and I had this idea. Make a rope and climb out like in that fairy tale with the hair. I told her to make a rope and she listened. She used the short ropes by the bed and some shirts in the closet to make a sort of chain. Then, she heard the trash truck and climbed out just before he caught her. But she wasn't strong enough, couldn't hold on, and she slipped. That's when she broke her leg. Fortunately, the two trash men were there and helped her."

"Why did they just leave her in the ER and not tell us where that awful man was?"

"They were hiding from the law too."

"What?"

"They had fake names and were hiding from police. They couldn't let anyone see them and recognize them. They had to hide. At least they did the right thing by bringing her in. They saved her life."

"I wish I could thank them."

"Me too."

"Robbie, I'm so glad you and Missy were with her."

"I wish there was more we could have done."

"You did everything you could, and those things you did saved her life. I'm sure of it. The doctors could not believe she was still alive, and definitely couldn't believe she had the energy to escape on her own. She was missing too much blood. Almost half. It's supposed to be impossible to live with that amount of blood missing."

"It's truly a miracle, Jules."

"Yes. I feel like we have a second chance. And I'm never letting her out of my sight again. Well, once she's home."

"I don't blame you."

"Robbie, thank you so much."

"You don't need to thank me. I did what I could to help because she's my daughter, too, and I love her just as much as you do."

Julia nodded. "I know."

"You were okay while I was gone, though. Paul helped you."

"Yes. He did. He was a huge help to me."

"I'm glad he was there. Sometimes it takes a crisis to show a person's true identity, what they're really made of. He's a good man, Jules."

"He is."

"You trust him?"

"Yes."

"Then let it happen, Jules."

Julia held her head. "I would miss you."

"I'd still be here for you."

"You would?"

"Not as often, but yes. You wouldn't need me as much. I could be with the kids more."

"You talk to them? I thought they didn't talk back to you?"

"No, they haven't talked to me. I've seen them in dreams, but they are afraid. I don't push it, but I will keep trying."

CHAPTER FOURTEEN

Relieved, Julia slept until the middle of the day the next day. Billy had gone to school and had come back. When he came in and slammed the front door, she woke up. She turned over and checked her clock. It was after three, and the afternoon sun peeked from around her thick window shade. "Oh, no," she muttered as she hopped up and ran to the door, stumbling on the way from her sleepiness. "Billy?" she asked as she yanked the door open. He was there with his fist in the air, ready to knock. He laughed. "Oh, my goodness. You scared me."

"Sorry. I just wanted to make sure you were here. Did you just wake up?"

"Yeah. You went to school?"

"Yeah."

Julia shook her head then patted her son's head. "I'm proud of you, little boy. Well, not so little anymore." Billy chuckled as he stood proudly in front of her. "I heard Paul promise you last night to take us both to see Rachel today. You want to go now? Or soon? I have to take a shower and change first."

"Let's go, then."

"Can you track down Paul for me? He's in our barn or his. Someone can give you his number if you need it."

"Okay, Mom."

Paul came to get them, and they went to the hospital together. Billy approached Rachel cautiously, Paul's words from the previous night still echoing in his mind. They had warned him how sickly his sister looked, that she didn't even look like herself. But when he saw her, he was floored. No words could have prepared him for the sight. He was afraid to touch her for fear of hurting her. She looked to be in so much pain, even in her sleep.

He glanced at his mom, who was touching one of Rachel's legs and looking on with pity. Paul had the same expression. Julia finally caught Billy's gaze. "She'll be okay, though, Billy. She is going to get better. It'll just take a while. The worst is over. She's going to be okay."

Billy nodded as he pressed his lips together in a fine line. "Rach?" He had finally summoned the courage to get close enough to talk to her. She didn't move. He checked with his mom.

"She's on some heavy pain meds and probably asleep. They drug her heavily, so she will sleep well and hopefully not have nightmares."

Billy shook his head, wishing his sister didn't have to go through this. No one deserved this, especially not Rachel. He sat on the bed next to her and took her hand. Her hand hung limply in his. Such a contrast to what she was just a few weeks ago. She was the strongest person he knew. And now she would have to be even stronger to get through this.

"You look a lot better today," Paul said turning to Julia.

She grinned up at him. "Thanks. I feel better. I have hope again. She really is going to be okay."

"Yes, she is."

Rachel began stirring in the bed, shifting her head back and forth. Julia noticed and ran to her side. "Oh, no," Julia muttered. "Please, no."

"No! No!" Rachel screamed repeatedly. A nurse rushed in to check on her and went to her legs to make sure she didn't twist out of the straps, as she almost had done the night before. Billy backed away from her, afraid to hurt her, or to get hurt. Rachel began flailing her arms around in front of her. The nurse tried to hold her arms down, but all that did was make it worse. Rachel screamed for help. "Let go of me! Get off me! Help!" The nurse let go, afraid it was scaring Rachel. Rachel's tearful eyes were open, but they were sure she was not fully awake.

Julia went to her side and took one hand. "Rachel," she called. "Rachel, wake up." Rachel cried and begged for help a few more times, but then quieted as she heard her mother's voice. "Rachel."

"Mom?"

"Yes, honey. You're okay now. You're safe. I'm here."

"Don't leave me, Mom," she cried and opened her arms. Julia bent down and held Rachel as best she could.

"I won't, honey."

∪∪∪

"I need something to go on, Rachel. We need to catch this guy."

"I know, but..." Rachel bit her lip and then rubbed her eyes, which were perpetually blurry lately.

"You don't have to describe him, okay? Tell me, did he say anything about where you were?"

Rachel shook her head.

"Did you see anything outside that would have told you where you were?"

"No. Well, the alley."

"Alley?"

"There was an alley behind his house."

That narrows it down to about fifty thousand households. "Was it a house, a brownstone, townhouse type place, or do you know?"

Rachel thought about it. She had only seen it from the back as she crawled out the window, but she wasn't paying much attention to her surroundings other than keeping an eye out for the trash men. "I don't know. I, um, I g-guess it was like townhouses. They were connected." She remembered then her view from the window and remembered seeing the houses on the other side of the alley. They were connected. "Yeah. Connected."

"Did he give you his name?"

Rachel paused to think. "No. I don't think so. I was delirious most of the time. He kept shooting something in my hip. I don't know what it was. I don't know why he did it, but I'm glad he did because I missed a lot of what he..." She couldn't finish her sentence.

"It's okay. You don't need to talk about that too much, unless you want to. I want to know how you got away, Rachel. We know two trash men brought you to the hospital. How did you happen to run into them?"

"I made a rope and climbed out when they were coming to get the trash."

Those words echoed over and over in Julia's head. She covered her mouth with her hand and she realized something. Robbie had told her the exact same thing last night. There was no way Julia could have been making Robbie up in her head. He told her what happened before Rachel had even mentioned it. Robbie was...

"He told me he had killed other women."

When Julia didn't think her eyes could get any wider, they did. Every word coming out of Rachel's mouth not only horrified her, it also proved to her that after all these years, Robbie had truly been with her. She would never doubt again.

ᴜᴜᴜ

After a few more days, they finally let Rachel go home. After two weeks being held captive and two weeks in the hospital, she was finally home again.

Julia knew Paul was taking care of things at the track and she had been there to check on the horses a few times. Things seemed to be going well, but she felt absolutely awful about all the extra work Paul had taken upon himself to do. She knew she would have to pay him back somehow and tried to come up with some way to repay him. She didn't have a lot of money, though she really had no idea how much she had in her account now. She hadn't paid attention to how many wins she had earned while away, if any.

After staying home with Rachel for a day, she decided to go back to work. Grandma would be there for Rachel if she needed anything. Rachel was on crutches and unable to get around very well, and her hysterectomy scar was hurting whenever she tried to move, but Rachel insisted she would be fine with Grandma.

Julia showed up at the barn at five the next morning. Hordes of friends and workers asked how Rachel was doing, and Julia was especially glad to be able to give them good news for a change. She hadn't been here regularly for a month now, so she dove in, reorganizing things the way she liked them.

Paul visited her in her office as she was going through her books. She forgot to restrain herself and jumped up and into his arms.

"I'm happy to see you, too," he joked as he tightened his arms around her for a second.

She pulled away, keeping her gaze down. She went right back to her chair but mustered up the courage to look him in the eye again. "Sorry. Just...a little emotional lately. I guess."

"It's okay. Perfectly understandable. I wanted to stop by and see if I could help. I'm not used to only working in my barn. I keep thinking about things over here, too."

"Ugh. I'm so sorry, Paul."

"Stop apologizing," he said as he sat in the chair next to her desk. "That's what friends are for, right? I was glad to help."

"You seem to love to help people."

"Not all people. Just people I like."

Julia blushed slightly, despite her attempts at stopping it. Unfortunately, he seemed to notice, further embarrassing her. She bit her lip and swallowed noisily. "Um, I want to repay you somehow."

"Jules, come on. You don't need to repay me."

"I do. You begged me to let you help. Now I'm begging you to let me repay you."

He tilted his smile slightly but nodded. "What have you got in mind?"

"Well, that's the problem. I don't know yet."

Paul laughed.

"Give me some ideas."

"Are you serious?"

"Yes. How else will I know what to give you?"

He grinned a wicked grin and wiggled his eyebrows. She knew immediately what he was thinking.

Julia opened her mouth in a wide O and tapped his arm. "No. Not that," she said, then blushed and lowered her face again. Although, somehow, she kept her smile.

"Darn it. Well, I can't think of anything else."

Julia rolled her eyes and shook her head. This was a bit weird, flirting with him. She hadn't flirted with somebody since she met Robbie at the tender age of sixteen. She wasn't sure how a thirty-six-year-old woman was supposed to flirt. Or were they even supposed to? It felt natural to. This was one of those times she wished she had a girlfriend to talk to. Sadly, she had no one. She was going to have to wing it.

She reminded herself, though, that they had agreed only to be friends. So, she knew she'd have to put a cap on the flirting and stop it before it happened again. Also, before she jumped into his arms again. She couldn't have that happen. That was horribly embarrassing.

"Yoo-hoo. Anyone home?" he asked, waving his hand in front of her face.

She shook her head out of the clouds and focused on him again. "I'm sorry. What were we talking about?"

Paul took a breath. "You need some more sleep, I think."

"Do I look that bad?"

"You don't look bad. You never look bad. You're thinking about something else, though. Your mind is elsewhere. On Rachel?"

"Mm hm." Seemed like a likely excuse.

"Understandable. Therefore, I will be around to help today again. Gotta make sure things are going smoothly. It's been a while. Things have changed a bit."

"I've noticed," she said, lifting her recordkeeping book.

UUU

Julia was thrilled to have her routine back. She didn't know how to function without one. The last month had been crazy. She was glad it was over. She was also glad that the two-year-old season was starting soon. This year, the farm was sending them a promising colt, one they were extremely excited about. He was perfect in conformation and was fast. He loved to run and was a well-behaved colt, too, which meant he was smart and aware. They called him Chivalry and told Julia they would have him down at Belmont by the end of March. In a couple more weeks she'd have this colt in her hands, ready to work.

The pressure was enormous, though. For them to have such high expectations was a little disconcerting for her. What if the colt couldn't perform the way they expected? They would surely blame her or maybe her training style. She told herself to train him the way she'd train any other colt. The rest would be up to the colt.

She had to hire another exercise rider to take over for Rachel. They had been strapped and left searching for help every morning lately. So, she put an ad in the *Daily Racing Form*. She had several applicants, but none who seemed to be very good at riding or handling horses. Then, one Sunday, she watched an eighteen-year-old kid named Erick ride and decided he was perfect. He had experience, almost as much as Rachel, was the same size, was aspiring to be a jockey, and he even sat like Rachel in the saddle. She couldn't ask for anything more and hired him on the spot. He was so excited.

He came back the next morning and got right to work. He worked twelve horses that day. Paul was amazed.

"We have a routine set up and we're quick to go from horse to horse. Only way to get them all in, especially considering he's going to have to go to school. He's only going to be able to work half that many tomorrow."

"Why'd you hire a kid that can only do half of that?"

"That's all Rachel did. We'll be fine. Don't worry."

Paul nodded. "I'm not worried. I know you know what you're doing. You're a smart cookie."

She smirked at him. "School will be out in a couple months, anyway."

"How long do you think Rachel will be out?"

"She's a mess, Paul. I don't know. Physically, she could be ready in two months, I suppose. But mentally, I don't know. Now she's experiencing flashbacks, like what you'd expect from a Vietnam War vet."

"You're kidding."

"No, unfortunately, I'm not. She's seeing things."

"You need to get her to a psychiatrist."

"That would be wonderful, if I could get her out of the house. She doesn't even want to go to the doctor for a checkup."

"She's afraid to leave the house?"

"Yes." A soft sigh escaped her lips. "But we're working on it. I suppose all we can do is be patient with her and let her know those things she sees are not real. Which, she knows. She knows it's not real, but only after it happens."

"That's awful. Poor Rachel. I feel awful for her."

"Me too. She's really suffering."

"Get her back here. She'll feel much better around the horses. Don't you think?"

"Yes, definitely. I've thought of that, I've suggested it, and she wants to come, but she's still too afraid. I'm sure she'll come around, though. It'll take time."

Paul shook his head. "I can't imagine what she must have gone through. Has she told you yet?"

"She doesn't want to talk about it too much, but a detective came and talked to her while she was still in the hospital. She told him she tried to run from a man in a black van, but he cornered her in an alley, picked her up, and threw her in the van. He tied her up, took her to his house, and tied her to his bed. He...you know. Did horrible things to her. She nearly bled to death because of it but she managed to escape. She tied shirts together and climbed out."

"That's incredible."

"Paul, the most incredible part was something else."

"What do you mean? What could be more incredible than that?"

"I was kind of afraid to tell you, though I wanted to tell you sooner." With her face lowered, she glanced up at him sheepishly.

"What's that?" Paul leaned in closer.

Julia took a breath and straightened in an attempt at looking more confident. "Robbie told me that he and Missy were with her."

"You're kidding." His eyes were huge with amazement.

"No. He said they couldn't interfere with what was happening, but they did talk the man into giving her water from time to time. And they put ideas in Rachel's head, like to take a shower to get more water, and to tie the shirts together. Paul, he told me all of this before Rachel told that detective the story. So, when Rachel told the very same story, I knew for a fact that Robbie was real."

Paul was speechless and shook his head as he considered her words. His eyes glazed over and drifted.

"I have proof now. Robbie and Missy are really with us."

Finally, he recovered. "Why didn't you tell me this before?"

"Well, honestly, I wasn't sure if Rachel would want me to tell anyone else what happened to her. Don't let her know that you know, okay? I'm sure it's embarrassing to her. It would mortify her to know that you know she was...Oh God, I can't even say it. That you know what happened there."

"I understand, Jules. It's all right.

"Has Missy said anything?"

"She said she was trying to help, and that's where she was, but she didn't want to tell me anything else because it was private, and she wasn't sure Rachel would want me to know."

"Understandable. She's very thoughtful. Robbie said they told her to make a rope and climb out, and she listened. Only, Rachel thinks it was her idea. She didn't actually hear them or talk to them."

"That's interesting. So, they can control things, but only if they can convince people of doing something."

"Yes. Exactly. Robbie made sure to tell me he wasn't magic." One weak corner of Julia's mouth raised.

"Well, they saved her life. That's the most important thing."

"I can't help but think that Rachel wouldn't be here right now if I hadn't been talking to him this whole time, keeping him here." Julia clenched her jaw as she normally did when trying to control her emotions.

"True."

"And if you hadn't been talking to Missy, I wouldn't have had the support I had. You saved my life, in a way, Paul. I couldn't have gone through this without you." Her voice shook slightly as she spoke.

Paul nodded and touched her hand. "You're welcome. I hope you know that I did it for me as much as for you, you know."

"What?" She laughed, embarrassed.

Paul straightened again and withdrew his hand. "To help me cope, too. I had to keep busy. I was worried, too."

"They're not even your kids. How could you be so worried?"

"I guess because they're yours. They're part of you."

Julia blinked and was speechless. He hardly knew her kids. Although, lately, he had been working with Billy. It was to keep the teen occupied, Paul had said. Julia admired Paul for that.

"But, don't worry. We're still just friends. Right? Nothing to worry about."

What? What's that supposed to mean? "Okay."

Paul tapped his hand on the desk and stood up. "Gotta run. I'll be back in a bit to check on you."

"Okay."

When he left, she almost hyperventilated. She leaned over her legs wishing he could come back and calm her down again. He was so good at that. He'd kept her calm through one of the toughest times of her life. Fighting the urge to run into his arms, she did all she could to calm herself in case someone came into her office. She had to look normal again, as she always did before. Hiding everything.

At the same time, she had to think about this. Again, she wished she had a girlfriend. She almost wished she could talk to Missy. That thought was amusing. Certainly, she couldn't talk to Robbie about this, though she was sure he knew.

Robbie knew so much more about her now than he ever had in their five-year relationship before his death. It occurred to Julia that she had now known him longer in her dreams and in her mind than she had in real life. On top of it all, Robbie was able to read her mind. That part was very scary. Was he reading her mind now? Part of her appreciated his protection while part of her wished for a little more privacy. Privacy. That was another thing she would need if she were to be with another man.

There were times she had lay in bed aching for a man, not doing anything about it for fear Robbie would see. She would wrestle within herself knowing that he was aware of her need and knew she was embarrassed to do anything about it. Most of those nights, Robbie had visited her, and they had made love in her dream. She would wake up out of breath, throbbing inside, thrashing around the bed, sweating, sometimes catching a moan or cry before it escaped. She always wondered how many had slipped through. Had the kids heard?

The unfulfillment was painful. Dreaming about it and experiencing it physically are two different things. Many times, the realization that she did not have a real man with a real body hit her like a brick wall. The loneliness poured over her, weakening her, taking her resolve, taking her will to stay strong. There had been times when she had considered having mindless sex with a man to curb the physical pain as well as the mental.

What would Robbie say? Inevitably, that thought was what stopped her every time. That and not wanting to be perceived as someone who slept around. It brought everything to a screeching halt. Everything but the ache.

She glanced at the door through which Paul had vanished, wondering if he was going through the same thing. Surely, he was. He was a man. Men can't live without sex. How was he coping? Maybe one day she would muster up the nerve to ask him. He would love that question.

"So, Paul. I was wondering. How do you cope with the lack of sex? Do you even have to cope? Do you make use of prostitutes? Promiscuous women around the backside?"

"I haven't had sex in fourteen years, Jules. I'm bursting at the seams, as you can imagine."

"So am I. Maybe we could remedy that. Together."

Julia laughed aloud this time at her ridiculous fantasy. Disappointed with herself, she shook her head at her choice of words. It was like a bad movie. *Yeah, real sexy, there, Jules. He'd fall for that in a heartbeat.* This reminded her how little she knew about sex, about men, about flirting, how to attract a man, how to be sexy. She shook her head. Was she really considering this? No way. It couldn't happen.

Why not?

What would Robbie say? He'd probably be happy for her, though it would still hurt him.

Julia's shoulders slumped, and she fell back into the wobbly seat back of her old office chair. One of these days, she'd have to replace that thing. It had been here as long as she had.

CHAPTER FIFTEEN

Paul did his best to keep his distance. Julia had enough on her plate without worrying about dealing with a lonely old man such as himself. *Old? Oh, God.* Had he gotten old? No, not yet. He still felt young, felt fine, had energy, kept himself trim and fit. No, he wasn't old. He had plenty of years left in him. Years he was doomed to spend alone if he didn't do something about this.

The only way was to distance himself from Missy. It had to be. Missy couldn't be around if he were going to be with another woman. It couldn't happen. He didn't want her knowing about it, let alone watching. Oh, how awful that would be. For both of them.

Herein lies the problem - the conundrum he had been dealing with since she had died. He loved Missy with his whole heart and soul. She was a part of him, he was a part of her; they were soulmates. But she was dead. Her body was dead, anyway. Relationships were not supposed to be this way. Paul longed for the touch of a real woman. Soft, gentle, loving, caressing... He ducked into his office before anybody could see his suit pants sticking out awkwardly. He groaned and held his head as he fell into his desk chair.

His body needed a real woman. Not his hand. Not a prostitute. And no, he would never let himself give in to one of those. It would be like cheating on Missy, and he couldn't do that to her. While she had given him permission to have a relationship with a real woman, he wasn't sure that was best for her. Would it hurt her feelings? Would she cry at the sight of him with another woman? Even Julia, who she swore she liked?

He was tired of going back and forth. For fourteen years now, he had not been man enough to make a decision. He groaned internally, hiding the sound from an employee walking by.

"Missy, I'm sorry. I'm going to have to do this. For both our sakes."

There it was. It was said, aloud too, further cementing his decision. He couldn't go back now. He had already said it. "I'm sorry," he whispered as he rubbed his neck and squirmed in his seat. "I'm so sorry."

OOO

The chilled air whooshed from his fan and over his steaming body. He wore nothing and lay with his arms and legs spread over the queen-sized bed. All day, he'd felt hot, despite the cold weather outside. His own thoughts disturbed him as he realized what he had done today. Essentially, he had told Missy to leave him alone. His heart ached, and he missed her already. He did not feel her presence. Could she have left him without saying goodbye? Was she mad he had said it that way?

He covered his eyes with one hand. "Missy, I'm sorry. I'm sorry. Please talk to me." He knew there was no chance to hear her voice unless he was asleep, but he was too anxious to sleep. As he eyed her brush, the same one he had slept with so many times, the same one that seemed to bring her back to him, he wondered if he should put it away.

One more night, he told himself. With a sharp pain in his heart, he stood from his bed, cradled the brush in his hands, and brought it back to his bed. With one finger, he caressed her soft blonde hair, finding it more brittle than before. He wondered how long it would last before disintegrating and falling from her brush. Some of the hair already had. He had gone to great lengths to keep anything from touching it over the years, for fear of losing another hair.

He set the brush on the pillow beside him, and then crawled under the covers as he kept his eyes on it. "Missy," he whispered, touching the brush's handle, careful not to touch the hair. "Missy, I'm scared. Don't tell anybody, okay?" He chuckled. "Right. Like you could tell anybody. Well, I guess you could tell Robbie. Don't tell him, okay? I'm worried about what might happen if I try to embark on the rest of my life without you. I've been with you for so long now that I don't know if I can do it without you. But I know I can't have you *and* Jul...another woman...at the same time."

He sighed. "I guess you already know how I feel about her." He shook his head into his pillow and closed his eyes. "I'm so sorry, baby. I didn't mean for this to happen." His heart ached for Missy as he wondered if she was hurting, and if he was the cause of that pain. One finger drifted lazily over the brush's handle, caressing it as if it were her milky white arm.

She never tanned, she used to joke. Only burned, and then promptly turned white again once the dead skin peeled away. At the beach, she always wore a huge brimmed hat, some sort of cover-up, and always sat under an umbrella. He would tease her and ask her why she bothered to come to the beach. "Because of the waves," she always said. She loved to go just past the breakers and jump with the waves as they rolled by.

He remembered one time they were doing this, body surfing, and some sort of fish touched her leg. She screamed bloody murder and latched onto him with her arms and legs. The lifeguard stood up on his chair, whistle in his mouth, ready for action. Paul had waved to him, signaling everything was okay as he laughed hysterically. She had smacked his shoulders until he was able to stop his laughter. He kissed her and jumped as a wave rolled by, making her giggle. With her legs wrapped around him, he couldn't help but fill with desire for her, and he pressed against her. They held each other's gaze as he wiggled his swim trunks down, pulled her bikini aside, and then slipped inside her.

Their desire and need overcame the annoying dryness the salt water caused. They decided staying still was the best option, though it made it more difficult for him. Despite the challenges, the dryness, the waves, they found their release, then held one another as she rested her head on his shoulder.

Finally, she found the courage to let go of him, and they waded back to the shore. It was at that point they realized how many people were on the beach. Did they know what they had done? Missy had laughed and told him not to worry about what other people think. They certainly could not have known for sure. The water was too dark to see. And if they had known, the life guard would have been sent in to interrupt them. They laughed about what might have happened if they'd been caught.

"You can have that again, Paul. I won't stop you."

"Missy?"

"Why not have that again? Why are you keeping yourself from living life to its fullest?"

"For you, baby. I don't want to hurt you."

"I promise you, I will be fine. You will not hurt me. In fact, you will make me happy. I want you to be happy, too."

"But I don't know if I can be without you. I don't remember what that's like. We've been together for so long."

"I won't disappear forever."

"How can I be with another woman knowing you're near? Knowing you can see us together? Won't it hurt?"

"Maybe a little, but you can't think about that. This is the way things have to be. It's not natural for you to be so attached to me like this. It's natural for you to be with a real woman."

"You are a —"

"You know what I mean, love."

"I don't think I can say goodbye."

"Then don't."

"I can't give my heart to two women."

"So, you want me to leave? Forever?"

"No."

"What is it that you want?"

Paul slammed his fist onto something, whatever was next to him. He didn't know what it was. Everything was the same shade of gray. It was as if he were standing on the handle of her hairbrush. However, he knew that was impossible. He looked down at the marbled, smooth ground he stood upon, and then met Missy's blue eyes again. They were so blue. So bright. They lit up the whole room. And his heart. "I can't do it. I can't say goodbye to you."

"I see now. You're still torn, love. It's okay. You'll work through it, I'm sure."

Paul let his head drop almost in shame at the realization. How could he not be ready? After all this time? It had been fourteen years. *Years!* No one waits this long.

Except Julia.

ʊʊʊ

He stormed to the barn from his car the next morning, still torn, still undecided, still in the dark. There seemed to be no answer. Well, the only answer now was to keep things in the status quo.

"Hey, kid." Paul waved and walked by the new groom. He couldn't remember his name.

"Good morning, Mister Holton. I have a message for you."

Paul stopped and faced him.

"The lady trainer wants to see you about something."

"Lady trainer? You don't know her name?"

"No, sir. My memory's not what it used to be."

"Used to be? You're what, nineteen?"

"Yes, sir." He lowered his gaze to the ground, his long hair falling to hide his face.

Another damned hippy. Paul sighed and thanked him, then walked to his office to call Julia. Then he decided it was too impersonal. He should walk.

He saw her from a distance, the morning sun glistening on her hair. It was perfectly straight today and seemed longer than she normally kept it. Maybe she hadn't had time to get it cut lately. Of course, she hadn't, with everything going on. He loved it like that, though.

Her eyes lit up when she saw him, and she walked toward him. "Sleep okay?" she asked.

He chuckled and shook his head. "You?" She shrugged. "You requested my presence?"

She laughed loudly as she touched his arm. He couldn't help the smile on his face. When she recovered, she responded, "Well, yes and no. You really could have called. I had a question about your notes on this horse." She waved her hand for him to follow, and then walked to her office with Paul close behind.

Julia ruffled through papers on her desk. "I swear, I am so behind. I can't keep track...Here it is." She pulled out a piece of yellow paper that had been torn from a legal pad. "It says, 'Left behind, hated dogs.'" She looked up at him with an expectant look on her face. "I'm supposed to know what that means?" Paul was glad she was grinning. He hardly remembered this workout.

"Uh," he stalled. He took the paper from her hand. There was a list of horses that had worked that day with scattered bits of information. Some had times, some had notes, some had both. "Oh, wow. I wasn't very organized this day, was I?"

She snatched it from his hand. "Well, don't worry about it. If you can't remember..."

He snatched it back and wrinkled his nose at her. One corner of her mouth raised. "Oh, I can remember, all right." He pressed his lips together as he studied the words. "He uh, broke from the gate, but uh, didn't. He didn't run. Just balked. He saw the dogs...wait. You know what the dogs are, right?"

"Paul!" she shrieked, then slapped his chest and laughed.

Amused, he continued. "They're those little cones, they keep the horses away from the rail when it's too wet and deep."

"Oh, stop it. I know what the dogs are, silly. I take it he shied?"

Paul took a breath. "Well, honestly, I had so many horses..."

"It's okay. It's fine. I'll just assume he shied and go from there."

Paul put one hand on his hip. "What are you going to do about it?"

"Depends on how bad it is. Guess I'll have to try to see for myself. It's not raining today. No dogs out. We'll start with the gate. I'll work with the gate crew. They know what they're doing. Maybe they'll remember what exactly happened."

"If you say so." She tapped his arm and let the paper fall onto the pile on her desk. "Lunch later?"

Julia tried not to let the other corner of her mouth raise but couldn't help it. She nodded in reply. Paul winked and walked away.

Julia groaned internally. She was acting like a silly teenager.

ʊʊʊ

"What's the craziest thing you've ever done?" Paul asked her over their pizza.

Julia finished her bite then answered. "Me? Crazy? I don't think so."

Paul chuckled and waved a finger in her face. "Now, now. I know better. You've got a wild side. I can tell."

Julia opened her mouth in an O. "Are you quite sure?" she asked with her hand over her heart.

Her proper tone reminded him of Missy. He quickly dismissed it in favor of keeping their conversation going. "Come on. You can tell me. I can keep a secret."

"Well," she started, but stopped, shaking her head. "No. I shouldn't."

"Aw, come on. You can't start that way and then stop."

Julia pursed her lips to extinguish her grin, but it wouldn't stop. "Well, it's really not all that crazy."

"Give me something juicy. Come on."

"Are you going to tell me one? Because I'm not gonna —"

"Of course," he said, waving his hand to interrupt. "Go on. Do tell."

Julia sighed and rested her chin on her hand as she kept her eyes on him. "Okay. Well, I was young and stupid. I was still a groom." Paul raised his eyebrows with interest, but he was silent. "This trainer came to town, saw me, and assumed I was an exercise boy. At the time, I was sort of dressing down. You know. I didn't want to look too feminine."

"Of course."

"He did figure out I was a girl, but no one else in their barn ever did, I don't think. So, long story short, he asked me to work his horse for him while he was in town. Didn't see me ride first or anything. He just thought it would be funny. 'A gas,' he called it. And, well, I'd only been on a horse a few times at that point, and never faster than a trot."

"What?" Paul shouted, attracting the attention of several others in the track kitchen.

Julia shushed him and laughed. "Yes. Well, I rode the horse. On the track. Every morning for two weeks. The whole time, I think the other employees thought I was a boy, and that my name was Jules, as in Jules Verne."

Paul's mouth was wide open in amazement and Julia laughed. "You're joking. You're not serious."

"I swear," Julia answered, trying to keep her voice down. She raised a hand. "Scout's honor."

Paul slapped his forehead with his mouth still open. "I...I...definitely can't top that one."

"You don't have to top it, genius. Just tell me the craziest thing you've ever done."

Paul shrugged. "Well, hmm..." He tried to think. There was the time when he was a kid and stole a peppermint stick from the candy store. He never got caught but felt guilty for years about it. Then there was the time he skipped school to go to the park with his friends. But everybody did that. Then, there was the fact that he had been married for a whole year and her parents never knew. He tried desperately to come up with something else. The time he almost shot himself in his dad's bedroom? He shook his head quickly to rid himself of that one. "I'm sorry. I can't think of anything."

"You can, too. You just don't want to tell me."

He narrowed his eyes at her. She saw right through him. He was silent for several long seconds as he came up with something. "Well, okay." He shrugged. Julia nodded as she perked up. "My friends and I got a hold of some fireworks." His eyes wandered with the memory.

Julia leaned forward. "Oh, oh."

"A whole box full. My friend, Jerry, took them from his dad's shed. We went behind Mr. Barton's grocery store. Started with the easy ones. Sparklers. Harmless. Then the snakes. Then we graduated to the fountain type. Set a bunch of those off at one time. That was fun. Then we decided to try the ones that shoot up into the air and explode."

Julia covered her mouth.

"We lined them up near this dumpster. Alex came up with this plan. If any cops come, we just take our bikes and run into the trees. No problem. I decided I didn't want to blow my arm off, so I made Alex light them. He went down the row and lit as many as he could, about four, before the match went out. We ran back to watch."

Julia leaned forward.

"Nothing."

"Nothing?"

"Nothing. Fizzled out. We tried the rest. All fizzled. So, we tossed them into the dumpster and went on to the other ones that we had. More fountain type things. Well, about ten minutes later, we smell something burning. We look up and there's smoke coming out of the dumpster."

"Oh no."

"We didn't know what to do. We didn't have a fire extinguisher or anything. Before we could even decide, though, they started exploding inside the dumpster."

"What?!"

"BANG! POP! Then the flames."

"No!"

"Shooting from around the lid and the side door. Well, by then, we were on our bikes and racing from the scene."

"Did you call the fire department?"

"We were afraid to. We figured it was just a giant incinerator at this point, and wasn't hurting anything, so we let it go. We went to the park near my house and hung out there. We could see the smoke over the trees. We argued about who was going to get a fire extinguisher, but I kept saying that a fire extinguisher isn't going to put that fire out."

"Of course, not," Julia laughed.

"Then we heard the fire department."

"Oh boy."

"A fire engine is far too exciting for a pre-teen boy to resist. So, we followed and went back to the store. We watched them put the fire out pretty quickly, but we didn't stick around for anyone to ask us questions or perhaps identify us as the kids who were there before."

Julia bent over, laughing.

"I guess aside from my marriage to Missy for a year before her parents knew, that's pretty much the craziest thing I've ever done."

"You were married for a whole year without her parents knowing?"

"Yep. We couldn't wait. Then we got married again in England the following year. In York." Paul's face lit with the memory. His heart swelled as he remembered how beautiful she was that day. It quickly faded when Julia asked the next question.

"Paul, what happened? Were you in the accident, too?"

"No one's told you?" He was surprised. No rumors? Around here? Everybody loved to gossip at this track.

"No. But if you don't want to talk about it..."

"No, it's okay. It's been many years now. I guess the sting has faded some." Paul took a breath, blew it out while Julia silently waited. "I was driving. The truck came from the opposite direction. We were in England, and you know. They drive on the left there." Julia nodded. "Well, I could have sworn I was on the left. But the truck driver said I crossed the line and was on the wrong side. Missy said that once he found out I was American, he quickly made up the lie to protect himself. He was actually the one on the wrong side."

Julia's mouth opened in horror.

"Of course, Missy's parents believed that man. I was in a coma for three weeks and couldn't defend myself. They completely cut me off. I never even got to go see her gr–" Paul groaned and ran his fingers through his hair. "You know." He couldn't continue.

Julia touched his hand, then withdrew. "That's awful. How could they do that to you? That's absolutely not fair. Did you ever tell them it wasn't your fault?"

Paul shook his head and took a few seconds to compose himself. "I had no proof. It was his word against mine. More than likely, being on the wrong side would have been the case with any other American. But you know me, at least well enough to know that I am very careful. Every few seconds I reminded myself to stay on the left."

Julia couldn't help the angry frown on her face. "That's unfair."

Paul shrugged. "I can't do anything about it. So, no sense in dwelling on it, I suppose. I had to let it go. It was killing me. Almost lit–, well, let's just say it upset me a lot."

Julia's eyes were wide now as she realized what he had almost said. "That's when you thought about being with Missy?"

After almost a minute, he finally nodded. "The whole United Kingdom hated me."

"Why? Was she famous?"

"Her father worked in security for Queen Elizabeth. Her Majesty even gave us a car as a wedding present. In fact, that's what I was driving at the time."

"Wow!"

"Yeah. I wish sometimes they all knew the truth about me, but there is no way to prove it."

"Oh, Paul, I am so sorry."

"But, like I said, just gotta let it go. Right? It'll eat you up, if you don't. Might as well let it go. Gotta forgive and forget. Well, I can't forget, but I can forgive."

"I guess we'll have to forgive that son of a bitch that almost killed my daughter, too."

Paul nodded and took her hand. He noticed a spot of pizza grease, picked up the napkin and wiped it off for her. She smiled. Somehow, their fingers became weaved together as they sat gazing into each other's eyes. Paul's thumb brushed over the back of her hand, still slightly soft from the grease.

The realization hit him. What about Missy? He wasn't ready for this. He withdrew his hand and set it on his lap. Julia blushed and smiled like a young girl, which he found cute. She hid her eyes from him for several seconds, but finally looked up and into his eyes. "Sorry," he whispered. The word came out almost in a whisper.

"It's okay, Paul."

"I feel like I can tell you anything."

"Me too."

"Of course, you can tell you anything. You're you."

Julia reached over the table and pushed his shoulder, lightening the mood again.

"I uh," he started, and then scanned the dining area for people who might overhear. Again, anything to avoid rumors. Although, they had been seen together a lot lately and people had their suspicions. "Sometimes I feel ready, sometimes I don't."

Julia nodded, knowing exactly what he meant. Ready to move on.

He wondered if that nod meant she felt the same way. She probably did, given the circumstances.

"You know what I mean?"

She nodded again. "Yes. I am going through the same thing, Paul."

"So, sometimes you think...maybe we could...you know, date. But then you wonder about Robbie. What would he think? Truly? Would it hurt his feelings? Would he feel less wanted or needed? Is that what you are thinking, too?"

"That's exactly what I'm thinking. Yes. I worry that I couldn't go on without him, too. I wouldn't know what to do."

Paul scooted forward in his chair and reached across the table again for her hand. She slipped one hand into his. "Jules, will you be patient with me? I mean, I would be patient with you. I *will* be patient, I mean. If you want. Am I making sense?" He shifted nervously in his seat.

"Yes. We're not ready. We still have some thinking to do, some things to work out with our...spouses."

Paul nodded. "Yes, I suppose, but I don't want you to feel like you're a consolation prize. You're not. It's just that, well, I got myself into this mess, and I want to get myself out."

The comparison seemed a bit silly to her, but she understood.

"Listen, if it ever happens, I promise you, you'd be my first priority. That's why I want to make sure I do this right. You deserve to be first."

It was quiet for a few seconds as their eyes connected, and as they thought about the future. She thought about all he had done for her while Rachel was missing and in the hospital. "Paul," Julia started.

"Yes?"

"I'd never make you choose. Never. But all you've done for me lately, you put my needs ahead of yours. You sacrificed your time, your strength, for me. Was I already your first priority? Or am I still?"

He narrowed his eyes thoughtfully.

"Paul, who would you choose if you had to? Right now. And don't be afraid of telling me if it's Missy. Because that just means you're right. You're not ready to move on."

"Who would you choose?"

"I asked you first."

Paul chuckled, and then thought about it. "I don't want to choose. I don't think I can. I don't want to choose her, or you."

Julia nodded. She felt the same.

"Who would you choose?"

"I wouldn't be able to. I can't let Robbie see me with another man, even though he says he wants that for me. I would feel too self-conscious. I would think about him too much."

"Me too." Paul sat up straighter and Julia thought she saw a light bulb over his head. "What we need to do, Jules, is say goodbye to them both. Whenever we're ready, I mean. Not yet. When we're ready, we'll say goodbye. For good. They're supposed to pass on anyway. They're not supposed to be here."

"What?" Julia's eyes filled with horror. "What are you talking about?"

"I read this in another book. It doesn't say whether there's a heaven or hell, but it does say that their spirits need to move on, that it's not good for them to be here for so long."

"What?" Julia was horrified. "Wh-why didn't you tell me this? I've ruined him! I knew it. I knew it was bad for him."

"No, Jules, it's not going to ruin him. In fact, I think the book is sort of wrong in some respects, because Robbie and Missy seem fine, don't they? But just in case, I can't help but wonder if it would be better for them. Are we holding them back?"

"We'll have to ask them."

"Think they'll answer? You know how they avoid answering questions about how things are over there."

"Maybe. We can ask them what is best for them. Would it be best to stay? Or go? Let's ask them. If it's better for them to go, well, then it will give us the strength to let them go."

"You're right." Paul dropped his gaze to the table as he considered her words. "Do you think they know, though?"

"Of course, they do." A sudden fear swept over Julia's face as she realized something.

"What's wrong?"

"They've protected us. What will we do without their protection? Robbie helped save Rachel's life. What if something happens later and we need him? Or you need her? And they're gone?"

"Is that what we're afraid to lose? Their protection?" Paul narrowed his eyes and tilted his chin toward the ceiling. It was silent for nearly a minute.

"I don't know."

Paul scoffed at himself. "I'm overanalyzing everything again." He sighed and sat back in his chair, withdrawing his hand from hers. "I guess I need time to digest this. To think."

"Me too."

One corner of Paul's mouth raised. "Do we agree on everything?"

"Not on how to take workout notes."

OOO

Talking to Robbie would solve everything. All she had to know, basically, was if she was harming him in some way by keeping him here. If it were harming him, she would say goodbye. She would have to, for his own good. She would have to do what was best for him. What if it did not hurt him, though? What if this was his mission? Like the angel in "It's a Wonderful Life," being sent back for a second chance to make everything all right again? Was this his job now to watch over them? And if so, she could not very well say goodbye or dismiss him in any way.

That would mean she could be doomed to spend the rest of her life without a real companion. For the first few years after his death, Julia had so often told herself she would grow old alone, that she came to believe it. It became fact, and such a fact that it no longer saddened her. *That's not the way it's supposed to be, though.* That's not normal, and she knew it.

Robbie had told her that even her mother, who had only been widowed for one year, had considered remarrying. Julia knew her parents loved each other, though they were not overly affectionate, at least not that she could see. Did her mother not love her father enough to mourn the way

Julia had fifteen years ago? Was her marriage to Robbie that much stronger? Selfishly, she wanted to tell herself that yes, it was. That they had a storybook marriage made in heaven, and all was perfect. Though they were happy and never did have a fight, they hadn't been married long enough to suffer through any of the turmoil that ordinarily affected marriages.

She remembered overhearing her mother from time to time saying that she loved her husband more now than she had the day before. Could her love with Robbie have grown like that, had they had the chance to be together all these years? Well, they were together. He was with her. Sort of. Julia groaned as she flopped herself backwards onto her pillows.

The faint whiff of the clean sheets hovered in the air, and she turned her head to look at the pillow on her right. That had been Robbie's pillow. It had been here the whole time. After a few years, she had given up trying to find traces of his scent leftover in the pillow. She had also kept a few items of his: handkerchiefs, socks, and an undershirt. Those items soon took in the aroma of everything else, leaving no trace of him anywhere.

As she traced a wrinkle in the pillow case, she still remembered him lying next to her and the way he would touch her. Though she would occasionally feel him in her dreams, it wasn't real, and she knew it. Waking up in an aching and desperate sweat was the biggest clue. It could never be real. Her body could not respond to him the way it should. They were not made to do that.

"Oh, Robbie. I don't know what to do anymore. I'm so confused."

"You wouldn't be in this state of worry if you did not feel something for him, you know. And by the way, I have told you a thousand times that I want you to be with someone else. A real man. You don't deserve this, Jules."

"Robbie, I have to ask you something."

Robbie sighed. Julia could hear him, but not see him. He was saving his energy for her again. "You know what I'm going to ask you?"

"Yes. Without telling you too much, I can tell you that it does not hurt me to be here with you."

"Are you my guardian angel? And the kids' too?" Julia bit her lip.

"In a way. I don't have to be, but I would like to be, very much. Jules, it's not an all or nothing decision. If you begin a relationship with him, it doesn't mean I have to disappear."

"But…"

"No, I won't watch."

Julia writhed with embarrassment. Fortunately, Robbie laughed with her. She wished she could slap his arm or tousle his hair. Yet another thing missing from their relationship, another thing she could do with a real man, and had done with Paul. "So, if I need you, you'll come to me?"

"Yes. Definitely. But you won't need me, I promise."

"Won't you miss me?"

"Of course. Things will be different, but, like I said, I won't be gone forever. I will still be around."

"I'll miss you, though." Emotion came from nowhere, choking her words, drowning them with tears. "No. I can't do it."

"Anybody who loses someone will miss them from time to time, but that pain lessens gradually. You've put that pain off." Robbie sighed again. "And, I let you. This is partly my fault because I couldn't bear to see you in so much pain."

Julia sucked in a shaky breath. "What?"

"Jules, you know I had just as much a hard time with this as you, but now, practicality has to take over. You are a practical woman, Jules. You do things that make sense. Does this make sense to you? Our relationship this way?"

She glanced at her left hand, noting the absence of her wedding ring, which she had stopped wearing several months after his death. There was no longer an indentation, no longer a tan line. No evidence of it at all. In a way, she had said goodbye to him while making the decision to take it off and leave it in her underwear drawer. She had said goodbye to his possessions, too, giving away his clothes to charity, and everything he owned that she couldn't use or didn't need.

She had said goodbye again the day she went back to the track to get her old grooming job back. She had said goodbye the days Rachel and Billy started school. School plays. Boyfriends, girlfriends, good friends, bad friends, learning to ride, learning to drive, and soon, graduation. They will get married. They will move out. She had said goodbye many times but hadn't said goodbye in the most important way, in her heart.

No, this was not at all practical. It was very unlike her to do something that made no sense, and even more absurd to keep a relationship with a spirit, not a human being.

It was time.

OOO

"I don't think I can do it, baby. I can't be with her and keep you here, too. I couldn't do that to you. Or me. It's just not right."

"No, it's not right, but you are not keeping me here, either. I can leave anytime I want."

Paul was silent with his mouth open in surprise. Would she leave him now?

"I'm here as much for you as for me."

Paul sighed and nodded. "I know, baby. I know. Do you want me to end my friendship with Julia, then? Because I will. Anything you say."

"No, love. I want you to be with a real woman. We can't do this forever."

"Only until I die. And then we can be together again."

"You're in such a hurry to die and I hate that. I want you to enjoy the life you've been given. Look at all the wonderful things in your life. Look at everything you have and look at what others don't have. Do you know there are people in the world who live in cardboard houses? Dirt floors. No running water. No clean water. They get rotten bits of food to eat. They die of diseases. Paul, you really don't know how good you've got it."

"What's that got to do with anything? I know what it's like for those people. I mean, I haven't seen it for myself, but I've heard. So, what am I supposed to do? Go live like that?"

"You should enjoy your life. You've been given a good life. You should enjoy it. Now, it would be wonderful if you joined the Peace Corps, gave up everything, and rescued an entire village of starving people. But is that what you're designed to do?"

"I don't think so." *Am I?*

"That kind of life is not for everybody. You're a good person, but you wouldn't last a whole day in those conditions."

Paul chuckled as he pictured himself in the desert, upset that there's no bathroom, bed, hot food, or a shower. Missy was right. He would not be able to survive without those things. He was really too spoiled. "Maybe I should, though. Maybe I should force myself to do that. I could become a humanitarian."

Missy sighed and laughed loudly. "Very noble, good sir, but I assure you, you were meant to be a trainer. Also, as a real human being, a real person with flesh and blood, you should not be alone. You should be with Julia. Or somebody. I would choose Julia, though."

"Why?"

"Paul, my dear, she is absolutely perfect for you. In fact, I dare say she is a better match for you than I was."

"Oh, no. Don't say that."

"You are a different person now than you were fourteen years ago. You are more practical, you're smart, you are more set in your ways, you've tried things, failed, learned from those things, and you've matured. Am I right?"

"I suppose."

"Julia is the same. In fact, I believe if you were in her body, you could fool everybody into thinking it was still her in there."

"What?" Paul laughed. "That's ridiculous."

"What I'm trying to say is, you two are so alike it's scary. It's positively ridiculous some of the things you two say and do. In fact, I wouldn't put it past you to sit her down and discuss the pros and cons of kissing her before you even did it."

"Oh, Lord." Paul smacked his forehead.

"Well? Would you? And don't lie. I can read your mind, you know."

"I'm not going to..." *Then again, knowing me, I just might.* "You're right." Paul laughed with her. Then he thought about it. Kissing Julia? That would be weird. "I haven't kissed anyone since you." Paul was more musing to himself than speaking to Missy.

"It's like riding a bicycle. It's perfectly natural, and you will not have any trouble. Trust me."

"Won't it hurt you to see me with someone else, though? I know it would positively kill me to see you with another man."

"I will be fine. I promise."

"So, you're saying you're not in love with me anymore?"

He heard a soft sigh and chuckle. "I love you enough to allow you to have a better life."

"You're not leaving me, are you?" A slight sense of panic washed through him. He wasn't sure if he could do this.

"I will be here whenever you need me."

The panic dissipated. "Promise?"

"I promise."

ᘮᘮᘮ

They could not help comparing notes the next morning. Paul saw her in her usual spot, watching workouts. Without a word, he slipped closer and into the seat beside her. She glanced over, flashed a quick grin, and turned back to her horses on the track.

Paul let out a relaxed groan and leaned back in his chair. He clasped his hands together behind his head.

"You're awful relaxed this morning," Julia remarked as she peered through her binoculars.

"Yup. You?"

"Just fine."

"That's nice." It was silent for a minute, until the horse Julia was watching galloped easily past them and continued around the clubhouse turn with Billy trying to slow him down. "How's Rachel doing?"

"Same. I can tell she's anxious to get back here, though. I expect any day now she'll be ready. Only for a visit, though."

"Probably not too easy to ride in a cast."

"Her foot wouldn't fit in the stirrup." They shared a laugh. "Oh, but I guarantee you, if she could get her toe in, she'd ride."

"You know it. She's not one of these ones who would soak off her cast, is she?"

"No," Julia chuckled. "She's smart. She knows trying to ride when it's not healed all the way will hurt worse down the road. She's seen what the other jocks have tried to do over the years. Many have soaked casts off out of necessity of money, but even so, she sees now how it affects them later. She's a smart kid. She thinks ahead."

Paul nodded thoughtfully, noting silently that Rachel wasn't thinking ahead while walking in a bad neighborhood by herself that night.

Of course, Julia was thinking the same thing. She let her binoculars rest in her lap on her yellow legal pad. "I guess she's not perfect, though, huh?"

"Teens. Not that I know much about them, but I remember being one. And I remember thinking that nothing would ever happen to me."

Julia nodded. "We were invincible."

"That we were. And she's learning, well, she has learned now, she's not. She will be more careful from now on, I assure you."

Julia took a breath and nodded. "I hope so."

Paul couldn't help but unclasp one hand and pat her shoulder. She smiled weakly up at him. "Speaking of learning, what did you learn from Robbie last night?"

"I would be willing to bet the exact same thing you learned."

"I bet you're right, but we need to compare notes." He pressed his lips together, smothering the grin from thinking about Missy's statement last night about them talking about kissing before doing it. And here they were. He fell right into the trap, too. In an instant, he decided to be unpredictable. He wasn't going to talk about kissing her first. He was just going to do it. Not yet, though.

"Okay. You first." Julia glanced over with a smirk.

"Well..." He sat up twisted his body toward hers. "Okay. Missy said I should sell everything and join the Peace Corps."

"Ha!" Julia rolled her eyes. "Did she, now?"

"Absolutely. She said I'm a natural born humanitarian."

She tilted her head at him, glanced at the gap as she waited for a horse, and then back to Paul. He was still looking at her with expectancy, so she slapped his arm.

"Ow!"

"You deserve it. You liar." Julia frowned, sticking her bottom lip out as she had seen Rachel do.

Paul laughed at her and resisted the urge to touch her lip. He shook his head to rid himself of it the instant that thought hit him. "Well, she sort of said it."

"Uh huh..."

"She said the opposite. Ha."

"How does that work? You take things from the poor?" Julia couldn't help but snicker at her own joke.

"No, that's not what she said," he said in a mocking voice. "She said to enjoy the life I've been given. Real profound, I know."

"Good advice."

"I know. So, is that what Robbie said?"

"Basically, yeah."

"She also said she wouldn't go away completely. She'd still be here, but only if I need her, but that I won't need her." He wished suddenly he could take those words back. Too presumptuous. Way too presumptuous. Julia's eyes widened with what he thought looked too much like fear. She swallowed heavily but didn't speak. "Sorry. I didn't mean to assume..."

"No, no. It's okay. I, uh, I know what you mean. Robbie said the same." Julia glanced from Paul's face to the floor, to the track, back to him, then to the paper on her lap.

"So, uh, then, um, maybe we should, um, go on a..." He cleared his throat and adjusted in his seat. "D-date?"

"You want to?" she asked *sotto voce*. Paul thought she might be shaking but was afraid to get close enough to find out.

"Do you?"

Julia ran her fingers through her hair, scratching her head slightly. She bit her lip, then answered, "Y-yes?"

Paul nodded. "Okay."

"Okay."

A heavy weight fell over them. Though they each knew the other was scared, it was of no solace. The thought of going on a date was utterly paralyzing.

Paul felt an actual pressure on his chest. Was he supposed to come up with a place? Or should he ask her where she wanted to go? How does this work? Do they agree on a time and date? Does he pick one? She was looking at him, waiting now. He wasn't sure what to do.

"When?" she asked, finally.

"Um, how's Monday night? Dark day, we won't be too tired."

"Okay."

"S-six? Six o'clock?"

"Okay."

"It's a date." *Yikes.*

"It's a date." *Lord, help me.*

CHAPTER SIXTEEN

It only took a few more days for Rachel to find the bravery to come back to the track. Julia was petrified for her, knowing her reaction to being outside the house, but she did her best to stay strong and let Rachel know that everything was going to be fine.

Everyone on the staff greeted Rachel, and while they surrounded her, she shook like a leaf. Julia kept her hand on Rachel's back for support as one by one, barn workers greeted her and welcomed her back. She saw Erick standing in back, occasionally talking to people, and then craning his head to see Rachel. Julia wondered what Rachel's reaction would be. Other girls around the track had swooned around this kid, flirting and giggling, each trying to vie for his attention. He was a good-looking kid. Today he was wearing a black cowboy hat, which was different for around here. He was from Texas. Normal there. Not normal here, and it got him a lot of attention.

Sure enough, Rachel's eyes bugged when she saw him. Julia almost laughed, mostly because she was relieved that Rachel wasn't scared of him. She hoped this meant she would not be afraid of men in general, as she had proven to be in the last month. Erick looked a little shell-shocked himself, but he already had a girlfriend. *Oops. Drama.* Julia could see it coming.

Later that morning, though, Rachel had a complete meltdown. Julia had tried to step into her office for a few seconds, out of Rachel's sight, knowing she was okay with Mike, a groom in their barn. She heard screaming and ran out, wishing she hadn't left Rachel's side. Rachel was on the ground on all fours, clawing at the dirt floor. Mike stood over her with his mouth agape, utterly confused.

Julia fell to her knees next to Rachel and took her hand. "Mom," Rachel cried. Julia helped her stand again. Rachel wrapped herself in her mother's arms and quivered. Everyone looked on with horror and concern, but Julia tried to smile and put them at ease as she attempted to relax Rachel at the same time. She felt as though she had fifteen kids all needing her at once.

Rachel finally recovered, but soon after, her friend, Peggy came. *Great. Erick's girlfriend, Rachel's friend. Here comes the drama.* Julia did her best to keep an eye on Rachel as the three of them talked yet stay out of the way at the same time. Rachel was, of course, nervous. Julia wondered if it was because she wasn't close enough, so occasionally, she wandered by. Rachel always looked up and watched, always keeping a close eye on her mother.

At least Julia knew the bulk of Rachel's nervousness was not because Erick was there. Or was it?

A half hour went by, and it was almost lunchtime. Julia wanted to take Rachel home before the races, so she could be ready for them without having to worry about her daughter. First, she had to pick up the workout reports from Paul. He had promised to keep track of her horses that morning, so she could spend that time with Rachel in the barn. She left Billy in charge of Rachel and left, heading for Paul's barn.

"Hey," she greeted softly from behind.

He spun around on his heels. "Hi."

"Got something for me?"

"Huh?" He blinked. "Oh. Okay. Here," he said, waving his hand for her to follow. They went to his office. Once at his desk, he sifted through a few papers as Julia stood beside him. He found the piece of paper with the list of workouts and turned to her.

Julia eyed the paper, which he had not yet given her. Instead, he held it close to his chest. She blinked and looked up into his eyes. He looked petrified, and almost as though he wanted to say something. "What's wrong?"

"Nothing," he said quickly, then shoved the paper toward her.

She looked at it as she took it from him and stood her ground. "Thanks." Again, she caught his eyes, and then caught him glancing at her lips. *Oh no. Not here. Not now. It's too soon.* "Thanks, Paul," she said, and then vanished through the door.

On her way back to her barn, she stepped as quickly as she could, her heart pounding with fear. "I can't do this. I can't do this," she mumbled. But she didn't have time to think about it anymore. She heard someone calling for help inside the barn. It was Erick's voice. She ran inside to find Rachel unconscious and on the ground. Erick met Julia closer to the door and walked with her as he tried to explain what had happened. She had just fallen, no warning, but hadn't hurt herself because Erick caught her in time. Julia kneeled at Rachel's head.

"Rach? Rach?" Julia patted Rachel's face and hands until she finally awoke. Rachel looked dazed and confused for a minute, but finally realized what had happened. They got her up again and back on her crutches. She swore she was feeling fine, but Julia had her doubts. Obviously, something had to have caused this. Julia offered to go get the car for her and had to leave her with Erick in the meantime. She didn't want to do that, but she had no other choice. Billy was off somewhere, though he was supposed to be helping her with Rachel.

As she hurried to her car, thoughts of Paul came back to her. This date was going to be harder than she could ever imagine.

ᴑᴑᴑ

The weekend flew by without seeing Paul anywhere, not even from a distance. Julia mentally slapped herself for running from him like that. Surely, he knew why. He had to have seen her confusion. Her nervousness. Now, it was Monday, date night, and again, she hadn't seen him all day. Of course, it was a dark day, there were no races, so chances were, unless they made deliberate attempts, they would not have seen each other. Were they still on for tonight?

Julia's stomach rolled with nervousness as she debated calling him or waiting at the house to see if he showed up. She touched the phone, and then drew away from it quickly. As she stared at the black rotary dial, she pictured herself picking up the phone and dialing the number in his barn. She let her hand fall close but could not make it touch the phone. With a fit of rage, she slammed her palm flat onto her desk.

It stung. She picked up her hand with the other and cradled it.

"You okay?"

His voice made her jump for several reasons, and she very nearly jumped into his arms as she had done a couple of weeks ago. Instead, she managed to stand and hold her place. "Hi."

Paul stepped inside. "What'd you do to your hand?"

"Huh? Oh, nothing. It's...it's fine." She shook it out quickly. "Um, we still on for tonight? Or are you..."

"Yeah, we're still on. If you want."

"Yes." She nodded just to make sure he understood her completely. She very much wanted this. Although, she was deathly afraid. She'd never been so scared to do anything in her life. It was all new. It was different. It was something she hadn't done in almost twenty years.

"Great," Paul said, looking relieved. Julia was relieved, and relieved that he was relieved, and tittered nervously. "See you tonight."

Julia made sure to smile before he left. She noticed that he had walked out at a normal pace, not nearly as quickly as she had left his office three days ago. When he was safely out of earshot, she let out a huge breath of air and bent over, then fell into her desk chair.

ꙮꙮꙮ

She stood in front of her mirror inspecting her well-fitting, square-necked, sheath dress, decorated with a patterned scarf and a circle pin to keep it in place. The belt was thin, and the same color as her dress. Her tan heels complimented the outfit perfectly. He seemed to like her hair straight, so she styled it straight and long. She thought it odd that she would not do it the way she wanted to do it, curling it up on the ends, but rather do something to please him. That was not her way at all. Pursing her lips and shrugging, she took a breath and sat on the bed.

Though she knew Robbie would probably not talk back, she had to talk to him anyway. "Robbie, I hope you're here and you can hear me." She made sure to talk softly so no one outside her room could hear. "I know you're okay with this. I guess. But I'm scared to death. I don't know if I can do this. I'm just going to ruin it all. I'm going to panic and mess it up somehow, I know it."

She thought she heard him say, "No, you're not. Just be yourself. Everything will be fine."

Julia nodded, wondering if she had heard his voice, or was hearing things. Was it only in her head? Was she making it up? Was she making him speak in her head? Crazy to think, after all these years, she still could not tell sometimes.

There was a knock at the door. "Mom?" It was Rachel.

"Yes, honey?" She stood and made her way to the door, took another breath, and opened it.

"Mom? Where are you going? Is something going on tonight?"

She berated herself for not telling Rachel about this earlier. "I, um, I'm just going out with a friend, that's all."

"A friend?" The corners of Rachel's mouth raised slightly.

Julia rolled her eyes and walked past her daughter, stepping around her crutches. "Yes, a friend."

"Okay." She could hear the smile on Rachel's face and did not dare look for fear she would giggle like a teenager, too. She couldn't believe she was doing this. Rachel followed as Julia went to the kitchen, wishing they had wine or something alcoholic in the house. Vodka. Bourbon. Anything. Instead, she opted for a glass of water.

Rachel was seated in a kitchen chair now, and watched her mother, with her shaky hands, pull out a glass, grip it tightly to avoid dropping it, then hold it under the faucet for water. The water shook visibly as her mother sipped it, and the glass clunked on the counter as Julia sat it down. "Mom, you're white as a ghost. What's wrong?" The smile was gone from Rachel's face now.

"Nothing," she said with her voice husky after the drink. She took one more sip, set the glass down again, then went to the table and sat with Rachel. Rachel touched her mother's hand. It was ice cold.

"Mom, you're freezing."

"It's cold in here." Julia looked around for her coat. She found a sweater draped over the back of a dining room chair, but it didn't match. Blowing out a puff of air, she stood and went to the coat closet. She pulled on her dress coat and went back to the table, wrapping it tightly around her. She shivered.

"It's not that cold. Geez."

"Well, I am cold." Julia rocked forward and back.

"You're scared to death. Mom, don't be scared. He's not going to bite. Is he?" Coming from her, it was a valid question.

"No." She shook her head without looking directly at her daughter. "He's not going to bite."

"See? So. Is it Paul?"

Julia tilted her head but couldn't hide the truth. "Yes."

Rachel lit up. "It is. That's great, mom. I'm proud of you."

Instantly, Julia wished the conversation were going the other way. This was strange. She would much rather be saying those words to Rachel.

"What time is he coming?"

"Six." Julia glanced at the clock on the wall above their green refrigerator. It was six. Where was he?

In that instant, there was a knock on the door.

"Six on the dot!" Rachel proclaimed, then stood and made her way to the door.

Julia sighed and hurried directly there, unable to wait for Rachel to get there with her crutches. She opened the door to find Paul there in his suit. He looked like a younger Frank Sinatra. Funny. She had thought the same thing about Robbie on their first date. The thought made her shake and almost cry. As she reminded herself that she was good at controlling herself, she cleared her throat and smiled politely. "Hello. Come in."

"Hi." Paul hesitated a second, checked the door threshold for anything he might trip over, and stepped inside. "Hi, Rachel." His voice was soft, almost inaudible. "Uh, need her home by a certain hour?" he asked louder.

Rachel bit back a grin. "She goes to bed at nine, but I think it'll be okay to stay out a little later tonight."

Paul laughed as Julia shook her head. "Okay, Mother. I'll be home soon. Don't wait up." She kissed Rachel's cheek. "Tell Billy I'll be home by nine, okay?"

"Mom, seriously. You don't have to be."

"I know." Julia waved dismissively as she turned. Paul touched her back as they walked through the door, leaving Rachel beaming with joy at the sight.

"Bye," they heard before closing the door. Julia finally let out the laughter, though quietly, as they walked down the path to Paul's car. Paul hid his face from their curious onlooker inside the house, opened the door for Julia, then went to his side and slipped in.

"I've never been so embarrassed in my life," Julia admitted.

Paul chuckled. "Oh, it's not that bad."

"She's been trying to get me to go out for *years*. I mean, for*ever*. To her, she feels like she's won some sort of a prize."

"That's okay. Good. She needs something to be happy about."

"True," Julia said, catching his gaze.

They drove to a restaurant several miles farther up Long Island. He held her chair for her, she scooted herself in, and he sat at the table in the seat nearest to her.

"Nice place," Julia remarked, noting the tablecloths, silverware, glasses, and waiters in tuxedos and clothes draped over their arms.

"Only the best for a first date." Paul slipped his napkin onto his lap.

Julia barely had time to smile at him when their waiter interrupted. They ordered wine and steak and sat back to wait. Julia sampled her wine, looking for something to talk about. "It's good," she noted.

Paul tried it, too. "Yes, it is."

As Julia tried to think of something else to talk about, she kept her eyes on him. He looked just as nervous. Directness had been useful in the past. She decided to try it again. "Nervous?" she asked boldly.

His eyes widened for a second, and then he smiled at himself and wiped his moist hands on his napkin draped over his leg. "That obvious, huh?"

Julia shrugged. "Me too. If it helps."

"You don't look nervous. You never look nervous. Always cool as a cucumber."

"Ha. I'd like to think that was true, but it's not. Rachel saw right through me."

"Well, she does know you a little better than I do, I guess."

"She's very perceptive. Always has been. Ever since she was little." She touched her glass and straightened it. "I'm sorry. I guess you're not supposed to talk about kids on a date, are you?" Julia wrinkled her nose slightly.

"What? No. Who said that?"

"I don't know. 'They?' You know. Those mysterious people who always know everything."

"Well, 'they' are wrong. We can talk about anything we want. Besides, it's probably only married couples who aren't supposed to talk about their kids when they go out."

"Married couples still go on dates?"

"Well, I wouldn't know, but from what I've heard, yes. It's good for a marriage."

"Really? Well, that's good. I agree. It would be good. And you're right. Probably not good to discuss the kids, since they discuss the kids at home. Right?"

"Absolutely." Paul nodded unceasingly for several seconds. "I guess that means we can't talk about our horses, then, does it?"

Julia froze just before taking a sip of her wine. "What?"

"Well, they're like our kids, aren't they? In a way?"

Julia sipped her wine and nodded. "I suppose so. You're right. Well, then. What else is there to talk about?"

"Other people's horses."

Julia caught a loud laugh before it sounded.

Finally, they were able to relax and spend the evening talking and eating. Julia hardly wanted to eat, shy about eating in front of him suddenly, since it was a date. She also did not want to stop talking long enough to take a bite. She did so only to make sure he was able to talk some, too. She'd never been this talkative before. *Must be the wine*, she figured.

Her only real concern popped into her mind from time to time – the after-date kiss on the front porch. Would it happen? She hoped not. She *really* hoped not. Although, as she glanced at his lips, she found herself wondering what it would be like. Would he be soft, warm, gentle? Or would he be rough from nervousness over having not kissed a woman in fourteen years. *Fourteen years.* She could hardly believe it. It had been fifteen for her. The thought made her unconsciously shake her head. Fortunately, it fit with what he was saying.

Paul filled up her glass again. How many glasses had it been, anyway? She had completely lost count. Her head spun. She hadn't had so much wine in a long time. In fact, well, for her father's funeral, where there had been a Catholic wake with wine, she'd had only one glass. Rachel had tried it. Didn't like it, thankfully. She wouldn't be allowed to drink wine legally until she was eighteen, anyway. Before the wake, Julia had had some at some other funerals, maybe a glass or two. She didn't think she'd ever been drunk before. Was this what it felt like to be drunk?

Oh no. He's not going to take advantage...no...not him. He'd never...

Paul was waving his hand in front of Julia's eyes. "Hello in there." He had a silly grin on his face and for some reason, Julia felt the same on her face just then. How did that happen? "Too much wine?"

"We can't go home drunk. Am I drunk? Is this what it's like?" She looked around, noting the blurry nature of things around the room. "Wow," she sighed.

"You've never been drunk." He stated it but asked it at the same time.

"N-n-nope." She swung her head back and forth a few times, but got dizzy, so she grabbed the table and stopped moving. "Oh, wow."

Paul chuckled. "Don't do that, now."

"Are you drunk, too?" Julia whispered, leaning forward so no one would hear. It would be scandalous.

"Not much. Maybe a little buzzed."

"How are we gonna get home?" Julia asked, her eyes so sad, she almost looked as though she would cry any second. "Rachel will be mad." Tipsy as she was, or drunk, whatever, she could not let Rachel see her like this.

"You could just act normal."

"How does one go about doing that?"

"Sit up straight. Walk straight. Talk clearly. You'll be fine. Besides, Rachel and Billy will be in bed."

"Billy," Julia said, almost in a whisper. "He'd be mad at me, for sure."

"Why?" Paul was trying his hardest not to laugh.

"Well, he's young, you know. Impress-shin-impressionable. His voice is changing. He's becoming a man." Julia slammed her hand over her face to hide as tears came out of nowhere. After a second, she wiped her face, sat up straight, and pretended to be fine again.

"Wow. You're good at that."

"You don't become a lady trainer at Belmont by showing emotions. Wait. I said that wrong. You can't show emotion when you're a lady. No. I said it right. Right?"

"Yes," Paul chuckled. "That's very admirable of you to be so strong."

"You have to be, too, to, to, to be a boss. Do you not?"

"Of course."

"And bosses don't get drunk. I can't believe I did this. I can't believe I shamed my people. I've shamed my children. I've shamed –"

"Julia," Paul laughed. "Why don't we get you home?"

"What? No. You can't...well...I mean...what about...you...ugh..." She slammed her back against the seat back and nearly knocked the chair over in the process. Her eyes widened as she caught Paul laughing at her. He stood and took her hand. "Oh, my God. I've got to get out of here."

"Let's go get some air."

"It's cold," she stated as he helped her don her coat.

"That's what coats are for, my dear. You'll be just fine."

"Don't call me that."

"Okay, okay." Paul put up his hands in defense.

Julia realized how silly she was acting. And telling him not to call her that only made her look like she was thinking about that sort of thing, and she was supposed to not think that way. *What way? Oh, pet names.* "We haven't gotten to that point in the relationship. Yet," she said aloud, and then slapped her hand over her mouth.

"No, not yet. I promise. No pet names until we've both agreed that it's an appropriate time." They were outside now, and Julia cackled with laughter at the thought.

"We'll draw up a contract."

"Have it ratified."

"Witnesses."

"The whole works. It'll be epic."

Julia leaned over, slapping her bare knees as Paul tried supporting her with his arm around her waist. Quickly, she straightened when she realized he was touching her. She straightened too quickly and lost her balance. Laughing, Paul wrapped his arms around her, saving her from falling off the sidewalk and into a parked car. "Oh, my goodness, Paul. I am so sorry. I don't even know what's going on. I mean, I do. I mean, but I can't see straight. Or think. I need to get to bed before I wind up eating my feet."

Paul was still laughing at her. He was going to have some fun stories for the morning. If she even made it to work. He helped her to his car, and they drove home with Julia talking non-stop.

"Rachel's doing much better. She can't wait to get the cast off and start riding again. Of course, she's worried that Erick has replaced her, but of course, he hasn't. Obviously, I'd choose my own daughter over somebody else. Right? Poor Billy, too. With all this stuff with Rachel going on, he's not getting enough attention. He's so quiet, though, that I hardly notice. I mean, I really must think about making sure he's okay too. You know? My mother. Oh, my goodness. My poor mother. She has tried so hard to pick up the slack. She did well, though, while Rachel was gone. Came by every day to help with Billy. She and Billy are really close. As you can imagine. She used to watch him more when the kids were little."

There was a slight pause, and Paul took a breath to speak, but Julia interrupted.

"I wish I could tell the author of that book how wrong he is. He has no idea what he's talking about. Nobody knows except us. I feel like we're the only people in the whole world that know it's true. There is something after we die. We don't know what, but there is. For that man to sit back in his easy chair and write stuff that he knows nothing about, and to preach it like he's right and everybody's wrong, well, that's just wrong. Right? I mean, he has no right. He's wrong."

Julia laughed hysterically for a few seconds. Paul scrunched his face at her, snickered, and continued driving.

"Speaking of wrong, this dress…this dress is all wrong. Don't you think? Well, never mind. You wouldn't think about things like that, would you? Do you see how it's wrong?"

"Not re –"

"It's too dark for my skin. It makes me look too white. See, people as pale as me cannot wear dark colors."

"You're not pale. You spend so much time outside."

"I am, too. I'm pale. I'm white as a ghost. Okay, maybe only a little. Maybe I'm not as white as a ghost. Maybe just… You know, ghosts aren't really white, are they? They have clothes on, just like we do. Robbie's still wearing his silks. Sometimes the helmet too, sometimes not. I wonder where he puts it. Do they have homes? Where do they live? Do they eat? Do they drink? Do they feel things? How does he get from place to place?"

At that point, shaking his head and smothering laughter, Paul pulled up to her house and noted that the front porch light was on.

"Here we are," Julia announced. He was a little worried about leaving her, knowing her kids were in bed and couldn't help her. It was ten, and they'd surely be asleep by now. Julia was fumbling with her purse, looking for her keys. She couldn't find them and shook her purse to see if it jingled. It didn't. She gasped as she looked up at him. "No keys."

"What will we do? You think it's unlocked?"

"Are you serious? Rachel's probably barricaded the doors and windows. I'll never get in now." Julia stared longingly at her house.

Folding in her lips, she reached into her purse one more time, and then stopped with her hand buried in her small clutch. She met his eyes, smiled, then pulled out one key. "Spare. See? It pays to be sensible, doesn't it?"

Paul laughed heartily. "Yes, it does." He got out of the car, helped her stand, walk to the door, and took the key from her shaking hand. "I'll do it."

"Oh. Okay. Doesn't mean you're coming in, though."

Paul raised one eyebrow at her. "Jules, I promise I won't touch you. I just want to make sure you get in okay and to your room. I'll help you to you room and then I'll leave. Okay?" He raised both hands.

Julia pursed her lips to one side as she considered her options. "Well, okay. I suppose that couldn't hurt. Right?"

"Absolutely not. Besides, I'd never hurt you anyway."

Julia hesitated, glanced at him, and decided she didn't understand what he meant, if anything. It was too hard to figure out, so she continued into her house. Rachel was asleep on the couch, so Julia put her finger over her lips. Paul nodded. They tip toed down the hall to her bedroom with Paul holding one of her arms to keep her steady.

Her door was already open. She took a few steps inside and stopped. After a second's hesitation, she turned abruptly toward Paul, who jumped. "What?" he asked.

"You're in my bedroom," she whispered, flabbergasted at the thought, then burst into a fit of giggles. She was even giggling at the thought of giggling.

Paul covered his mouth to keep his laughter quiet but wound up snorting as a result. Julia laughed, and then covered her mouth as well. "Shh," they scolded together.

As soon as the laughter died down, Paul, with his eyes on her, touched her arm. She held his gaze, by some miracle, and wondered if he would kiss her. After all, it was a date. Were they supposed to kiss? Instead, Paul nodded and frowned slightly. It was apparent he had changed his mind. He started to pull away, but Julia wrapped her arms around his neck and pulled him closer. They were face to face now, their lips only an inch apart, the sweet scent of Merlot thick in the air between them.

"You said..." Paul started.

Without thinking, Julia closed her mouth over his. After a few seconds to realize what was happening, he relaxed, wrapped his arms around her, and kissed her back. He adjusted one hand behind her head and moaned softly as their tongues touched, tasted, played. Julia felt safe in his arms, warm, secure, and she found his lips to be soft and caring. He caressed her mouth with his, but it felt as though he were caressing her whole body. It felt so good, igniting her all the way down to her toes. She wanted more, never wanted to stop. She hadn't felt this for... *Don't even think about that.*

Several minutes passed as they stood in her doorway locked in a heated embrace. Then Julia realized that Rachel was just down the hall in the living room. *She could see. She would positively...freak, to use her word.* Julia pulled back, panting for air, as was he. His eyes were wide and wild with need. He was eyeing her wet lips, desperately needing to touch them again. And she needed him.

After taking a few breaths, Julia reached over and pushed her door closed as silently as she could.

"Jules..."

At that point, she realized what was happening. She pulled completely free from his arms and stood staring up at him. Her swollen lips were parted in surprise, her eyes were puddled with confusion.

Paul stepped closer and held her arms, steadying her. "No, Jules, I can't. You've been drinking. I don't want you to think I took advantage of you."

"I invited you in." Her words meant two things at once. It was a bit of an argument to convince him to stay. Then again, she couldn't believe she had done this, and stood dazed and confused in his arms, staring at the floor at their feet.

"Yes, but, well, let's just say goodnight, okay? Are you gonna be okay?"

Julia looked up at him and nodded slowly to avoid making herself dizzy. It was time for bed, but she was still in her coat. She slipped off her coat and let it fall to the floor as she kept her eyes on his.

Paul let his shoulders droop with disappointment as he could see her shape now beneath her dress. All he'd have to do is slide his hand up... He lowered his hand, almost touched her hip, but pulled away again. "I should go." Her hips were his favorite part. It killed him to do this, especially since she appeared to want him.

Julia looked sad but nodded. She lowered her eyes to the floor in defeat and embarrassment.

He couldn't leave her like this. He stepped toward her again, touching her arm. When she lifted her eyes to his, he leaned in and kissed her, but only for a second. "See you in the morning," he whispered. He touched her hair and then ducked through a narrow opening in the doorway and down the hall. Julia heard him fiddle with the lock, then close the door behind him.

That was nice of him to lock the door for me. That was the last thing she remembered until morning.

CHAPTER SEVENTEEN

"How was your date with Paul, Mom?" Billy asked on their way to the track. It was still dark as they walked, but streetlamps made it look more like twilight. Every crack in the sidewalk, every tree, fence, every blade of grass, they had memorized, as they had made this walk so many times.

"Oh, it was fine." Julia had never had a hangover before and never wanted to experience this ever again. Her head pounded, and she wondered if it might explode or leak some sort of fluid from her ears. Every step on the concrete felt like a giant bass drum pounding from on top of her head, though she stepped as lightly as she could.

"How late were you out?"

She couldn't help the slight chuckle. "Does it matter?"

"Just curious."

"Honestly, I didn't look at the time. I guess around ten?"

"Oh, okay. That's good."

Julia reminded herself that he was getting older now and probably trying to take on a roll of the man of the family. It was cute, but what if she married Paul? Oh, that was thinking way too far ahead. It had taken fifteen years to find the courage to go on a date with another man. How much longer would it take to find the courage to actually marry someone? She'd be in her seventies, at least.

$\upsilon\upsilon\upsilon$

Billy was tacking up a horse when Paul walked up sporting a huge, wicked grin. His teeth were bright despite the pre-dawn darkness. Julia did her best to keep the smile from her own face, but resistance was futile. Seeing him made her cheeks flush pink. She was glad for the darkness.

Julia shook her head with her gaze lowered.

"Are you okay?" he asked, stifling a laugh.

"No," she stated matter-of-factly with her nose in the air. "I believe I have a hangover. I suppose. I'm barely functioning and it's not easy to pretend I'm not sick as a dog. Ugh."

"Take a couple of aspirin and drink plenty of water. You're dehydrated. You'll feel better in a few hours."

"Oh. Okay. I take it you have a lot of experience with hangovers?"

He laughed. "No. Just a few. I don't make a habit of getting drunk. I wind up embarrassing myself."

Suddenly it hit her. Embarrassing? Embarrassing wasn't a strong enough word for it. Mortified? That was more like it. "Oh, God." Her face turned redder than it ever had.

"Oh, don't worry, Jules. I won't hold it against you." He winked.

She had no idea what he was talking about. She remembered kissing him...but...was there more? "Paul, I'm so sorry. I don't know what came over me."

"A strong desire for a good-looking man in a suit?" he asked, leaning in so only she would hear.

She opened her mouth wide and slapped his arm. Hard. He ducked and laughed. She tried to hit him again, but he caught her arm. "Oh, my God," she whispered, still mortified with herself. "Paul, please be honest with me. We didn't..."

"You kissed me," he whispered, then winked.

That was bad enough. Hopefully, that was the end of the story. "And that's, um, it?"

Paul nodded with a false frown. "Sadly, yes."

"Oh no. Paul, you were in my bedroom, weren't you?"

Paul chuckled with his hand over his stomach. "Yes. So? Are we in boarding school? We're two grown adults. It's perfectly fine."

"It is?"

"Yes, Jules. It's fine. Besides, we didn't go any further than kissing, anyway."

"I kissed you in my bedroom. Robbie...Oh no..." She covered her cheeks with her hands.

"Oh, Jules. He said he wouldn't watch. Right?"

She looked up at him hopefully. "I am so embarrassed. Paul, I'm so sorry. I didn't mean −"

"Jules, yes you did, and so did I. It's fine. No need to apologize. Nothing to apologize for. Unless you've decided you were sorry you did it. In which case, I should be the one who's embarrassed. Not you."

"What? No. No. That's not what I mean."

"What are you sorry for, then?"

"I don't even know." She made a sound something like a whine. "I don't feel good, and I can't believe I let you...Wait. I kissed you first."

Paul nodded like an eager child being offered a chocolate bar.

Julia felt her stomach turn.

Paul patted her arm, and then let his hand slide down to take her hand. He ran his thumb over her knuckles. "So, does this mean we're going steady?"

She met his eyes, noted the goofy grin on his face, and couldn't help but laugh. She glanced around for prying ears or eyes, but everyone was busy with their work, keeping their eyes on their horses, which is where they should be. "We'll need to draw up a contract first."

"How's tonight, then? We'll make some notations on cocktail napkins, the bartender can witness it, and we'll make it official?" He winked.

Julia nodded. "So, you're not mad at me for the way I acted? I was awful silly last night."

"No," he said as he laughed. "No, Jules. It was fun. I had fun last night."

"I'm not doing that again, though." She waved a hand in the air dismissively.

"Not doing what?" he asked with one eye half-closed.

"Drinking. No way. Not worth the way you wake up the next morning." *And do things without thinking about the consequences first.*

"Gotcha. We'll drink water."

ᴕᴕᴕ

"Mom, I didn't get to talk to you about your date last night." Rachel scooped Grandma's cheeseburger casserole onto her plate. "So? How'd it go?"

Julia was forcing herself to eat so she didn't look ill in front of the kids. It was becoming increasingly difficult with each bite. She was torn between feeling glad for the excuse not to take another bite and dreading answering this question. "It was fine."

"Fine? So, does that mean you're going out with him again?"

"Yes." Julia tried her hardest to keep her eyes lowered as Rachel searched her face for clues.

"When?"

"Later tonight."

Rachel's face lit with joy. "That's great, Mom." It was evident Rachel was trying her hardest to control herself and not irritate her mother. Or embarrass her. Julia appreciated it.

Rachel, Billy, and Grandma all waited anxiously in the living room while Julia got ready. Again, she wore a dress and looked very sharp. Too sharp, she thought as she checked herself in the mirror.

"Robbie, honey, I'm so sorry. I feel so guilty. I was such a whore last night. I shouldn't have done that." Before she could control them, tears slipped down her face, making streaks in her makeup. "Oh, Lord," she mumbled, then grabbed tissues and tried to blot her face. Just then, she heard a knock on the door. It was Paul. She hoped her mother would get the door, so she could have another minute to cover the tear tracks. "I'll never drink again, Robbie. I promise. I don't know what came over me. I never would have done that. Especially not in front of you. I hope you weren't here. I hope you didn't see." She pressed the tissues against her face to blot more tears, and then cursed herself for allowing them to fall in the first place.

By now, her eyes had reddened. She sighed, wadded up the tissues, and threw them in her trash can.

"Mom?" Billy asked through the door.

"I'll be right out." She scurried to her bathroom and fixed her makeup, then wished she had eye drops to hide the redness. Surely, he would see it. She would have to make sure to keep her eyes down. With a deep breath, she took one more look in the mirror, yanked the door open, and went straight for the front door, grabbing her coat from the rack without stopping. "Ready?" she asked, keeping her eyes down and putting on her coat at the same time. Paul tried to help her but she was too fast for him.

"Yeah. Okay, folks. See you later, then," Paul said, then followed Julia, who was already out the door.

"You okay?" he asked as he hurried to catch up.

"Yup." She lowered her face to hide her eyes and kept walking. Finally, she was in, and waiting for him to get in on his side. She tried smiling at him, squinting her eyes at the same time, hoping it was enough to hide the red.

Once they were driving, he asked, "Dooley's tonight? How's that?"

"That'll be great."

The rest of the ride was in silence. Julia bit her lip and tried to distract herself, held her breath, anything to keep her guilty tears at bay. She knew at some point, she would lose control. Paul would feel awful, too, as if he had caused it. She knew he would feel responsible. She didn't want to hurt his feelings and didn't want to hurt Robbie's either. Imagining how much it would have hurt to see her with another man that way got to her, and a sob slipped out. She hadn't even felt it coming on. She covered her mouth.

Just then, they pulled into the parking lot. Julia hid her face from him. He turned to her and touched her arm. "Jules?" he asked softly, handing her his handkerchief.

"I'm so sorry."

"About what? Are you breaking up with me already?"

Julia hid her face in the handkerchief and bent over her knees, sobbing, without answering him.

"Why? Is it Robbie? Was it last night? Jules, if you're not comfortable..."

Bravely, she sat up, stopping his questions in their tracks. "I just feel...guilty. It's not you, Paul. I don't know what to do. I don't know how to feel. I'm so torn. I'm so confused."

"Jules, it's very admirable that you care so much about his feelings. You care more about his feelings than you do your own." He lowered his gaze. "Or mine."

Julia blinked. Paul withdrew his hand from her arm, but she grabbed it. "No. No, it's not like that."

"What is it, then? Who would you choose? Me or him?"

"We weren't supposed to choose. We said we wouldn't make each other choose."

"We might have to."

"What? No. Why? Why would you say that?"

"You will feel guilty forever or until you let him go."

"Have you let Missy go?"

He shrugged. "Maybe a little. Not completely. I guess it'll take time. She helped me realize that life must come first. I have to let her go enough so that I can live in the present. You have to do the same. Don't you?"

Julia dried more tears and took a wobbly breath. "Yes. I know. But knowing it and doing it are two different things."

"It's a lot like what Rachel's going through, isn't it?"

"In what way?"

"She knows she's safe at home with you and Billy and your mom. Despite that, she keeps the doors locked. She's afraid to leave the house because the house is safe. Don't you see? You're doing the exact same thing, and you have been for *fifteen years*."

Absently, she stared out the window behind him as they sat in his car. He was right. He had been doing the same but seemed to be doing a better job of getting out of that rut once he realized what was going on. She knew she had to get out, too. She had to let Robbie go. It hurt to think about, but it was necessary. She was too reliant on him. It was holding her back. She wasn't living life.

She had become afraid to live.

"You're a very brave and strong woman, Jules. I know you can do this."

"I sure as hell don't feel very brave right now. Look at me. I'm a bumbling fool." She slammed her hands into her lap.

"You're not a bumbling fool. You're a beautiful woman. You're a strong woman. Look at everything you've accomplished in your life so far."

She shrugged. "Big deal."

"It is. You're saying that, though, because you're not enjoying it. You've accomplished your goals, but you don't let yourself enjoy the results."

"Why not?" she asked herself, as well as him.

"I can't say for sure, but if you're anything like me, and I think you are, then you feel like you should still be grieving the loss of your husband. And if he can't enjoy life, then neither should you. You feel guilty for the ability to enjoy things he cannot enjoy."

"I guess."

"But you don't need to, Jules. No one expects you to grieve another day, not even Rachel and Billy. Not even Robbie."

"I know."

"You do know. And now you have to do it. Remember? Like you said, 'Knowing it and doing it are two different things.' It's time for you to do it."

"I'm going to have to avoid him. Avoid talking to him. How do I do that?"

"He will understand and try not to talk to you. Missy's already backed off."

"Really?" She met his gaze.

"Really."

Julia wondered how he felt about that. She searched his face and could see that he was disappointed but knew that it was necessary. It was something he needed to do in order to move on. She knew that she would have to do the same. "I have to say goodbye."

"You can still talk to him if you really need to, Jules, but you should try not to. Try to stand on your own now."

She nodded solemnly, lowering her eyes again.

"I have no doubt that you will be able to do it. Like I said, you are strong. One of the strongest women...no...people I know. In fact, I wonder if you really know how strong you are."

She shrugged.

"You know what you want, and you do what you need to do to get it. Any other woman would never have had the strength to do what you did, moving from groom to head trainer when almost everybody was against you, and in such a male-dominated sport. But that didn't matter. You did it anyway. Your horses are doing so well. And this new two-year-old, he could bring your barn to new heights. What if he wins the Kentucky Derby? Preakness? Belmont? All three?"

Julia chuckled. "I don't dare dream about that."

"It could happen. It very well could happen."

Finally, a smile grew on her face, gradually. "Can you imagine? The Triple Crown."

Paul laughed. "No, I can't. I don't dare dream about something like that either. But you could now that you have Chivalry. He's another Kelso or Northern Dancer, Jules. I know it. You do too, don't you?"

Julia nodded. "I'm so scared of screwing him up, though."

"You won't. You know what you're doing. Just do things the way you normally would, and everything will work out fine. I promise."

"I guess you're not superstitious, are you? No superstitious person would say that for fear of jinxing it."

Paul snickered. "No. No way. Neither are you. We're too practical for that." He straightened his jacket.

"You're right." After a few seconds of silence, she asked, "Paul?"

"Yes?"

"Let's go in and draw up that contract."

EPILOGUE

Everybody around them was getting married. Not them. Why not? What was the problem? Was he still nervous about Missy's feelings? He couldn't be.

The first time they'd made love was on his couch in his living room, and Julia quickly figured out why. Just as she had done with Robbie, the place where he had talked to Missy the most often was in the bedroom. Missy had said she wasn't going to watch. Robbie too. What did it matter which room they were in? The living room was close enough.

Finally, Julia had convinced him it was okay to go to the bed to make love. Then came the discussion about sleeping in Julia's bed. Well, of course, Julia used the excuse of her children being in the same house. At their age, they knew what was going on in there. Paul had laughed but finally relented and agreed they would only spend the night together at his house. Paul was quick to point out that the kids surely knew what was going on during the nights she stayed over his place, too. "Not the same," she had said.

Julia ran her fingers through her hair as she sat in her office contemplating her life and the direction in which it was going. She knew they were in love. They wanted to be together as much as possible. They had agreed that if they had to race against one another, they would treat each other like anybody else. And if he won, fine. If she won, fine. There would be no jealousy or ill will. They'd have to accept it, just like any other married couple around the track.

It had been over a year since their first kiss. Why hadn't he proposed? Was he jealous of her success? She had recently won the Triple Crown with Chivalry. Men everywhere were upset with her, especially since she had done it with Rachel's help as Chivalry's jockey. He had never seemed jealous before. Paul had seemed ecstatic about her win.

She let her head rest on the heel of her hand. Certainly, he wasn't still worried about Missy. Julia knew she certainly wasn't worried about Robbie's feelings. Robbie had let her know many times that he was fine with this new relationship. He'd even let it slip that he thought they would get married.

"I don't know if I can do that to you. You would watch me become married to another man?"

"Well, if you think about it, Jules, we were only married for three years. Together a year and a half before that. Here, you have the potential to be in a marriage that could last twenty, thirty, forty years. Maybe more. It'll make our marriage seem like a one-night stand."

They had both laughed.

"It would be weird."

"…at first," Robbie finished for her. "You'd get used to it, just like you have become used to going out with him." Robbie sighed. "And…you know…doing more than just going out."

"Do you hate that?"

"No. I understand, completely. You have a body, and a nice one at that." Julia blushed. "And you need things that I can't give you. We could never be together that way again. As sad as it is for me to say it, it's the truth, and we can't change that fact."

Julia nodded. "It is sad, baby."

"We can't live in the past."

She shook her head. "Nope. I guess we can't. I will always love you, though." She bit her lip to curb her emotions. "It's sad that I can't be with my first love, but at least I have another chance."

That conversation had only been a few weeks ago. That was the last time she had talked to him, too. Their conversations had become less and less frequent, mostly because she spent less and less time alone. She and Paul might as well be married for all the time they spent together.

She went to his place that night, again. She wondered if they ever did get married, would she move in here? She already had half of her things here anyway.

They made dinner together, ate, then watched television and relaxed on the couch, which soon turned into making love.

They never did much of anything other than this anymore. Julia wondered if this is what she really wanted. Sure, she loved Paul. They had admitted their love to each other after a few months of careful deliberation. They were both sure they were in love. However, now, they'd gotten stuck in a rut, and it made Julia wonder if her married life would be the same.

As they lay together in his bed, her head on his chest, him drifting his fingers up and down her arm, she found herself saddened by the thought of that routine, even though she needed some routine to feel safe and secure. Her heart beat faster and he felt it.

"Something wrong?"

She cursed herself for being so transparent. He always knew. Always. It was almost like having Robbie reading her mind again. "I don't want to be in a rut," she said simply, as if that would explain everything.

It did. He knew exactly what she meant. "Neither do I. Let's change things up."

"How?" She lifted her head to meet his gaze.

"Have you ever been on a vacation?"

Julia's eyes widened, and she sat up even more. He scanned her body appreciatively and grinned until she covered herself with her sheet, opting for keeping the conversation going. "Not really."

"Where would you want to go? We have the money. Might as well."

"What about the horses? Trainers can't take vacations."

"We have assistants."

"You think they could handle it?"

"Absolutely. Especially if we prepared them beforehand. It's summer, we're not racing at Saratoga this year, we're in limbo anyway. We'll give them a few weeks' notice and they'll be more than ready for us to leave so they can take over."

"Oh, no."

Paul laughed. "It'll be fine, Jules. I promise. Where would you like to go?"

"I don't know. I've never thought about it. Never thought I would actually go on a vacation."

"I kind of thought Europe would be nice. France? Or England. We could go to Royal Ascot. Or we could go to Canada. Woodbine. Or California. Santa Anita. Wherever you want."

"You just named all race tracks. How is that a vacation?"

Paul laughed loudly and for a long time. "You're right," he admitted. "I didn't even think about that. That's ridiculous."

She poked him, and then relaxed onto his chest again. "Vacations are supposed to be on a beach or at a resort, or mountains, or a lake. Something like that."

"You an expert on vacations now?"

"Or a cruise."

"Okay, Miss Travel Agent. Where will we be headed?"

"Florida."

ᗝᗝᗝ

A month later, they flew to Florida. Julia had never been on an airplane before, and was nervous, but she tried not to let the other passengers know. As if that weren't enough cause for concern, some people recognized them and asked for autographs. Julia, being the trainer of a Triple Crown winning horse, was easily recognized. She hated it because she did not like attention. Although, she told herself repeatedly that it was all good for the sport and tried her best to be accommodating.

After picking up their rental car from the airport, they drove to Tampa from Orlando and checked into their hotel. First, they collapsed onto the bed and slept without changing out of their traveling clothes. Hours later, they stripped them off and made love. They stayed in bed the entire next day, ordering room service and staring at the beach outside their window. They didn't set foot on the beach until the third day.

Paul carried some plastic beach toys he had bought in the gift shop in the hotel. Julia laughed as she watched him proudly swinging his plastic bucket and shovels.

"You're embarrassing me," she whispered.

"Oh, fiddlesticks. Let's build a castle."

"Fiddlesticks, huh? Okay then. Let's build this."

Paul was quiet as he worked, seriously and methodically. He planned and designed, with Julia's help, an entire fortress. In the middle, he made two small, round bumps.

"What are those supposed to be?"

"Me and you."

Julia bit her lip and smiled wide, glancing at him. "That's so sweet. I look positively...uh...shapely. Just...round...shaped."

Paul laughed and pointed. "This one is you."

"How can you tell?" She looked closer.

"Well, I'm not sure, actually. You'll have to stick your finger inside to see." Paul pursed his lips thoughtfully.

"How's that supposed to prove which one is which?"

"I'll show you." Paul poked his finger into the top of his round lump and felt around for a few seconds. Then he pulled out a gold ring.

Julia's eyes bugged. "Where did you find that?" she gasped with her hands on her face. "Did you find that?"

"Yeah. Wow. Maybe there's another one in the other pile. You'd better check." Paul looked closely at the ring, dusted it off, held it up to the light while she knit her eyebrows at him.

Curiously, she poked her finger into her lump. She hit something hard. She swallowed heavily as she realized what it was. With her finger and thumb, she pulled out a plain gold ring.

"Wow," Paul exclaimed, though softly.

Julia looked at her ring, then his. They matched.

"Maybe there's another one in there."

Holding her breath, hoping she didn't pass out, she reached into the pile again and found a diamond ring. "What...?"

"Jules," Paul took her hand and drew closer to her. He took a breath and held it as he realized she was shaking. "Jules, are you ready? Are you ready to move on? With me?"

She nodded quickly as her eyes filled with tears. Paul scooted closer and took her ring.

"Really?" she asked.

He pressed his forehead against hers, and then kissed her. "Really," he whispered. He held up the ring near her finger. "Julia, will you marry me?"

"Yes," she managed to say. She nodded to affirm and cuddled helplessly in his arms as he slid the ring onto her finger.

ABOUT THE AUTHOR

Raised in Southern Maryland, Kristie Higgins grew up as a horse lover, riding friends' horses whenever possible. Short stories written as a horse-obsessed teenager have stuck with her and are now emerging as novels.

She is a graduate of Indiana University, Bloomington, and a retired instrumental music teacher. She taught in various elementary schools in Maryland for twelve years before retiring. No musician can ever give up music, so she plays keyboards in her church, with her two teenage sons playing guitar and bass alongside. At the end of the day, she relaxes, watching horseracing and writing with the help of her cat, Cookie.

Would you like to learn more about Rachel, Erick, Candy, Julia, and the Hanover Farms team?

Follow Kristie's blog on http://kristiehigginsauthor.com and her Amazon author page for updates.

The Backstretch Series:
Chivalry
Wounds into Wisdom
Turn of the Tide
How (not) to Grieve

(**Blame**, the only horse to beat Zenyatta, at
Claiborne Farm, June 2017.
Photo by Kristie Higgins)

CPSIA information can be obtained
at www.ICGtesting.com
Printed in the USA
LVHW09s0437240818
588003LV00001B/234/P